XY-Girls and More Stories

Derwin Mak

Milton, Ontario

First edition, August 2025
Published by Brain Lag
Milton, Ontario
https://www.brain-lag.com/

ISBN: 978-1-998795-22-2 (softcover)
ISBN: 978-1-998795-23-9 (ebook)

Library and Archives Canada Cataloguing in Publication

Title: XY-girls and more stories / Derwin Mak.
Names: Mak, Derwin, 1963- author
Description: Includes bibliographical references.
Identifiers: Canadiana (print) 20250173190 | Canadiana (ebook) 20250173255 | ISBN 9781998795222
  (softcover) | ISBN 9781998795239 (EPUB)
Subjects: LCGFT: Science fiction. | LCGFT: Short stories.
Classification: LCC PS8626.A4225 X92 2025 | DDC C813/.6—dc23

Content warnings: Blood ("Willpower"), death (various), gun violence ("Flying Devils"), sexual assault ("All Dancers Go to Heaven")

To Jim Wong-Chu (1949-2017)
Co-Founder of the Asian Canadian Writers' Workshop

Jim, thank you for inviting the science fiction and fantasy writers into the Asian Canadian literary community.

Contents

Ham and Cheese and Other Observations

Derwin Mak is not someone who draws attention to himself while simultaneously living the kind of life that attracts attention. He's quiet, soft spoken, and although I've never seen him dressed down in the ubiquitous SFF uniform of jeans and a T-shirt, I have seen him costumed as such an excellent replica of Jessica Rabbit (from the movie *Who Framed Roger Rabbit*) that I wasn't aware it was him until he spoke. He has master's degrees in Accounting and in Military Studies, is a chartered accountant, and writes non-fiction on a variety of subjects as well as award-winning science fiction. There's a lot going on beneath the surface.

Between 2004 and 2018, Derwin was nominated for six Aurora Awards—the Canadian Science Fiction and Fantasy Association's awards for excellence in the genre—and won two. In 2004, "The Siren Stone" was nominated for best short-form work in English and in 2006 "Transubstantiation" won for best short-form work in English. He was also nominated for long-form work in English in 2008 for *The Moon Under Her Feet*, won in 2011 for *The Dragon and the Stars* in the category "other work in English", short-form nominated in 2015 for "Mecha-Jesus", and nominated for related work in 2018 for *Where the Stars Rise: Asian Science Fiction and Fantasy*.

Two of the stories on that list are in this collection: Aurora nominated "The Siren Stone" and Aurora winner "Transubstantiation".

"The Siren Stone" is an almost old-fashioned, Bradbury-esque tale of asteroids and spacers and tying up loose ends with the dead. "Transubstantiation", however... Most sf authors either ignore humanity's religious preoccupations, or they blur the details into a generic "faith". This story embraces it. When a character transports the Host (communion wafers) through a barely understood device, that device transubstantiates (the process of bread and wine becoming the actual body and blood of Christ) into a physical manifestation. Jesus is back—as Jessica, a teenage girl in a Catholic schoolgirl outfit. Definitely a tricky concept to pull off, but Jessica's so *joyous* that it works. Science, faith, and the evidence of our own eyes (which can be both science and/or faith) battle it out as Jessica tries to complete her mission.

If you have any background in Christianity, you have to love her reaction after the salmon fillets miracle.

"Thank you," Jessica said, grinning. "I'm very good with fish."

At first glance, it seems these two stories have little to do with the title stories of the collection, that being the stories of the XY-girls, until, that is, "Wedding on Southern Comfort", the fourth of the XY-girl stories, when the same accidental transubstantiation brings Jessica back and she matter-of-factly points out, *"Transubstantiation, transfiguration, transgender."*

The XY-girls themselves are exactly what it says on the label. Transgender women who have come to the planet Southern Comfort because of a military contagion that targets and kills people with XX chromosomes. Does everyone accept them? Of course not, humanity will always throw up a few unmitigated assholes, but the women stand together and overcome because no one gets to tell them who they are. In fact, they make it quite clear that everyone—androids, weapon systems, Jessica—should be the person they believe they are and not settle for being the person someone else says they are.

"A Girl Like Us", the second of the XY-girls stories (order is important because these stories are chronological and build on each other) has my favourite interchange in the entire collection. Business is slow so Crystal, a sex worker, ends up cruising the bar...

Then she turned to Carl and purred into his ear. "Do you want to have some fun again? What would you like today?"

Carl shrugged and said, "A ham and cheese sandwich?"

Sometimes, you just want lunch.

At a time when transgender rights and transgender people are under attack around the world, these are stories we need.

When women returned to Southern Comfort, they all had XY chromosomes.

Because transgender women are women.

The five post XY-girl stories include:

"Willpower", a different take on vampires—and different is difficult given the multitude of vampire varieties out there—with a working class protagonist and a truly obnoxious fanboy.

"Bite me, turn me into a vampire!" he demanded.

"You're an idiot!" I replied.

"Flying Devils", a quiet, almost elegant piece written for a Chinese themed steampunk anthology where it's made clear that history looks entirely different from the viewpoint of the colonized.

"The Room Where We Hid", in spite of being in a collection that includes the resurrection of Jesus as a teenage girl, is quite possibly one of the weirdest things

I've ever read. Which isn't that surprising when you consider it includes *Pence: An American Musical, Winner of 11 Tony Awards* and time travel. Time travel itself isn't intrinsically weird, but this particular application...

"The House of Hagfish", fact-based science fiction by way of the fashion industry. I, personally, admire Derwin's restraint in not calling it "What's It All About, Alfie".

And "All Dancers Go to Heaven", about making peace with your dead, thematically revisiting "The Siren Stone", the first story in the collection. Rather than "Siren"'s space opera and empathic geology, this final format is strongly rooted in both science and human frailty. In a collection involving different styles, different challenges, different points of view, there's a lot to appreciate about a story order that takes the reader back where they began; albeit here at the end, things are a little more sophisticated and a lot more dangerous. But ultimately, there's still the chance to say unsaid words.

There's still hope.

Is it possible to sum up *XY-Girls and More Stories* in a few words? The sort of words that Cathy, the marketing director in "The House of Hagfish", could have stencilled onto a slime-eel T-shirt?

Kind? Yes. Accepting? Yes. Aware? Yes.

Derwin Mak makes weird work? Absolutely.

Still waters run deep.

Tanya Huff
April 2025

The Siren Stone

The Siren Stone

*   *   *

Colonel Matthew Chang sat aboard the spaceship *Long Island* and stared at the sensor map, which showed asteroid 20 521 Odette de Proust flying steadily towards Space Station Reagan—and the two hundred and ninety people he'd had to leave there.

A video transmission from General Boyd on Olympus appeared on a monitor.

"Colonel," said Boyd, "all our fleet—what's left after the Mars disaster—is still carrying refugees away from Olympus. The soonest any ship can get to Space Station Reagan is seven weeks."

"Odette will hit Reagan in six," said Chang plainly.

"Are you confident the demolition crew will blow up the asteroid well before that?" Boyd asked.

Chang shook his head. "They're still behind schedule. Two days now. Something's wrong." In the asteroid demolition business, rock blasters did not linger on an asteroid by choice. If they were late, they had run into trouble. A failed bomb, a premature explosion, a crashed ship, a collision with another asteroid, an injured crew... there were endless possibilities on how the mission could fail.

But these problems occurred on asteroids that wobbled erratically in orbits crowded with other rocks. They seldom occurred on asteroids like Odette, rocks that rotated smoothly in orbits with few neighbours.

"Rock Blasters, Inc. are the best in the business," said Boyd. "But if they've failed, you and the *Long Island* must be in position to blow up the asteroid."

"I should be evacuating the station. It's not worth risking anyone—" Chang protested. "We're not the experts—"

"I'll take full responsibility. I've put the order in writing," said Boyd. "Remember, the *Long Island* holds only ten people. Time isn't on your side—to save the personnel or the station itself. That's why I'm sending you to make sure that asteroid is destroyed. It's the only way to save all three hundred people."

After Boyd's transmission ended, Chang muttered, "We should've blown up Odette years ago. Those stupid civil servants don't take anything seriously until it becomes a crisis."

A lieutenant turned to Chang. "Sir," said the lieutenant, "we've re-established contact with the *Rocky Road*."

"Finally," said Chang. "What's going on now?"

"The crew is still acting crazy. They insist there are people living on the asteroid."

"Impossible," Chang growled. "How can anyone live on an airless rock?"

The lieutenant pointed at a monitor. "We're getting a transmission from the blasters now, sir."

On the monitor, the image of Andrew Lundman appeared, beamed from his ship the *Rocky Road*, now on Odette.

"Lundman, when are you going to blow up that rock?" said Chang.

"Not while there are people here," said Andrew.

For Andrew Lundman, owner of Rock Blasters, Inc. and captain of the *Rocky Road*, the project had seemed clear and simple: land on Odette, bore a hole into its core, plant a couple nuclear bombs, leave, and detonate the bombs. Odette would break into pieces of varied trajectories instead of slamming into Space Station Reagan six weeks from now.

Scavengers would follow to pick up the chunks of iron ore and pay a commission of five million gold units to Rock Blasters, Inc. Along with the twenty million gold units for blowing up the asteroid, Rock Blasters, Inc. would make a good profit.

20 521 Odette de Proust, named after a character from the novel *Swann's Way* and the novelist who created her, should have been a routine assignment. Odette was small and deemed safe enough that the United Nations Committee On Asteroid and Meteor Collisions had simply outsourced the job to Rock Blasters, Inc. On schedule, Andrew Lundman, George Hodding, and Ed Benton had landed on Odette without problems. Just another asteroid demolition. Or so they'd thought.

The first ghost had appeared when they were drilling into the asteroid. Andrew remembered the moment in every detail. They all did.

"Oh, God, look over there!" George shouted.

Ed gasped and pointed at the figure. "What's that?"

"Then you see her too?" demanded George.

Andrew turned off the drill. "I see it too," he said. "What is it? An alien?"

"No, it's Rachel," said George, both mystified and excited. "Rachel, my wife."

As he watched the figure walk closer, George muttered, "Rachel, Rachel. But Rachel is dead."

Andrew turned and stared straight at her so that his

helmet camera would capture her image. "Reagan Mission Control, there's another person on the asteroid. I'm aiming my helmet camera at her. Do you see her?"

"Negative, Lundman," Mission Control replied warily from Space Station Reagan. "We don't see any person other than you and your crew."

George began walking towards Rachel. As he passed by, Andrew saw the dumbfounded look on George's face and the hesitant way he approached Rachel.

Mission Control addressed George: "Mr. Hodding, why are you moving away from the drill operation?"

"Investigating an anomaly," said George as he approached Rachel, who was now smiling.

Rachel put her arms around him. "Oh, George, it's been too long," she cooed. "Don't look so shocked. Look happy."

"Rachel, how—how on Earth did you get here?" George blurted.

"We're not on Earth," Rachel reminded him. "Just hold me for a little while."

Over his helmet radio, Andrew heard George and Rachel talk. "Mission Control, Hodding is talking to his wife. Do you hear them?" he asked.

"Negative on that. We hear Hodding talking to someone, but we don't hear anyone talking back to him," said Mission Control. "What's going on over there?"

Even if she were alive, she should have been dead because she had no spacesuit and no air. Instead of any protection from the cold and vacuum of space, she wore a red jacket and short black dress and high heels. It was the outfit she had worn on their first date twenty years ago.

She also looked as young as she had been on their first date. Behind her, the stars shone like bright white pinpricks against the black fabric of space. The searchlight from the *Rocky Road* lit half her face, leaving the other half in shadow.

"George, it's so wonderful to see you again," she repeated.

George shook his head. How could she talk through the vacuum of space, and how could he hear her voice on his helmet radio? How could her wavy black hair blow in a wind that couldn't exist?

"Rachel, is it really you?"

Rachel smiled. "In the flesh."

George reached out and touched her again. She was solid.

"How can you stand there without a spacesuit, how can you talk to me?"

Rachel shrugged. "I don't know. I was suddenly here. I don't know how I got here or how I can live here." She swung her arms around and danced. "But I feel so alive!"

Even though you died seven years ago, remembered George.

"George, how is Megan?" she asked.

"Megan's well. She turned fifteen a month ago. Listens to those Euro-rock groups. She got an A in English. Her teachers like her..." he rambled.

Rachel squealed. "Oh, how I wish I could see her grow up! And how about Crystal?"

George smiled. "She's well too. Crystal's an athlete, pretty good for a twelve-year-old. Came in second at a school track and field meet. She got a ribbon."

Rachel pointed at the *Rocky Road*. "Can we go inside the ship? Did you bring photos of the girls? I want to see them!"

As they walked to the ship, George wondered how he would tell his wife's ghost that he had betrayed her.

Ed's father, who had died of lung cancer five years ago, appeared next. Ed had seen photos of his dad's last days, when he looked scrawny and wasted by disease inside an ill-fitting green hospital gown. But here on Odette, he looked healthy and fit, as he was in Ed's childhood, and wore his favourite red plaid shirt and blue jeans.

Ed walked slowly, cautiously, to his dad. Ed felt his throat go dry with fear and surprise, but he managed to talk.

"Dad, how did you get here?" Ed asked.

"I dunno. Suddenly appeared here. Glad I'm alive again, though."

"So you know—you know that you're—dead?" Ed asked.

His dad threw a pebble. It soared silently through the beam of light from Ed's flashlight and into the black depths of space.

Dad nodded. "Yeah, I know I'm supposed to be dead. I don't know how or why I'm here with you."

The final ghost to appear to the rock blasters was Sally, Andrew's sweetheart at the University of Oregon. She had died when terrorists bombed her train in their last year at university. Yet on Odette, Sally was alive and well, as young as she had been in her senior year, wearing the white, green and yellow uniform of a University of Oregon cheerleader.

"Go, Ducks!" she yelled, referring to the University of Oregon's football team. After dropping her pom-poms to the ground, she jumped into a pike, a jump where she kicked her legs up parallel to the ground and bent at the waist to touch her toes. When she landed in front of Andrew, a small cloud of rock dust rose from her feet.

With a gasp, Andrew stumbled and fell backwards onto the ground. Up and down his spine, he felt both the heat of shock and the cold of fear. As he looked up at Sally, he saw and heard her laugh.

"Klutzy, just like at the spring dance! You haven't changed a bit!" she teased him. She bent and reached down to help him get up on his feet. He felt her solid hands grab his arm.

"Hey, Andy, let's go into the ship," she suggested. "You can take your spacesuit off in there. You'll be more comfortable. Yeah." She smiled. "Why don't you take some clothes off?"

Back aboard the *Rocky Road*, Andrew took off his spacesuit and led Sally to the control room. Used to a mere three-man crew, Andrew suddenly felt crowded in the control room, with George and Rachel holding hands in one corner, Ed and his dad huddled over a monitor at another area, and now he and Sally walking into the room.

Andrew had never seen George's green eyes so happy and bright as now, as Rachel ran her hands through his brown hair. Andrew also noticed that Ed's blond hair was thinning in the same spot, at the back of his head, where his dad had gone bald.

He turned around and saw Sally put her pom-poms down beside a computer console. As she sat down in a chair and stretched, he noticed how life-like these ghosts were. Unlike the transparent spirits of horror movies and stories, these looked opaque and felt solid.

He saw his reflection in a shiny metal control console. Gray hair, induced by time and hard living. He'd aged so much since Sally died. What a contrast with her ghost's hair, still as blonde and shiny as it had been in college.

"How can you exist?" Andrew demanded. "Without air? Without food? Without, uh—"

"Without life?" said Sally. "Yes, I know I'm supposed to be dead. I don't know how I got here. But why does it matter? We can just pick up where we left off." She rose from the chair, put her arms around Andrew's shoulders, pulled his lips towards hers, and kissed him. It was a deep, wet kiss, full of love and longing and hunger.

Andrew gripped her and returned the kiss. Her skin felt warm and soft and smelled of the lilac perfume she had worn on their last date, two weeks before she died.

On Space Station Reagan, Mission Control still could not see Sally, Rachel, and Ed's dad through the *Rocky Road*'s cameras, nor could Mission Control hear the ghosts' voices. After Mission Control and Andrew had argued for hours, Colonel Chang, the station's commander, was called in. Like his staff, the colonel could not see the ghosts either.

"All I see are you, Hodding, and Benton," said Chang. "I can't see anyone else."

"How can you not see them? They're right here beside us," said Andrew. He turned to Sally. "Sally, say something to the Colonel."

"I can't explain this, sir, but I am here," said Sally.

Chang said nothing. Hadn't he heard Sally? Andrew wondered.

Finally, Chang spoke. "Lundman, who were you talking to a minute ago?"

"Sally," said Andrew. "Didn't you hear her?"

"Hear who?" Chang asked. "I heard nobody."

Over at another corner, Rachel sighed. "It's so stuffy in here, George. Can I go back outside? I feel more comfortable on the asteroid surface."

"Soon, Rachel, soon," said George as he rubbed Rachel's shoulder to soothe her.

On the monitor, Chang looked puzzled. "Hodding, what are you doing? Rubbing the air?"

"My wife," George said. "Her shoulders are a bit sore."

"Your wife? But Abby's in New York," Chang protested. "She called Mission Control last night."

"Not Abby. Rachel," explained George. "I was talking to Rachel."

"Rachel?" Chang said. "No, that's impossible."

Ed's dad waved dismissively at Chang's image on the monitor. "He doesn't believe we're here," he said. "He just wants you to blow up the asteroid."

"Don't worry, Dad. We won't blow it up," said Ed.

"Mr. Benton, did I hear you tell someone that you're not going to blow up the asteroid?" Chang erupted.

Ed nodded. "You heard correctly," he mumbled.

Andrew looked at Chang's image on the monitor. "Colonel, I know how incredible this all seems to you. We're very shocked and surprised, too. I think we shouldn't destroy the asteroid until we've had a chance to study it."

Chang looked alarmed. "You *must* blow up that rock."

"We can't blow up this rock. It's different."

"What do you think you've found?" Chang protested. "A Siren Stone? You know they're just a deep space myth."

As mermaids had been to ancient mariners, Siren Stones were to modern spacers. They were a way to explain the space crews who turned crazy and disappeared without a trace. In the vast deepness of space, what lonely spacer could resist the beautiful spirits who haunted the Siren Stones? Andrew hadn't taken the myth seriously—until now.

"Maybe there's some truth behind the myth," said Andrew. "That's more reason to preserve the rock until we learn more about it."

"What about the three hundred people on Space Station Reagan?" said Chang.

"We can still save them. Let's not blow up the asteroid. Let's move it instead," Andrew suggested eagerly. "We'll plant bombs on the rock's surface, and when we set off the explosives, the blast will nudge the rock into a new orbit, one that won't threaten Reagan or anything else."

Chang shook his head. "Attempts to move asteroids into safe orbits have a lousy success rate. The procedure is too complicated. That's why we blow up the damn rocks. I can't take the risk. I won't gamble with three hundred lives."

"We *can* move the asteroid into a safe orbit," Andrew insisted.

"You have your orders, Mr. Lundman. Blow up that rock."

Ed and his dad went outside the ship, back to the airless surface of Odette. Ed wore a spacesuit, but Dad did not.

"How is the family?" asked Dad.

"Mom's okay. She moved to California about two months ago," Ed replied. "Joan's not at Georgetown anymore. She chose a contract position at Stanford because she likes it there. And Trini and I had a son last year. His name is Norman."

"Wow, I'm a grandfather! Whoo-ee!" his dad yelled. "Too bad I couldn't be there for the boy, Norman's his name? It's bad enough that I missed a few years of your life, and now I'm not around for my grandson's."

A few years of your life: the words echoed in Ed's ears.

Ed's dad quit his job at the car factory when Ed was five years old and spent the next five years moving from one bad business deal to another. During that time, Dad never had money, and Mom never smiled. After five years of financial failures, he had simply walked out. To support Ed and Joan, Mom worked two jobs, one cleaning an office building and another waiting at a restaurant.

Dad returned five years later, paler and thinner than ever before, but with a small amount he had earned in odd jobs in California. He was ready to lead his family again, he announced sheepishly. Mom wouldn't take him back, though. Without any argument, he gave her the money and moved into an apartment across town. He had exiled himself from his family when they had wanted him, and now they were exiling him when he wanted them.

He came to visit them from time to time, though. By the time Ed left to work on the Moon, Mom and Joan were just warming up to Dad again, starting to close the chasm in the family. Eventually, Mom and Joan forgave Dad for his disappearance. About seven years after his return, Dad and Mom renewed their vows; in essence, got married again, with Joan as bridesmaid. But Ed was away on the Moon and couldn't come back. He had said that his employer had no room for him on the next shuttle back to Earth. In fact, he had not even asked for a seat on the flight.

Ed visited his mom and dad only twice in the next five years. Unlike Mom and Joan, he could not forgive his dad for leaving him when he was ten years old.

And then his dad discovered he had cancer. When Ed got the space transmission from his mother, he realized that if he wanted to see his father again, he was running out of time. But Ed was on a rock blasting team heading for Mars. By the time the ship returned to Earth, his dad had already died.

Ed wanted to tell his dad that all is forgiven—but was this ghost really his dad?

"Before you arrived here, what was the last thing you remember?" Ed asked.

"Dying," said Dad.

Ed looked at the stars above them. *Is this what heaven looks like?* he asked himself. *Is that where they were? In heaven?*

"INCOMING TRANSMISSION" flashed on the monitor. Andrew watched the words fade out and Colonel Chang's image fade in. The transmission was coming from the *Long Island*; Chang had left Space Station Reagan and was heading to Odette.

"You are now three days behind schedule on the demolition of Odette," Chang said. "Do you intend to blow it up?"

"I repeat, not while there are people here," said Andrew.

"There are no people there!" said Chang. He sounded agitated; Andrew had never seen him unnerved before.

Chang tried a more reasoning tone. "They're all in your imagination," he said.

Andrew looked at Sally. She straddled the floor, legs wide apart, and raised her arms over her shoulder to touch her feet. That was how cheerleaders stretched their hamstrings and calf muscles. He remembered seeing her do those stretches on a football field in Oregon many years ago.

She looked so warm, so lively. When they had kissed, he realized that he had never kissed as passionately as with her. Sally was a real woman again.

Andrew turned back to Chang. "No, sir, they are not our imagination. They are real."

"So are the two hundred and ninety people now on Space Station Reagan," Chang reminded him grimly. "That's two hundred and ninety dead if you don't blow up Odette."

"We're working on a way to move the asteroid into a safe orbit," Andrew said. "I'm confident we'll succeed."

"You know that's the riskier procedure." Chang scowled from the monitor. "You leave me no choice, Mr. Lundman. I will demolish Odette and arrest you and your crew."

"Arrest us?" questioned Andrew. "On what grounds?"

"*United States Space Stations Code*, section 52, 'Willful Endangerment of a Space Station,'" Chang stated. "Minimum sentence, ten years. Don't make this mistake. Obey your orders."

George and Rachel strolled outside on the asteroid's surface, talking about the girls. Rachel laughed when she heard how her daughters had grown up.

"Oh, how I wish I could have seen all of it," she said finally. "Oh, if only I could have been there for them."

George nodded. "That has been the greatest sadness of my life, that you aren't there to see them grow up."

Rachel shook her head. "George, don't feel sad anymore. I'll always be with all three of you."

"Are you in heaven?" George asked.

She took his hand and placed it over his heart. "I'm right here, in your heart."

"You always have been," said George as they continued walking.

"I got to hand it to you, George," said Rachel. "It must have been hard to raise two girls by yourself for seven years."

George sighed. "There's something I have to tell you. I wasn't alone all that time."

"Oh?" said Rachel. "My mother has been helping out?"

"No. I remarried four years ago. Her name is Abby."

Rachel stopped walking and looked at George. "Abby. Is she a nice girl?"

"Yes."

"And how does she treat the girls?"

George said nothing.

"George, how does she treat the girls?" Rachel asked again, anxiously.

George took in a deep breath. "Extremely well. Abby loves them deeply, treats them as if they were her own daughters."

Rachel crossed her arms and shifted her gaze to a rock beside them, as if to avoid looking him in the eye.

"Oh, I see," she said softly.

For Andrew, Sally's death had ended all of their plans: getting married, getting jobs, and starting a family.

"So you never went to that job you had lined up after graduation, the one with the City of Eugene?" Sally asked.

"No, I went into the Navy instead," said Andrew. Without Sally, he had joined the U.S. Navy after graduation, hoping to fight the terrorists who had blown up her train.

He had felt a brief sense of joy when Navy missiles killed the last terrorist commander in Sudan, but it couldn't erase the sadness of losing Sally. Afterwards, he volunteered for service on the furthest, loneliest space station, and later, went into rock blasting.

"No children?" asked Sally. "Why not?"

"Hard to do with my job," said Andrew. "I'm always travelling for months in space. No time to meet someone, much less raise a kid."

He paused. He knew he had been making excuses for years.

"But remember, I *had* wanted children," he continued. "That's what we had planned. We would get married after graduation. We'd live in Eugene. We would get jobs there. I would be a road engineer. You would be an accountant for the bakery. We would have children."

Sally smiled. "We had our whole lives planned, didn't we?"

"We sure did, girl," said Andrew.

"Things didn't go according to plan, did they?"

"No, they didn't." Words came out of Andrew in a rush. "I was looking forward to life with you. It was the most important thing in my life. Instead, I wound up alone, no kids, living anywhere but in Eugene, blasting space rocks for a living. It wasn't what we had planned."

Ed and his dad passed by the drill, now motionless but still stuck into the asteroid. His dad pointed at the drill.

"Is it deep enough to plant those nuclear bombs?" his dad asked.

"We're not going to do it," Ed protested. "How can we? We would kill you."

"I'm already dead," said his dad. "But think of yourself. That military spacecraft will be here any day now. If you don't blow up Odette, they'll arrest you and blow it up anyway."

"We'll fight them," Ed declared. "I lost you once, I

won't lose you again!"

"Ed, you can't have me forever. Stop clinging to me. Son, why do you keep clinging on to me?"

"Because, because," Ed started. He couldn't force the words out of his mouth. But it was time to tell him.

"Because I never got to tell you that I forgive you for leaving me and Joan and Mom," Ed said.

His dad put his hand on Ed's shoulder. "I know, son. I've known all this time."

A tear ran down Ed's cheek. "You mean, you died knowing I had forgiven you?"

"Sure did. Don't let that bother you anymore."

Ed heard a clicking sound over his helmet radio. He turned around and looked at the drill's sensor box. The sensor box's lights were lit up in red, blue, and green. He knelt down to read the display.

"My, oh my," said Ed. "Dad, you've got to see this."

He turned around to look at his dad, but his dad was not there.

Rachel uncrossed her arms. George remembered that she always crossed her arms when she was angry. Had she been angry? Was she still?

"Since Abby is the girls' mother now," she said, "does she do everything that a mother should do?"

"Yes," said George.

"Do the girls love her?"

"Very much. You should see the three of them together."

"Ohhhh..."

"Oh, no, I shouldn't have said that," George said. "I'm

sorry, so very sorry."

"No! Don't be sorry!" Rachel cried. "Oh, George, I'm so happy for you and Megan and Crystal! And Abby!"

She threw her arms around him and squeezed him. Even through his spacesuit, he could feel that it was the tightest hug she had ever given him.

"I'm thrilled that my family is happy," Rachel said. "Why wouldn't I want to hear that?"

George took a deep breath. "I felt I had betrayed you by marrying Abby. I'm sorry, I'm sorry."

"Stop apologizing." She kissed his helmet visor. "You haven't betrayed me. If anything, you've done exactly what I've wanted. You've raised our girls to be happy, confident young women. You've created a warm, caring family."

"Really?"

"If you're looking for my permission to love Abby and raise the girls with her, you have it. I wouldn't have it any other way."

They hugged, they kissed, and this time, George felt her lips press against his.

That's impossible, he thought. *I have my helmet on. Oh, God, I better still have my helmet on!*

He felt his helmet with one gloved hand; he was still wearing it. He looked around. He didn't see Rachel anywhere.

Inside the ship, Ed scrolled through the graphs and figures appearing on his computer monitor. A three-dimensional computer graphic of Odette appeared, showing how animated waves poured from the core of the asteroid.

"Incredible!" Ed exclaimed. "The drill's sensor detected electrochemical signals below the asteroid's surface. The asteroid is hollow, and it's emitting electrochemical signals."

"Like a battery?" said Andrew.

"More like a brain. Look at this." Ed pointed at the animated image. "It's also absorbing electrochemical signals."

"From where? The only other source of electrochemical signals are us, from our brains," said Andrew.

"I can't prove it without further tests, but I think the asteroid is absorbing our brain waves and sending its own signals into our brains," Ed guessed.

"Holy smokes. Sally, Rachel, your Dad. Could the ghosts be based on our memories and thoughts?"

Ed nodded. "That's possible. Dad's ghost knew how I've felt since he died."

They heard the sound of metal doors swinging open and boots pound upon steel as George emerged from the airlock. After entering the control room, he began to take off his spacesuit.

"Funny thing happened out there," he said. "One minute, Rachel is standing there, hugging me, completely alive—"

"No," Andrew interrupted. "Rachel isn't alive. The *asteroid* is. This is a Siren Stone."

Aboard the *Long Island*, Colonel Chang returned to his usual calm, if humourless, mode after hearing Andrew's explanation of the ghosts. To Andrew, this was as close as Chang would get to showing happiness.

"Finally. Now that you've determined that there are no living human beings on Odette, proceed to destroy it," said Chang.

"Colonel, we still can't do that," said Andrew.

Chang glared at them through the thousands of miles of space. "Why not?"

"The asteroid is absorbing our brain waves and emitting its own brain waves. It's some kind of living being. We can't—we shouldn't—kill it."

"It's a rock!" Chang snapped. "Unlike Space Station Reagan. Reagan has two hundred and ninety permanent residents: scientists, tradespeople, artisans, farmers, settlers, and children born on the station. Don't forget that Reagan isn't just a space station; it's their home. You have to blow up the rock!"

"We've been working on the calculations for moving the asteroid. We'll know how many explosives to use, where to place them, and when to detonate them. We can do it," Andrew insisted.

"No, you won't. You're under arrest!" Chang yelled.

Andrew cut off the audio link to the *Long Island*. He could still see, if not hear, how Chang continued barking orders to restore the audio link.

"George, have you finished the prep for shifting the orbit?" Andrew asked.

"I've figured it out," said George, "but it's a complicated calculation. If I missed a variable, it might not work."

"It's a chance we'll have to take," said Andrew. "Ed, how's our flight plan coming?"

"Just finished it," said Ed, looking up from his computer monitor.

"Good, good," said Andrew. He moved towards the crew quarters. "Excuse me for a minute. There's one last thing I have to discuss with Sally."

"We should have died together," said Andrew.

"No, no," Sally said. "We should have *lived* together."

"But we didn't," he argued, "and that's what's haunted me for years. Life didn't go the way I had wanted. No house in Eugene, no job with the city, no cottage in the summer, no vacations to Disney World, no taking our kids to see their grandparents, no kids at all—"

"Hush," Sally ordered. "Listen to me. You've had a good life without me. You've beaten the enemies of our country. You've saved lives by blowing up asteroids before they hit people. You've been all over the world and beyond, from Oregon to Polynesia to the Moon to the asteroid belt. You've done things, seen things, helped and saved people. Don't ever think that your life was a waste of time."

"Even if I've lived it without you, Sally?" Andrew said.

"Even without me," she replied, smiling. "You've gotten on with your life, even if you don't know it. Stop mourning my loss and the loss of what could have been. What you made instead is great and wonderful."

"That's what I finally needed to hear," he said as his throat began to go dry, as the years of sadness ended with this moment of joy.

She kissed him, in the same deep, passionate way they had kissed in their college years.

Then suddenly, she was gone.

After they finished planting the bombs, Andrew, George, and Ed scrambled aboard the *Rocky Road*. An hour later, the *Rocky Road* soared away from the asteroid. They'd go beyond the range of the blast before detonating the bombs, but do it soon enough to not endanger the oncoming *Long Island*.

A day later, the *Rocky Road* reached a safe distance from Odette. As planned, the *Long Island* was still out of range. Andrew smiled; they had outrun Chang.

Andrew typed the detonation code into the transmitter. He hit the "SEND" button.

"It's done," Andrew said. He began the countdown under his breath.

"We have a strong signal from the probe watching Odette," said Ed. He sent the asteroid's image to all the monitors.

They watched the bombs explode. Although fragments of rock flew in all directions, most of the asteroid stayed intact. Amidst a grey cloud of pulverized stone, slowly but surely Odette shifted its path.

Aboard the *Long Island*, Colonel Chang and his crew silently watched Odette shift into its new orbit. Never before had they seen an asteroid move amidst a cloud of its own debris.

"This damn well better have worked," Chang said, breaking the silence.

"Colonel, your orders?" said Major Peters, the ship's first officer.

"Plot a course to intercept Odette in its new orbit," said Chang. "I want to be sure this trajectory is completely safe. We still might have to destroy it."

As the *Long Island* continued towards Odette, deep space probes monitored Odette and sent data to Space Station Reagan. With the data, asteroid trackers began mapping Odette's new orbit. Would Odette hit something sooner or later?

A day later, Mission Control sent the answer to Chang. "A one in a million chance, and they got it," he reported to General Boyd.

Back on Space Station Reagan, Mission Control sent the same relieved message to all ships and probes: Odette had changed its orbit and no longer threatened to strike Reagan or any other station.

The *Long Island* was preparing to head home, leaving Odette alone, when she received a distress signal from the *Rocky Road*. The rock blasters had returned to Odette for reasons unknown and now were in trouble. Calls to the *Rocky Road* only returned a recorded mayday message. Chang had no choice but to respond. What could be going wrong aboard the *Rocky Road* now?

Andrew looked around. George was telling Rachel about her mother's vacation to Spain last year. At his station, Ed explained to his dad how probes and beacons sent images back to Earth and travelling ships. George and Ed were making up for lost time with their loved ones, talking about family and friends, hopes and plans.

Sally, still dressed as a Ducks cheerleader, came back

into the control room. Andrew knew he could imagine her in other clothes, but he wanted to remember her this way. The college years had been the best time of their lives, when the present was full of life and happiness, when the future seemed eternally bright.

Sally sat down beside Andrew and took his hand. "Why did you return to us?" she asked.

"To bring Chang to the asteroid," said Andrew. "I've known Chang for several years, and he's always sad. I don't know why. Maybe it's someone in his past. If it is, he needs to come here."

Shortly after the *Long Island* landed on Odette, Colonel Chang and six commandos quietly boarded the *Rocky Road*. As the commandos took control of the engineering sections, Chang went to the control room.

Chang raised his helmet visor. "We received your distress signal," he said. "What's wrong, is anyone injured—oh, my God."

In addition to Andrew, George, and Ed, he saw other people on the ship: a woman in a red jacket, a man in blue jeans, and a girl in a cheerleader uniform.

"You're just figments of my imagination," Chang insisted.

"Captain Ross reporting for duty, sir!" someone announced from behind him.

Chang spun around. A soldier, dressed in green jungle combat camouflage, stood there. His name tag read "ROSS." He was unscratched and alive, the way he had been when Chang last saw him.

Chang put a hand on Ross's shoulder—his solid

shoulder.

Chang tried fighting back the tears, but a single drop rolled down his cheek.

"Oh, dear God, why can't you be real?" he asked. "Why couldn't I take you home to your wife? Instead, I had only your dog tags to take to her..."

One night in the U.S. camp in Haiti, Chang had heard strange sounds, like someone stumbling through the garbage dump just outside the camp. Chang had ordered Captain Warren Ross to investigate the sounds. As he walked into the garbage dump, Ross had stepped on a land mine and been blown to pieces. Ross had been married only ten months.

If only he hadn't ordered Ross to investigate the sounds...

Chang had never fully recovered from meeting Ross's wife Karen and their newborn son Daniel. He had given her Ross's dog tags, and soon afterwards, applied for space station service, away from Earth's fighting nations.

After Chang ordered the commandos to return to the *Long Island*, he talked to Ross in the control room, oblivious to the others, both living and dead. Finally, Chang heard the words he had needed to hear for nineteen years.

"Karen knew the risks, Major," Ross said, calling Chang by his rank during the Haitian War. "Her father and grandfather were both in the Army. She knew we could be killed in action anytime. I'm sure she never blamed the Army or you."

"Thank you, Captain," Chang said. "Let me say again that I was proud to have you under my command. I wish I had been able to tell you at the time."

Chang and Ross exchanged salutes. The colonel sighed and closed his eyes. When he opened his eyes, Ross was gone.

Sally, Rachel, and Dad left again, leaving the three rock blasters alone with their memories—and Colonel Chang.

"I'm going to drop the charges of wilful endangerment of a space station," said Chang, staring out the window at the stars above Odette.

Andrew joined Chang at the window. "Thank you, Colonel," said Andrew.

"It's the least I could do, considering you've lost five million gold units in scavengers' commissions," said Chang with a wry smile.

Andrew nodded. "That's a lot of money, but we can't put a value on this asteroid. It's priceless."

"And mysterious," said Chang. "We know nothing about it. Is it one of the legendary Siren Stones? Could there be more of them? Where did it come from? Did someone send it to us? Is it alive?"

"Do you think the asteroid is alive?" Andrew asked.

"I don't know," Chang answered, "but it doesn't matter. It does something wonderful, and that's what counts. You've done the human race a big favour."

"How's that?"

Chang gazed at the stars again. "You've saved something the human race desperately needs: a place where people can make peace with their pasts."

George and Ed joined them at the window. Up in the black sky, there seemed as many stars as there were lost souls in the human race, each wishing for a chance to say unsaid words.

"I have friends, family—we all do—who could be healed by coming here," said Chang. "Too bad it's so far from Earth."

"You brought more explosives, didn't you?" asked Andrew. "I think we can give Odette another nudge. Drop her in behind Mars, for instance. Not so close to Earth as to endanger anything, but close enough so people can come here."

"I have the explosives," said Chang. He gave Andrew a serious, questioning look. "Are you sure you can do it again?"

"Yes, I'm sure," said Andrew without hesitating. "We've done it once, we can do it again." Behind him, George and Ed nodded.

"Fine. You can have the explosives," Chang said. Then he became silent, deep in thought. "I have a problem, though," he said after his silence. "How will I explain this to General Boyd? He'll think I've gone crazy. I don't want to get discharged as a mental case."

"Don't worry about the General," Andrew said. "He'll understand after he comes here, like you did."

"Of course," said Chang with a smile. "And he will come here. This is a Siren Stone, after all."

About "The Siren Stone"

Thanks to Julie Czerneda again for inviting me to submit a story to an anthology about people working in space. She suggested the title "The Siren Stone". That was a great idea because it alluded to the sirens who sit on rocks and call sailors to their doom in Homer's *The Odyssey*.

I had not originally intended to create a universe with "The Siren Stone", but one grew out of it over time. An indirect sequel, the Aurora Award-winning story "Transubstantiation" (2005), led to two novels, *The Moon Under Her Feet* (2007) and *The Shrine of the Siren Stone* (2010). *The Shrine of the Siren Stone* had its own sequel, the short story "Mecha-Jesus" (2015), which appeared in *Mecha-Jesus and Other Stories* (2024).

Transubstantiation

The Catholic priest on the viewscreen looked bewildered. "So you're telling me that Jesus Christ, the Son of God, has returned as a Jewish girl in a Catholic schoolgirl's uniform on a space station in orbit around Mars?" said Father Kelly.

Paul Devane, director of Space Station Troika, looked back at the viewscreen and nodded. "That's who she says she is."

Paul heard footsteps on the metal floor of Troika's control room. He turned around and saw the teenaged girl standing by the entrance. The rhinestones on her silver tiara sparkled under a bright light above the entrance.

"You still don't believe me, do you?" she said.

Paul looked back at the viewscreen. "She's by the entrance. Do you see her? Did you hear her?"

The priest shook his head. "I don't see anyone standing by the doorway."

"But I can see her," Paul insisted.

"All right, maybe you can, and for some reason, I

can't," said Father Kelly. "Have you talked to her? What does she want?"

"She wants to crash our shuttlecraft onto the Martian surface," Paul said. "She thinks that's how God is going to create life on Mars."

All of Space Station Troika's sensors and cameras were aimed at the Martian surface below. As Troika orbited the planet, its crew searched for signs of survivors.

In Troika's control room, Paul Devane waited for the station to pass over Redsands Base. He looked at a shiny videoscreen and saw his reflection and cringed. Only forty years old, he looked like fifty, with grey streaks in his brown hair, a weary look in his eyes, and lines of age etched into his face. Living in space did that to some people.

He ran his hand through his greasy, dishevelled hair to try to comb it. He hadn't taken the time to wash his hair since the disaster on Mars.

He yawned and sighed. He hadn't slept much since he had killed that girl at Redsands Base.

The videoscreen suddenly flickered, and an image of Redsands Base replaced Paul's reflection.

Paul glanced at a woman wearing a yellow polo shirt with the Charging Duck mascot of the University of Oregon. Erin Malloy looked at him and turned back to her computer monitor. An aerial video image of a collapsed dome-shaped building appeared on the monitor. Nothing moved in the mangled mess of steel and plastic half-buried in loose dust and dirt. The only movement came from beside the dome: a geyser of water gushing from a pool created when geologists had dug into subsurface water.

"No body heat readings. There's nothing moving on the video," reported Erin. She turned away from her monitor. "There's nobody alive on Redsands."

Paul looked sadly at the video picture. "There were ten people down there. I was hoping to find at least one."

"Sorry, not at Redsands."

The video image began breaking up into static. "We're passing out of range of Redsands," Erin said.

"Thank you," Paul murmured as he returned to his chair and bit into a round hardtack cracker. The crumbs fell on his wrinkled blue shirt with the NASA logo.

All the combined nuclear weapons of Earth could not destroy the largest meteor to hit Mars in millions of years. The missiles and bombs had merely dented the rock. When the rock smashed into the Martian surface, it gouged out a gigantic crater, heated the surface a thousand degrees, and threw billions of tons of dust into the atmosphere. The shock wave and dust storm shook and smothered the Martian settlements. Now dozens of spaceships were evacuating the survivors to space stations in orbit around Mars.

Troika, being a small station carved out of a captured asteroid, had no room for refugees. Still, the disaster was keeping the three crew members busy. They usually surveyed the geography of Mars from their orbit, but now they had a new job: watching the Martian surface for signs of human life.

Another man approached Erin. She gave him a small smile. When Dr. Thomas Hall had arrived in Mars orbit a year ago, Erin had noticed how handsome the doctor was. A year later, he still looked like a buff, blond, Californian surfer dude. Living around Mars hadn't aged him prematurely, at least not yet.

He wore silver caduceus symbols of the medical profession on the collar of his clean, white shirt, and he looked at the brainscanner monitor in his hands. "The electrical activity in your frontal lobes went up while you were looking at the data coming from Mars," said Thomas.

"That's what's supposed to happen when I concentrate on something, right?" Erin said as she poured water into a pack of rehydratable tuna casserole. "God, this stuff is awful."

She looked at her reflection in the shiny metal control console. "This brainscanner is messing up my hair," she complained as she straightened the headpiece. It was a silvery band around her forehead with other bands arching over the top of her head. Small lights blinked on the bands.

"How long do I have to keep it on?" Erin asked.

"Another twenty-four hours," replied Thomas. "Then I'll have enough data. Is it uncomfortable?"

Erin shrugged and looked back at her reflection. "No, it's not too uncomfortable. It's lightweight. But I put waves into my hair to give it some body only to have you plunk this brainscanner on me."

"Ah, you still look beautiful, just like in that photo."

Erin glanced at a photo taped to her computer monitor: her wearing a white evening gown, silver tiara, and the sash of Miss Oregon. She was flanked by her Black American mother and her white Canadian father. They were all smiling on that night, when she had won the crown of Miss Oregon.

None of them could have predicted the tragedy that winning the beauty pageant would bring.

"Yeah, just like in the photo," she muttered, lost in her memories.

"Thanks for keeping the brainscanner on during the emergency," Thomas said. "This is a rare opportunity to study the neurological activity of deep space crews."

Erin looked up and smiled. "No problem. Scientific research: that's what we're here for."

Paul gazed grimly at the digital clock counting the seconds and minutes on his computer monitor. "It's been four days since we found anyone alive. There probably isn't anyone left."

"Probably not," Erin agreed.

"Are you okay?" Thomas asked Paul. "Get some rest. Doctor's orders."

Paul nodded as he slowly rose from his chair. "Maybe I should. I feel really tired."

He opened his eyes and looked at a small wooden icon that Troika's original crew, the Russians, had nailed to the wall. The multicoloured icon showed the Old Testament Trinity, the three angels who visited Abraham and his wife Sarah. In Eastern Orthodox tradition, the three angels represented God the Father, God the Son, and God the Holy Spirit.

When the United States took over Troika, Paul had decided to leave the icon on the wall despite Thomas's protests. "Oh, what harm can it do?" Paul had said. "It adds some charm to the place. Besides, it might bring us some good luck."

In a sense, Troika's crew had been lucky because the

meteor had missed them, but eighty-four people on the Martian colonies had not been so lucky. Whatever divine grace the icon attracted did not reach down to the Martian surface.

In his quarters, Paul called Father Raymond Kelly by video. Father Kelly lived on Space Station Exeter, which was circling Mars in an orbit lower than Troika's. Each week, Paul and Father Kelly would talk by video encoded to preserve privacy. Not even the Mars disaster could disrupt this sacrament.

The man on the video monitor wore the traditional black uniform of a Catholic priest and a European Space Agency badge. He was young for a priest, just forty-five years old, and though his face was still handsome and smooth, some of his brown hair had started turning white. The hardships of space colonization could age anyone prematurely.

"How are things on Exeter?" Paul asked.

"A bit messy and very busy," Father Kelly said. "We've got refugees all over the station. Our infirmary is overflowing with the injured, the medical staff is overworked, and we're running out of food."

"I offered our food supply to Bronson," Paul said.

"He'll want it, now that he's got more people than he had expected," said Father Kelly. "Okay, let's get down to business. Do you have anything to confess today?"

Paul cleared his throat. "Forgive me, Father, for I have sinned. I caused a woman to die three days ago."

He paused, took a deep breath, and continued: "She was on Redsands Base, and the interior of the dome building was on fire. She was trapped inside the dome. I tried to use the teleporter to take her out, but I failed."

Each Martian space station, surface base, and colony had a teleporter booth. An object would be placed in one booth, broken into an energy stream, transmitted to another booth, and rematerialize as the object: mass into energy into mass again. The technology was still in its primitive stage and prone to accidents, though. If spacers needed to send something important, they would send it by shuttlecraft or supply rocket, not by teleporter.

"Hush, Paul," Father Kelly ordered. "Bronson told me about Redsands. You don't have to confess to something that wasn't your fault."

Paul nodded but continued: "But it still bothers me. I tried to teleport her out of there. I knew the teleporter is safe only for non-living, inorganic matter. I knew I shouldn't have tried sending a human being by teleporter. But I tried anyway. Now she's just atoms scattered somewhere."

"You had no choice but to use the teleporter."

"I could have used the shuttlecraft."

"And you know why you didn't. You didn't have the time," Father Kelly reminded him. "There was plenty of pure oxygen on Redsands; the fire gutted the dome in twenty minutes. You couldn't have reached her in time."

"The University of Waterloo's been researching ways of making the teleporter safe for people. They say they might have developed a new program code for the teleporter, but we haven't received the new code yet," said Paul. "Maybe if I had a usable code—"

Father Kelly interrupted him. "But you didn't, and you

still don't, so stop speculating.

"Look at it this way," the priest suggested. "Be comforted in knowing that you had only one choice, and you had the courage to use it. She is with God now, and God does not blame you for her death, I'm sure."

Paul smiled weakly. "But I did violate transportation regulations by using the teleporter on a human being."

"Okay, if it will make you feel better, say three 'Hail Marys' as penance and consider yourself forgiven. Now be done with the matter." Father Kelly made the Sign of the Cross to bless Paul. "Now, anything else you want to discuss?"

"Yes. I haven't gone to Mass since I came to Troika a year ago," said Paul.

"It does get difficult to go to the only church out here. You do watch my televised Mass, though."

"It's wonderful, and I really enjoy watching it, but for me, something's missing. I miss receiving the Eucharist."

"The body of Christ," said the priest, referring to the Roman Catholic belief that consecrated bread becomes the body of Jesus.

"A TV show is no substitute for the real thing, especially after all that's happened," Paul said.

"Spiritual healing through the Eucharist. There must be some way I can help you," Father Kelly mused. He paused for a moment, pondering an idea.

"I can try teleporting a jar of consecrated bread to you."

Paul look startled. "You're going to try that?"

"You think there'll be an accident? Actually, accidents occur in only ten percent of attempts to teleport organic matter. That means I still have a ninety percent chance of sending the bread to you by teleporter."

"But it's the body of Christ."

"If anyone can survive the teleporter, it will be Jesus."

Paul returned to the control room just as another video message from Space Station Exeter popped onto his computer monitor. The image of Alfred Bronson, Director of Space Station Exeter, appeared.

Bronson, with his brown hair looking dishevelled and greasy, stared sleepily. Exeter's crew had been working over eighteen hours each day since the disaster on Mars.

"What can we do for you?" Paul asked.

"You said you have some food to spare," Bronson said.

"We've got enough for ourselves and nine extra people for two months, which is when the re-supply ship arrives."

"Every bit of food is essential. Could you please give us what you have in excess of your own needs?"

"We'll be happy to. How do we transport it? We can't use the teleporter," Paul said.

"No, no, even with the alleged ninety percent safety rate on organic matter, I don't want to risk it on food," Bronson agreed.

"Can you send a shuttlecraft to pick it up?"

Bronson shook his head. "Not for a week. Both our shuttlecrafts are in the search for survivors at the planet's poles. Can you fly over here in your shuttlecraft?"

"We could, but our shuttlecraft is low on fuel. We'll have to wait until we're at our closest position to Exeter. Then we'll have enough fuel for a one-way flight."

"How much longer until you're in range?"

Paul typed a few commands at his keyboard, and computer animation of the orbits of the two space stations appeared on his monitor. "Twenty-four standard hours."

"That will be okay, but what about you? Since it'll be a one-way flight, you'll have to stay here."

"Don't worry about three extra mouths to feed. We'll bring our own food supply, and we'll do work." Then, with resignation, Paul said, "I think NASA will let us abandon Troika. We've done all we can do to find survivors."

After Paul ended his video call with Bronson, he heard a soft chime. The message "TELEPORTER CARGO INCOMING" appeared on his monitor.

"That must be the consecrated bread from Father Kelly," Paul said.

"You're receiving consecrated bread from Father Kelly?" Thomas asked.

"Yes. I haven't received the Eucharist for months."

"It's all very silly if you ask me."

"Nobody asked you," Paul replied.

Erin looked surprised as she read the data from the teleporter. "That's a lot of bread: forty-nine kilograms or about one hundred and eight pounds."

"What?" Paul blurted. He looked at the computer monitor. "That's impossible. I'm going to the teleporter booth."

"I'll come with you," Erin said as she followed Paul out of the control room.

*   *   *

As they approached the teleporter booth, Erin gasped. Paul suddenly stopped and stared in surprise at the booth.

There was no jar of consecrated bread.

Instead, a slim teenaged girl stood in the teleporter booth. She looked pretty, had her reddish-brown hair tied into a ponytail, and wore a white shirt, green school tie, and a green tartan schoolgirl skirt. She wore a silver tiara with glittering gems.

"I haven't seen that uniform in years," Erin remarked.

Paul stared at the stranger. "What is it?"

"St. Joseph's College School in Toronto. My high school."

The girl looked bewildered as she stepped out of the teleporter booth. She hesitantly walked forward as she glanced around her.

She stopped a couple yards away from Paul and Erin. Her big brown eyes looked around in wonder.

"Where am I?" she asked.

"Space Station Troika in orbit around Mars," Paul replied.

"Yes!" the girl shouted as she clapped her hands together and jumped up. "Mars! Mars! I made it to Mars!"

She danced and squealed and swung her arms. "This is totally awesome! I have returned, glory, hallelujah!"

"Who are you?" Erin demanded.

The girl stopped prancing, smiled at Paul, and held out her hand so he could shake it. "My name's Jessica."

Erin noticed the gold necklace with a Star of David pendant around her neck. Why was a Jewish girl wearing a Catholic school uniform?

"Are you from Redsands Base?" Paul asked.

Jessica's eyes lit up. "Redsands! I belong there. I have to go there."

Paul shook his head. "No, no, you can't go back there. It's in ruins."

"That's not important. I can walk, I can talk, and I can go to Mars!" she chirped as she danced around again.

Paul whispered to Erin, "I think she's the girl we lost trying to transport up from Redsands Base."

"If she is, she must be suffering from some sort of strange shock," Erin said.

Jessica spun around in a pirouette and strolled back to Paul and Erin. She threw her arms around Erin, hugged her, and said, "It's *sooooo* good to have a warm body again!"

Erin laughed and gently pushed Jessica away. "You mean you know what it's like not to have a body?"

"Believe me, having flesh and blood feels better than being just a spirit floating around," Jessica said.

"Then you remember what it was like—after the teleporter accident?" Paul asked incredulously.

Jessica nodded. "Oh, yeah, for a long time, I was in a place of neither the living nor the dead but something in between."

"That's incredible!" Paul remarked. "And now you're back three days later!"

"Was it just three days?" Jessica said. "I thought it was two thousand years."

Erin showed the empty cabin to Jessica. "You can stay in

here," Erin said. "There used to be a fourth person on the crew, but she got transferred to Exeter."

Jessica smiled. "Thanks for your hospitality. It's *sooooo* decent. I'll be comfortable here, but I won't be staying long."

"Oh? Are you in a rush to go somewhere?"

"To Mars. I have work to do down there."

"Everyone's being evacuated off Mars. What could you possibly do down there?"

"My father's work."

"Your father? I didn't think people brought their children to Mars. Who's your father?"

"Yahweh," Jessica said casually.

Also known as 'God', Erin realized. How weird.

"So you must be Jesus, eh?" Erin joked.

Jessica nodded. "I am. Isn't that awesome?"

Holy Mary, Mother of God, we have a crazy one aboard, Erin thought.

Thomas stepped out of the shuttlecraft, through the airlock, and onto the floor of the shuttlecraft dock. On the dock floor sat boxes of food, all destined for Space Station Exeter.

Jessica walked to Thomas and smiled and waved at him. "You must be Thomas," she said.

"Yes, I am," Thomas replied. "And you must be our visitor, Jessica. Are you hungry?"

Thomas grabbed a box of crackers from a table, pulled a folding knife from his belt, cut open the box, and held it out to Jessica.

She was staring at the folding knife clipped to his belt,

Thomas noticed. But she quickly looked up, smiled, took a round cracker, and began munching it.

Thomas glanced at the gold Star of David on Jessica's necklace. He asked, "So what's a nice Jewish girl like you doing in a place like this?"

"Checking out the shuttlecraft," Jessica said, pointing at the small spacecraft. "Is it powered by a nuclear reactor?"

"You've done your homework. Yes, it's a Tsiolkovsky Service Shuttlecraft model 3, the first to be powered by nuclear energy."

"Cool. Awesome. It'll be perfect for taking me to Mars."

"Going to Mars?" Thomas asked. "Nobody's going down to the surface."

"I have to, totally. I have to finish my father's work down there, at Redsands," Jessica explained.

"Your father worked at Redsands? You can't go back. All its people are—dead. Except you."

Jessica's eyes lit up. "But that's the reason why I have to go there. From the dead of Earth, my father will create life on Mars."

"Huh? I heard of no such project."

"Not on your scientific stations, but it has been planned. Life has grown on Earth, and now it's time for God to create His other children on Mars."

Thomas smiled wryly. "God's your father? Come on, you really can't think that, at least not literally. I know you God believers call God 'Our Father', but you really don't think He's your *father* in a family sense, do you?"

"He is truly my father, and I am Him," Jessica declared.

Thomas shrugged. "Okay, if God is going to create life

on Mars, how's He going to do it?"

"With the same principles that He used on Earth," Jessica explained. "The bodies of the dead on Mars contain amino acids and proteins, the necessary substances of life. The ruined Martian bases also have oxygen and water imported from Earth. There's also subsurface water on Mars that has come to the surface by the digging of your geologists.

"When the shuttlecraft crashes into a ruined base, the nuclear explosion will start the chemical reaction that will convert the amino acids, proteins, oxygen, and water into living cells."

This is crazy, Thomas thought. The girl wanted to play God, Book of Genesis.

"I don't believe in God," he retorted.

"That doesn't matter. I believe in God, and that's good enough for me."

In the kitchen, Paul slid the tray of rehydratable salmon chunks into the oven. He looked at the box that had held the salmon. "One of the ingredients is salmon flavouring," he observed. "They actually have to add artificial flavour to make the salmon taste like salmon."

"There's a restaurant in Fisherman's Wharf in San Francisco, where the chef grilled fresh salmon in garlic and paprika," Thomas remembered as he poured a cup of coffee. "Too bad we can't get food like that in Mars orbit."

"It would take a miracle," Paul said.

"Speaking of miracles, where's our visitor?" Thomas asked.

Erin put down a fourth plate on the table. "She's taking a shower. She says she hasn't had a bath for over two thousand years."

"Cleanliness is next to godliness," Thomas said, repeating an old proverb. "Do we know who she really is?"

Paul shook his head and looked at his handheld computer pad. "When Redsands Base burned up, we didn't get a good video picture of the woman we tried to teleport up. I've looked through the personnel list of Redsands, and there was a Jessie Montega, a biologist, but she was twenty-seven years old."

"Our Jessica looks a lot younger than twenty-seven," Erin said. "Can you get a picture of Jessie Montega?"

"No. Our records don't have photos, but Exeter's might. I've asked Father Kelly to search for her photo," Paul said. "Here's an idea: could the teleporter have reconstructed her as a younger person?"

"I don't know," Erin said. "Anything is possible."

Thomas sipped his coffee. "Whoever she is, she's crazy. She thinks that she's Jesus."

Paul nodded. "Yeah, that's weird. Maybe Jessica had a weird, out-of-body experience when the teleporter lost her atoms, and now she thinks she's Jesus. Or maybe she had already gone loony on Mars. That happens to some people in space."

"The consecrated bread didn't arrive, but the girl did," Erin observed. "Could the bread have turned into Jessica?"

Thomas put down his coffee mug. "Oh, that's ridiculous. I usually think of you two as intelligent people, but sometimes your religiosity is too much. Any rational person knows that God doesn't exist."

"Not necessarily," Erin replied. "I believe in Him, and so do a lot of other people in the space colonies. Exeter Station even has a chapel."

"A waste of space if you ask me," Thomas complained. "I don't know why NASA let a priest come out here. Christianity is the last thing we need in space."

"I disagree, I think we need to bring our religions out here," Paul said. "That's what makes us human."

"It's what makes us morons. Think how ridiculous your religion is," Thomas snapped. "Do you really think a real Son of God would spend thirty years as a carpenter, unknown to everyone? And did the crucifixion really mean anything? If he really were a god, he could have used his godlike powers to come back from dead or his father could have brought him back to life, so the suffering was unnecessary and meaningless. It was just a publicity stunt to convert the superstitious. Jesus was probably just a guy who faked his own death—assuming he actually existed, and there's no real historical proof that he did. Christianity is just one big fraud."

"I am not a fraud," said a voice from behind.

They turned around and saw Jessica standing at the doorway.

"Don't take it personally," Thomas said. "I oppose superstitions of all kinds, not just the Christian kind."

Jessica frowned.

"Uh, dinner's almost ready," Erin said, hoping to change the topic. "Will you join us?"

The schoolgirl smiled again. "That would be awesome. I haven't eaten for a long, long time."

The oven bell rang, and Paul put on his oven mittens,

opened the oven, and pulled out the tray.

"Oh my God! What's this?" he blurted.

Instead of plain rehydrated salmon chunks, the tray held grilled salmon fillets bathed in a tomato sauce. The aroma of garlic and paprika wafted through the kitchen.

Paul, Erin, and Thomas stared wide-eyed at the fish. After a long, stunned silence, Erin finally spoke.

"You were saying it would take a miracle to get fresh salmon here?" she said to Paul.

Jessica grabbed the tray from Paul and put it on the table. "Don't be shy; everybody dig in!" she urged.

At first, Paul, Erin, and Thomas were reluctant to eat the fish, but with Jessica's prodding, they nibbled hesitantly at it. Then, when they tasted how delicious the fish had become, they ate it eagerly.

"This is wonderful," Paul said. Erin nodded, and even Thomas grunted in agreement as he chewed.

"Thank you," Jessica said, grinning. "I'm very good with fish."

"I must be dreaming," Thomas mumbled.

"No, you're not," Jessica said. "That fabulous gourmet dinner was real." She looked at each of them in the eye. "Now, can you do a favour for me?"

"What can we do for you?" Erin asked.

"Can I have the ignition key to the shuttlecraft?"

A stunned silence followed.

Erin reached out and touched Jessica's hand. "Dear, you're a special person, but you don't really believe you're Jesus, do you?"

"Like, yeah!" Jessica blurted with a sigh of

exasperation. "Look at the Jesus thing I did. I turned chunks of dry fish into—uh, fish with tomato sauce."

"Turning fish into fish," Thomas quipped.

"Okay, maybe that was a bit lame," Jessica admitted.

Thomas shrugged, raised his glass to his lips, and put the glass down. "I ran out of water."

"Oh, I'll get some," Jessica said as she grabbed the pitcher from the table. "Hey, water is so plain. Do you have any wine here?"

"You're too young," Erin warned.

Jessica giggled. "I know I look underage, but I'm a lot older than I look."

"We have no wine," said Paul. "We've got only water."

"Just water? How boring." Humming the old Jewish folk song "Havah Nagilah", Jessica skipped to the kitchen counter and filled the pitcher with water from the faucet.

She set the pitcher in the middle of the table. Thomas lifted the pitcher and began pouring water into his glass.

"Oh my God," he muttered as he saw red wine pour into his glass.

Paul took the pitcher, poured a glass of wine for himself, and sipped it. It tasted very sweet. He remembered a sugary red wine that a friend had given him at a frat party in university. It was a kosher sacramental wine drunk at Passover.

"Next time you drink wine, remember me," Jessica said.

"Do you need any help cleaning up?" Jessica asked.

Erin smiled and shook her head. "No, dear. We'll clear the table."

"Okay with me." Jessica yawned. "Wow, that was a lot of food. I feel tired now. I'll go to my room and take a nap."

"Sure. Sweet dreams," Thomas said.

"Oh, and think about letting me borrow the shuttlecraft," Jessica urged. "I really, seriously, totally need it."

The crew's eyes silently followed Jessica as she walked out of the kitchen.

Erin broke the silence. "Was any of this real?"

"It must have been real," Paul concluded. "All three of us can't be dreaming or hallucinating about the same thing."

"How did she do it?" Thomas wondered.

"It's a miracle," Erin said.

"No it's not," said Thomas. "She's not Jesus."

"She could be the woman I tried to teleport out of Redsands Base," Paul said.

"That still doesn't explain how she turned rehydrated salmon chunks into salmon fillets in tomato sauce," Erin said.

"Maybe she got superhuman powers when the transporter reassembled her," Paul guessed.

"Maybe she's an alien," Thomas suggested seriously.

"Whatever or whoever she is, one thing is certain: she wants to crash the shuttlecraft into Mars," Paul said. He took out a metal key from his pocket. "But she can't start the shuttlecraft's reactor without the ignition key. Do you know where yours is?"

Erin and Thomas felt in their pockets and pulled out their keys.

"Keep them with you at all times, and don't leave them

lying around," Paul advised. "We need that shuttlecraft to carry the food and ourselves to Space Station Exeter."

Erin returned to her cabin and lay down on her cot. She looked at another photo of her and her parents, this one from the night before the Miss America pageant.

Her parents had met at a tourism industry convention in Toronto, where her mother was a visiting American tour operator, and her father was an engineer who designed flying amphibious tour buses. They settled in Toronto, where Erin attended St. Joseph's College School on Wellesley Street.

After graduating from "St. Jo's," she went to study business administration at the University of Oregon in Eugene, her mother's hometown. In her second year of university, she entered the beauty pageants billed as "scholarship programs": first, she won the crown of Miss Willamette Valley, and then, the Miss Oregon crown. Her next step was the Miss America pageant, to be held in Salem, the state capital of Oregon, that year.

It was also the year of the Vernacular Wars, when the Sudanese declared *jihad* on the United States for allowing American Moslems to recite the Koran in English instead of Arabic. But despite the orange alert, ordinary life, including the Miss America pageant, continued in America.

Erin had just stepped off the stage in her evening gown when the terrorists charged into the auditorium. With their guns blazing, they slaughtered over a hundred people in ten minutes. Screams and moans filled the air. As the walls and floors turned red with blood, the police and National Guard unleashed their own storm of tear gas and bullets.

Erin found her father covered in blood but still alive. Her mother did not survive, though.

If only she hadn't been enthralled with the clothes, the gifts, the glamour, the attention, and the scholarships; if only she hadn't won Miss Willamette Valley and Miss Oregon; if only she hadn't entered the Miss America pageant, her mother might still be alive.

She dropped out of university and went to Toronto with her father. She returned to Oregon a few years later to earn a degree in science, and she volunteered to work in the space colonies, far away from Earth.

She sat up and felt the brainscanner still strapped to her head. When was that wretched headpiece due to come off?

She heard a knock on her door. She opened it and saw Jessica.

"Jessica," Erin greeted softly. "What can I do for you, dear?"

"You wish you could have had one last moment of quality time with your mother, don't you?" Jessica said as she strolled into the cabin.

Erin's eyes widened. "How do you know?"

Jessica smiled. "I know things. I can tell that her death has tormented you for years." She put her hands on Jessica's temples, as if trying to touch her mind. "Stop punishing yourself. You have no reason to feel guilty, no reason to flee out here."

"If only—if only I hadn't been so selfish, thinking only about myself."

"Hush. Will you believe me if you could speak to your

mother again?"

"How can you do that?"

Jessica grinned. "Oh, I can do all sorts of cool things."

"Erin, I'm so happy to see you again," chirped a voice from behind.

Erin spun around and stared at her mother.

She threw her arms around her mother and hugged her.

Her mother looked young and wore the blue tour guide uniform that Erin had seen in her childhood, years that they remembered over tea and crackers.

Eventually, they talked about the present. "How's your father?" asked Erin's mother.

"Oh, he's really happy in his retirement," Erin replied. "I just got a video message from him last week. He won a trophy at a model airplane contest. His glider flew over one hundred feet, farther than all the other gliders."

"Ah, he was always designing buses and boats and planes. I have to ask: did he ever remarry?"

"No, he never did."

"Hah, hah, I spoiled him for other women," Erin's mother bragged. "He would never find another one like me, I told him."

Erin laughed. "Oh, you were unique, and he knew that."

She suddenly stopped smiling. Her mother was unique. She had used the past tense because her mother had died.

"Mum, you died," Erin stated plainly. "How can you be here now?"

Her mother reached out to take Erin's hands. "Dear, I can only come back briefly, so let me say what I need to say."

She pulled Erin closer to her. "Stop blaming yourself for my death. It wasn't your fault."

"What are you saying?" Erin mumbled.

"Don't blame yourself. Blame the Jihadists."

"But if I hadn't entered the pageant—" Erin started.

Erin's mother interrupted her. "No, no, don't think that way. You enjoyed what you did, you didn't harm anyone, and your father and I were so proud of you."

"You were?"

"Of course, we were." Erin's mother smiled. "You looked so beautiful, so poised, and so confident when you were competing on stage. You grew up a lot in those two years at university."

"That's nice to know."

"So will you finally stop blaming yourself?"

"Yes, yes, I'll stop, I'll stop," Erin promised.

Erin's mother walked her to the cot and laid her down. "You've been tired for a long time." She kissed her on the cheek. "Get some sleep now."

Erin closed her eyes, smiled, and fell asleep. When she woke up, her mother was gone.

And so too was Jessica.

Erin felt inside her pant pockets as she rose from the cot.

The shuttlecraft's ignition key was gone too.

On the viewscreen, Father Kelly said, "God, Jesus, and the Holy Spirit are the same person in mainstream

Christianity. If this girl thinks she's Jesus, then she also thinks she's God."

"She does; she thinks she can create life on Mars," Paul said, glancing at Jessica and back to Father Kelly again.

"God does not wear a miniskirt," declared Father Kelly.

Jessica giggled and said, "Oh, but I do, especially with this schoolgirl uniform. Isn't it cute?"

"It's not unusual to find someone who thinks she's Jesus or Moses or Elvis or whoever; they appear in Israel all the time," Father Kelly commented. "But in orbit around Mars?"

Jessica joked, "Elvis has come back from the dead more times than I have."

"Be careful," Paul cautioned the priest. "You're talking about her as if she can't hear you, but she's right here."

"I'm not sure the girl is actually there." The priest paused for a moment and continued: "Paul, have you considered the possibility of mass hysteria? Or that something is controlling your minds?"

Paul looked back at Jessica and said, "I don't think it's mass hysteria or mind control. What could possibly do that to us out here?"

Father Kelly asked, "Did you say that Dr. Hall sees the girl too?"

"Yes, he does."

Father Kelly smiled weakly. "Dr. Hall is an atheist fundamentalist. If he sees the girl, she can't be God or Jesus."

Jessica laughed. "How ironic: the atheist can see me, but the priest can't."

"Then she's Jessie Montega from Redsands," Paul said.

"But if she is, why is she invisible to me?" Father Kelly asked. "Look, here's a radical idea: perhaps Troika was carved out of a Siren Stone."

Paul fell into a stunned silence. The Siren Stones were a modern myth: asteroids haunted by beautiful spirits who lured lonely spacers to their deaths. They explained why space crews went crazy or disappeared without a trace.

Father Kelly, Vatican astronomer, did not believe in myths and superstitions. He was a rational scientist—but so too were the first spacers to talk about Siren Stones.

"*You* believe in Siren Stones?" Paul asked.

Father Kelly shrugged. "No, but we're running out of explanations for what's going on."

The priest's cell phone beeped. He answered and listened to it, and then he looked eagerly at Paul.

"My friends found a photo of Jessie Montega," Father Kelly reported. "I'm going to my quarters to download the file."

He looked at his watch. "Paul, your launch window is coming in seventeen hours. You need to get off that rock and come to Exeter. Don't let anyone—or anything— hijack the shuttlecraft."

"Not even Jesus?" Paul asked.

"Especially not Jesus," urged Father Kelly as he ended the transmission.

Paul spun around in his chair and looked at Jessica. "Who are you, and what do you want?" he demanded.

"You already know," Jessica said.

"You've suffered a lot. You might have post-traumatic stress," Paul said. "There are people on Exeter who can help you. Come with us."

"Look, I don't have a lot of time. There's something you need to know before I leave," Jessica said. "Jessie Montega died for a purpose."

"What are you saying?" Paul asked. "You're not dead."

"I tell you again, I'm not Jessie Montega. Jessie Montega's body is dead in the ruins of Redsands Base. Her soul is living with God now."

Jessica walked to a computer monitor and began typing commands. Animated images of molecules, from *The Spacer's Encyclopedia*, appeared on the monitor. Paul recognized them from chemistry class: amino acids, proteins, and DNA.

Jessica pointed at the images of the protein molecules. "Jessie Montega's body contains amino acids, proteins, and DNA. When I crash the shuttlecraft onto her body, the nuclear reaction will start the chemical reactions that will create life. Her death has meaning and purpose. She died so that Mars can live."

Paul stared at the girl. "Now I know for sure: you're crazy," he said.

Jessica breathed in deeply. "You're the one who will go crazy if you keep blaming yourself for Jessie Montega's death. Believe me, it wasn't your fault, and she died for a purpose."

She marched out of the room, leaving Paul crumpled in his chair, alone with his memories of Jessie Montega's plea for help.

Thomas watched Jessica walk towards the shuttlecraft. He crossed his arms and moved to block her path to the airlock.

"Where are you going, young lady?" he asked.

"To Mars," Jessica replied.

"Sorry, but we need this shuttlecraft to deliver food to the people of Space Station Exeter. You wouldn't want them to starve, would you?"

"I'll find another way to get the food to Exeter. Just let me have the shuttlecraft."

"Can't you just wave your hand and make a one-celled organism?" Thomas asked. "Why does God need a nuclear spaceship?"

"I don't know," Jessica whined, her voice growing more agitated. "God works in mysterious ways. Only He knows."

"Did God crash the meteor into Mars? Did God want all those people to die? What kind of God is He?" Thomas accused.

"I don't know!" Jessica cried. "I don't know if all those people had to die. But I know that if I don't go down to Mars, at least one of those deaths will be meaningless!"

Thomas eyed her suspiciously. Her right hand was clasped shut.

"What are you holding in your hand?" he demanded.

Paul and Erin ran into the shuttlecraft dock.

"She's got my shuttlecraft key!" Erin yelled.

Jessica darted forward, but Thomas grabbed her. Paul and Erin rushed to Jessica, and they struggled to pry the key out of her hand.

"Got it!" Paul shouted as he held up the key.

Jessica stumbled backwards away from the crew and glared at them. "But I got this!" she hissed.

She unfolded Thomas's knife and held it over her wrist. "Give me the key or I'll kill myself."

"So what? If you're Jesus, you'll just come back from the dead," scoffed Thomas.

"Dear, put that down," Erin urged. "You don't want to hurt anybody."

Paul stepped towards Jessica. "Jessie, put down the knife. You need help that we can't give you here. Come to Exeter with us."

A chime sounded from a videoscreen. Erin went to the videoscreen and looked at the message scrolling in.

"It's Father Kelly," Erin said.

"Relay the transmission into this room," Paul ordered.

Father Kelly appeared on the videoscreen. "Hey, why are you all in the shuttlecraft dock?" he asked.

"We've got the girl here," Paul said.

Father Kelly looked puzzled. "I still can't see her, but tell me if she looks anything like this. Here's Jessie Montega."

A colour photo of a woman appeared on the screen. She was in her late twenties, had long black hair, and looked Filipina.

"You look nothing like your photo," Paul said to Jessica.

"Now will you believe that I'm not Jessie Montega?" Jessica pleaded.

"That means she's dead, she's truly dead," Paul muttered. His eyes grew sad. "I really killed her."

"Paul, you didn't kill anyone," Father Kelly said. "You have to trust yourself again."

The video transmission suddenly ended. Jessica looked at the videoscreen and said, "Forgive me, Father, but I don't need another person added to this balagan."

She turned to Paul. "Would it help if you talked to

her?"

Before Paul could answer, he heard someone say, "Paul, how nice to finally see you."

The voice sounded familiar. Paul turned around. Jessie Montega stood there, smiling.

"Do you see her too?" Paul asked.

Erin and Thomas, both looking shocked, simply replied, "Yes."

Thomas looked at the lights flashing quickly on Erin's brainscanner headpiece. He took the brainscanner monitor out of his pocket.

"Uh, maybe you should see this," he said.

But Paul wasn't listening to him. Instead, he stared at the ghost from Redsands.

Jessie Montega looked into Paul's eyes. "Thanks for trying to teleport me up. I know it didn't work, but I appreciate all that you did for me."

She held her hand out to Paul. "Feel my hand. That's the DNA, the amino acids, the proteins, the water, the carbon, and the oxygen that will become the first Martian life forms."

Paul took Jessie Montega's hand and gripped it. It felt smooth and solid and warm, not like what he had expected of a ghost. He marvelled at how human the ghost felt.

"Are you dead?" Paul whispered, barely able to speak.

Jessie Montega nodded. "My body lies on Mars, but my spirit is in heaven with God. It's a good place, so don't worry about me."

"Thanks for letting me know."

As Paul released her hand, Jessie Montega said, "There is a purpose of my life and my death. Let me fulfill my purpose." Then, looking at Jessica, she said, "Let her fulfill her purpose too."

With a wave of her hand, Jessie Montega faded away.

Paul looked at Jessica. "You really are Jesus."

"Finally, you believe me!" Jessica said. "Listen, you've done nothing wrong. Be at peace with yourself again."

Paul tossed the ignition key to Jessica.

"What are you doing?" Thomas shouted.

Jessica dropped the knife on the floor, caught the key, and dashed through the airlock and into the shuttlecraft.

"She's just a crazy kid!" Thomas yelled as he ran to the airlock.

He tried to pull open the door, but Jessica had locked it from the other side. The whirring sounds of machinery began. Thomas backed away from the door.

"She's starting the nuclear engine," Erin said. "Let's get out of here."

Back at the control room, they watched the shuttlecraft blast away from Troika and shoot towards the red planet below.

"We've got our cameras aimed over Redsands again," Erin said as she finally removed the brainscanner headpiece.

The viewscreen showed an aerial shot of the ruined station. The shuttlecraft fell quickly like a blur onto the broken dome. A blinding flash of white light erupted. A nuclear mushroom cloud arose.

In horrified silence, Troika's crew watched the thick radioactive smoke climb hundreds of feet into the Martian sky.

"Nothing could have survived that," Paul said.

Thomas scowled and turned away from the viewscreen. "We let that kid kill herself," he spat.

A tear ran down Erin's cheek. "Poor Jessica," she muttered.

Paul put his hand on Erin's shoulder. "I think she'll come back."

Thomas looked at another viewscreen, this one showing animated graphics of the orbits of Space Station Exeter and Space Station Troika.

"Exeter is now at its closest position to Troika," Thomas announced. "Well, we're stranded here. Neither we nor Exeter have a shuttlecraft. How are we going to take the food to Exeter?"

Numbers and words suddenly appeared on Erin's computer monitor and began scrolling upwards.

"This information's downloading onto our mainframe," Erin observed. "What is it?"

Paul looked at the monitor. "It's program code for the teleporter. Is the University of Waterloo sending it to us?"

"No, it's not coming from Earth," Erin reported. "It's coming from—Mars."

Paul looked at his computer monitor. Instead of the program code, it showed a message:

> *Your teleporter is now safe for people and food.*
>
> *XP*

Paul grinned at the signature: XP, the first and second letters of XPICTOC. Kristos: Christ in Greek.

All the food they teleported to Space Station Exeter

arrived complete and unchanged. "Just as hard and tasteless as it originally was, no miracle this time," Thomas joked.

Finally, the crew had only themselves to teleport to Exeter. But Thomas had something to show Paul and Erin before they abandoned Troika.

Thomas pointed at brain scans of Erin on a computer terminal. Different parts of her brain glowed and pulsated in red, green, and yellow.

Thomas pointed to an area that suddenly lit up and expanded in red. "That's the electrical activity in the left temporal lobe at the time when you first saw Jessica. It's all red, showing an increase in electrical activity."

He showed another brain scan with the left temporal lobe lit up in red. "And this is a scan of your brain at the time when you saw Jessie Montega's ghost."

Erin gazed at the brain scans. "And what about the time I saw my mother?"

"Same results," Thomas said. "The temporal lobe is where the emotions of religious experience, feelings like awe and joy, are created," he explained. "Religious mystics experience increased brain wave activity there when they see visions or go into altered states of consciousness."

"Does that mean Jesus and my mother and Jessie Montega really did come to us?" Erin wondered.

"Or something triggered these visions in our minds," Thomas suggested. He opened a three–dimensional computer graphic of Troika. Animated waves poured from the centre of the space station.

"I detected electrochemical signals from Troika itself," Thomas said. "The signals are coming from the core of the asteroid that the station is built in."

"Electrochemical signals?" Paul said. "You mean the rock is sending out brain waves of its own?"

"It seems to be. The rock could have planted visions of Jessica, Erin's mother, and Jessie Montega into our minds," Thomas said.

"And that's why Father Kelly couldn't see Jessica," Paul realized. "He wasn't here to receive the signals."

Erin leaned forward to look at the graphic image of Troika. "But my mother's ghost knew about me and my family. How could the rock have known all about our lives?"

"I think the rock is also absorbing our brain waves," Thomas said. "It's probably taking our memories and turning them into visions of people we knew."

"Incredible," Paul said. "Siren Stones are real."

Thomas shrugged. "I don't know if this is a Siren Stone or not." He paused. "But now I'm sure that God and Jesus are just figments of our imagination, created in our brains."

"Oh, I wouldn't say that," Erin protested. "Maybe God gave us temporal lobes so that we can experience Him."

"Oh, come on, you can't prove that," Thomas retorted.

"What about the missing shuttlecraft?" Erin mentioned. "Someone flew it into Mars. And that nuclear explosion was no illusion. Other space stations saw it."

"And then there's the new program code for the teleporter," Paul said. "Where did that come from?"

"Okay, I don't know how to explain everything," Thomas admitted, "but before we jump to conclusions about God, we need to look at all the possibilities."

"There'll be plenty of time to study all the possibilities,

but not now; Exeter's going to move out of range," Paul said as he looked at his watch. "Let's go to the teleporter."

As they walked to the teleporter, Paul said, "It's too bad we have to leave now. We don't know anything about this rock. How can it send and receive brain waves? Is it living? Is it intelligent? There's plenty for a future crew to study."

They teleported themselves safely to Space Station Exeter.

Later that day, Father Kelly celebrated Mass in the chapel. He gave the Eucharist to Paul and Erin, thanked God for the safe evacuation of Troika's crew, and included Jessica in the prayers for the dead.

Thomas also attended Mass that day, in memory of Jessica, the girl who had cooked a fish dinner in the way he loved from Fisherman's Wharf in San Francisco.

Nothing remained of Redsands Base except for hundreds of pools of chemical soup scattered on a charred red landscape. In one pool of chemicals, a geyser of water continued spraying up from the centre. Water, oxygen, carbon, proteins, and amino acids swirled together after feeling the burst of nuclear energy.

Long after the Earth people had left, membranes formed around proteins and chemicals, and the first cells appeared. The cells absorbed energy from the radiation and the sun, and chemical reactions began inside the cells. One day, a cell split into two.

Life had sprung on Mars.

About "Transubstantiation"

Northwest Passages: a Cascadian Anthology was published by the small, now-defunct publisher Windstorm Creative, later called Orchard House Press. It was a literary project of Cascadia Con, the 8th North American Science Fiction Convention, held in Seattle, Washington, in 2005.

The Siren Stone universe began with "The Siren Stone" (2003), but "Transubstantiation" kickstarted it. Cris DiMarco, the publisher of Windstorm Creative, liked it so much that she asked for a novel based on it, *The Moon Under Her Feet* (2007). I will always be grateful to Cris for giving me the opportunity to create my own science fiction universe and for publishing my first novel.

"Transubstantiation" won the 2006 Aurora Award for Best Short-Form Work in English (now called Best Short Story). That was my first literary award.

XY-Girls of
Southern Comfort

XY-Girls

"That's a nice dress," the new customer said to Susanna.

Susanna smiled and slid a glass of beer to him. She wore a long red gown with a slit up to her hip. The women working at Club Mandy had to look glamorous and sexy.

She flipped her blonde hair. "Thank you," she said. "I wanted to look like a Hollywood actress. Let's bring some glamour to this drab little planet."

The customer wore a blue jumpsuit with the logo of the Columbian Off-World Company, a golden eagle holding a spade in its talons. The jumpsuit meant that he worked in the mines or the smelting plants, not in the company's business offices. Susanna guessed that like most men here, he came to Southern Comfort for the high wages and would leave when his contract ended in two years. Southern Comfort offered nothing but a grey sky and an equally grey landscape. There was nothing to keep a man here forever.

The miner took a sip. "You look like a movie star," he

said.

He glanced around quickly, furtively checking out the other girls. Susanna thought, he's such a shy kid. Probably doesn't have much experience in bars like this.

Then he looked back at Susanna. "Uh, do you want to go upstairs?"

"Ah, no. I'm flattered that you would consider me, though."

"Oh, I thought all the girls in this bar are working girls," the miner said.

Susanna shook her head. "That's a misconception back on Earth. We're all working, but not all in the same business. But that's okay; you're new here. I'm in bar and restaurant management."

She pointed at a woman who was eating alone at a table. "That's Postie. She's the postal manager of the mining camp, which means she's Postmaster General of the entire planet."

"Wow, she's pretty," said the miner. "Is she a Thai ladyboy?"

"She's actually Filipina, and she prefers to be called a lady, not a boy."

"Oh, okay," the miner said. "I went to a bar like this in Vancouver once. Just once. The girls were beautiful."

"It's just the same here, only the chromosomes are different," Susanna said, "and sometimes the anatomy, but some guys like that, some guys don't, and some guys don't care. It's complicated."

"I was reluctant to take a job here when I heard that all the girls are XY-girls," the miner said, "but now that I've been here two weeks, I'm fine with it. Every girl here is like a girl back home."

"Though you probably didn't grow up next door to a girl like the one who's coming at you now," said Susanna.

Crystal, a brown-haired woman in a tight black minidress, approached them.

Susanna whispered to the miner, "If you're looking for personal services, Crystal is the girl for you."

Crystal had several skills, including hacking computer systems for fun and profit, but when she worked in the bar, she stayed honest. Crystal bought wristbands, thus helping Susanna increase her revenue. Despite her subversive hacker reputation, she never snuck guys upstairs without paying.

Crystal sat down beside the miner, leaned towards him, and rubbed his thigh. "My name is Crystal," she purred. "I'm from Colombia. Where are you from?"

"Medicine Hat," the miner replied. He gulped down some beer.

"That's in Canada, right? I hear it's really cold there. But I know how to make a man hot," said Crystal.

She rubbed the miner's thigh again. He squirmed and looked back at Susanna.

Crystal touched the miner's chin and turned his face. "Don't look at her. Look at me. I'm your girl 24/7."

Susanna grinned. Crystal knew how to get her clients.

After more of Crystal's flirting, the miner finally said, "Yes, let's go upstairs."

"Ah, great," Susanna said. "Crystal, I've got your wristbands."

Crystal handed some cash to Susanna. Susanna put wristbands on Crystal and the miner. Crystal laughed, grabbed the miner by the hand, and pulled him upstairs.

*   *   *

A little later, Susanna went upstairs to use the women's washroom. She tapped her employee card on the door. The words "ACCESS DENIED" appeared on it.

"Oh, it's broken again," Susanna muttered. "Crystal?"

Susanna looked around. The private room's door was closed. Crystal was still with her client.

Susanna wished she could get the money to renovate the washrooms and make them all single stalls. Until then, she had to make do with what the Company had built, separate washrooms for men and women. She also had to make do with Crystal repairing the IT systems in her spare time.

Susanna couldn't wait until Crystal had finished with her client. She pushed open the door of the men's washroom, which had no lock.

Several men stood at the urinals, and they ogled and whistled at her.

But one of the men said, "You guys think that's a girl? He's not."

Salvo was a miner. He frequently took XY-girls to the private rooms, but that didn't mean that he liked them.

"Hey, Salvo, leave her alone," said John, one of the Company's accountants. "*She's* the one who gives us beer and chicken wings and rehydratable processed fish-based food."

"I should never have come here," Salvo ranted. "You're turning me homo."

"Hey, chill out," John said. "Let's go to Texas Chuckwagon. It's pub crawl night, even if there are only two pubs on the whole planet."

After the men left, Susanna went into a toilet stall. When she left the men's washroom, some escort girls pointed and giggled at her. Susanna shrugged and walked downstairs.

Police Chief John Dunford entered the bar with a girl. Susanna had never seen her before. She looked about twenty years old, blonde bob hairstyle, very pretty, wearing a short green dress.

"Who's the new girl?" Susanna asked.

The girl held out her hand to Susanna. "My name is Helen," she said. "It's nice to meet you."

As Susanna shook Helen's hand, Dunford said, "She's a Victor Robotics L-10, Military Recreation Model."

Susanna gasped. Helen's hand felt warm and soft, like a real human's. She looked and moved so realistically. She had fooled Susanna.

"She's also programmed for pleasure," Dunford said. "I want to go upstairs."

Susanna quickly tied a wristband around Dunford. Dunford slapped Helen on her butt and pulled her to the stairs.

He turned and said, "I don't know why the Company allowed you freaks to come here. I would rather screw an android than a tranny."

Susanna glared at him. The government couldn't get decent police officers to work on Southern Comfort. That's how they wound up with a police chief who insulted the girls and fondled his sex robot in public.

"The men want us," Susanna replied. "Without us, they would have nothing better to do than get drunk and beat each other up. Or straight guys would be jumping each other like in prison. Either would be bad for Company shareholders."

Susanna closed Club Mandy and walked home. As she passed the Roman Catholic chapel, she heard the Filipina girls sing. The priest did not care that the girls had been born with boys' bodies. He liked them because they were his most loyal parishioners. He had trouble getting people to come to church on this God-forsaken planet named after a liqueur. Coincidentally, Southern Comfort was also the name of an annual conference for transgender persons in the late twentieth century.

There were no XX-women on Southern Comfort. The original two colonies, Pale Blue and Petit Rouge, fought each other in the Great Slaughter decades ago. Petit Rouge's President MacLeod, infamous for his disdain of women, created a bacterium that killed people with XX chromosomes and launched it at Pale Blue. The bacterium killed all of Pale Blue's women, but it also spread everywhere and killed Petit Rouge's women too. Society in both colonies collapsed, and MacLeod's own guards overthrew him. The United Nations put Southern Comfort under United States trusteeship with a Governor appointed by Congress. While the Earth nations argued over how to govern the planet, the United States leased mining rights to the Columbian Off-World Company.

XX-women could live on Southern Comfort if they took antibiotics after getting infected, but none wanted to risk dying before the antibiotics took effect. The colonization restarted without women. Without women, many men quit their contracts early and went home. The

Company tried entertaining the men with holograms of women, but that failed to stop them from returning to Earth. As a last resort, the Company recruited XY-women to the planet. The number of men who quit early fell by fifty percent.

The Company built Club Mandy, inspired by an XY-girl bar in New York. Susanna had worked there before going to Southern Comfort. She would work here for five years and return to Earth with ten times the money she would have earned there.

A crowd had gathered outside the Texas Chuckwagon. Susanna pushed through the people to see what was happening. She saw medics carry out a dead body on a gurney.

"May I see her? Or him?" Susanna asked. A medic nodded and pulled the sheet away from the body's face. Susanna gasped.

She was Miranda, one of the Company's office staff. She was the third girl strangled in the last two months.

Salvo walked by and said, "No big loss."

Police Chief Dunford and his android Helen walked out of the Texas Chuckwagon. Crystal ran up to them and said, "Someone is killing the girls." She pointed at a security camera on the lamppost. "Why can't you tell who it is when you have all these cameras?"

Dunford shook his head. "Someone killed the victim inside a washroom stall. We don't have CCTV inside the washroom out of respect for the privacy of you ladies. The security gap is all for you girls."

"And men too," Crystal added ruefully. "The last thing

a man wants is for another man to watch him unzip his pants on video."

Susanna asked, "But can't you check the video shot outside the washroom? You can see who went into the washroom with her."

Dunford shook his head. "There were so many people going in and out of that washroom that it's hard to tell who could have killed her. It's an all-gender washroom, so we can't spot anyone unusual, like a man entering a woman's washroom. There are seven hundred people on Southern Comfort. Half the population must have been here tonight for the video rodeo."

"There's a pattern," Crystal observed. "Cherry, Diana, Miranda. They're all XY-girls. The killer hasn't killed a man."

Susanna felt uneasy. She didn't think an XY-girl would kill another XY-girl. Could the killer be a man?

"Chief, please do something," Crystal pleaded.

Dunford guffawed. "The best way to protect yourself is to leave. Jump on the next warp ship, go back to Earth, and spend a week in quarantine for the bacterium."

He patted Helen's butt. "When we get more androids, we won't need you ladies anymore."

The next night, Dunford showed off his android to the other customers at Club Mandy. Helen laughed, talked, and moved like a real human.

"I wish I could afford to get one for myself," Salvo said as he groped Helen's breasts.

Susanna and Crystal watched the men admire Helen.

"That android is like a wind-up toy, just doing

everything Dunford tells it to do," Susanna said. "Aren't the L-10's supposed to have some artificial intelligence?"

"I don't know," Crystal said. "I thought they did, but this one is obviously just a programmable device. If it does have consciousness, I feel sorry for it. It has to live with Dunford."

"It won't be long before we're replaced by military-grade sex androids," Susanna said. "They don't need time off, don't need food, don't need money, and don't need hormones. They're the perfect girlfriends."

"I don't want to be replaced by a toy," Crystal complained. "In Bogotá, people treated me like a freak. But here, people treat me like a real girl."

"Well, most people," Susanna said, glancing at Dunford, "but I know what you mean. On this planet, XY-girls are treated like girls because we're the only girls here."

Crystal said, "You're a girl here, but when you go back to Earth, you become a boy again. Sometimes."

"Yes and no," Susanna said. "I can't explain it, but I can feel both female and male. On Earth, I was a girl half of the time. I know most people stay with being one or the other, but I'm not like that. If I can't be male sometimes, I would be missing a part of myself. If I can't be female, I would be missing another part of myself. But when I'm here, I'm a girl all of the time."

"Oh, a regular customer," Crystal said before walking to a man standing at the bar. Postie, wearing her post office uniform, came and gave a parcel to Susanna.

"Looks like another package of chocolate from your girlfriend," Postie said.

In high school, Susanna's girlfriend Naomi dressed

him in a prom gown and entered him in the school's womanless beauty pageant, a fundraiser for the cheerleading squad. Susanna insisted that was the last time he would wear girl clothes, a wig, and make-up. But Naomi dressed him as a winged female fairy for Halloween. He did not resist. By Christmas, Naomi regularly made him dress like a girl for sexual role playing. The cross-dressing excited Naomi, and Susanna discovered that he enjoyed it too. By the time he graduated from college, he had his own *femme* wardrobe and could put on make-up by himself. He also did mundane chores, like shopping for food or walking the dog, *en femme* half of the time, often without Naomi.

Dunford and Helen walked past them. The Police Chief whispered to his android, "Let's go home, away from these freaks."

Postie shook her head and turned to watch Crystal and her client. "Look at her flirt with that guy. Some sex workers like their work and some don't. Crystal's in the first category. She told me that she was never forced into sex work by pimps or poverty. She's just horny. She dreamt her first bondage fantasy when she was twelve years old, tied up her girlfriend at nineteen, transitioned to female at twenty, became a pro dominatrix at twenty-one, and came to Southern Comfort as an escort at twenty-four."

Susanna nodded. "And she found the time and a government grant for hormone replacement therapy, facial feminization surgery, and sexual reassignment surgery by age twenty-two. When she wants something, she goes after it and gets it."

"The hormones and surgery sure have worked

wonders on her," Postie said. "Speaking of which, guess what? The doctors approved me for estrogen and a testosterone blocker!"

"Oh, wow, great! When do you start?" Susanna asked.

Before Postie could answer, someone screamed from above. Susanna and Postie ran upstairs and saw an escort girl standing by an open door. She looked shocked.

Susanna entered the private room. A woman lay still on the floor.

"Oh my God, it's Jessie!" Susanna cried.

Postie knelt down to feel Jessie's pulse. "She's dead."

"She hadn't bought a wristband for a room, and she's not a sex worker," Susanna said. "She's an information systems engineer at the Company office. What was she doing up here?"

Postie looked at the ceiling. "There are no security cameras in here."

"And none in the hall outside either," Susanna added. "The men don't want anyone watching them come and go from the private rooms."

"Everything to protect them, nothing for us," Postie said.

Susanna picked up Jessie's handbag. Estrogen pills spilled out of it.

Diana, a truck driver, no surgeries, on estrogen. Cherry, a sex worker, with breast augmentation only, on estrogen. Miranda, an office clerk, with facial feminization surgery only, on estrogen. Jessie, a systems engineer, with facial feminization, breast, and sexual reassignment surgeries, on estrogen.

The only thing that the victims had in common was

that they were all women on estrogen.

"The killer killed Diana in her apartment, Cherry in a hotel room, Miranda in a washroom at the Texas Chuckwagon, and Jessie in a private room at Club Mandy," Susanna observed. "The killer knows where there are no cameras."

Postie watched the spaceship come through the space-bending warp at Main Station. The Company sent minerals to Earth on ships through the warp. Postie also collected mail from Earth here. It was faster to send mail on data drives through the warp than transmitting radio messages over thousands of light years.

When Postie was six years old, she played with her sister's dolls and felt strangely drawn to her clothes. Postie didn't have many friends; the boys bullied her for her girlish mannerisms, and the girls shunned her for being a boy. When Postie was twelve, she realized she wasn't really a boy. She grew her hair long, learned to put on make-up, and wore her mother's high heels and her sister's skirts. But her family had no money for testosterone blockers and estrogen, so her body changed from a boy's to a man's during puberty. It was the worst time of her life. After moving to California at age twenty, she joined the postal service and volunteered to go to Southern Comfort. Nobody else wanted the job.

As Postie pushed a mail cart to her office, Susanna came in, carrying a small parcel.

"I want to send this rock to Naomi," Susanna said.

Postie weighed the parcel. "Your girlfriend sends you chocolates, and you send her a rock?"

"It's a rock from Southern Comfort," Susanna said. "Astrogeology is her hobby."

"Ah, understood. Most girls would prefer a diamond," Postie said as she put the parcel into a bin.

She lifted a bag marked "UNITED NATIONS" to the counter. "Let's see what the U.N. gave us."

Postie took a data drive out of the bag, plugged it into her computer, and read the list of files. "Hey, this video is for immediate broadcast."

"What could it be?" Susanna asked.

Postie uploaded the video to the broadcast system. The United Nations logo appeared on the TV monitors. The logo changed to Pierre Laronde, President of the United Nations Trusteeship Council.

"Greetings to the people of Southern Comfort," Laronde began. "The United Nations and the United States Government re-affirm that Southern Comfort is a colony for all people, of all backgrounds, of all gender identities... We take your current crisis very seriously... I assure you that Governor Smith and Police Chief Dunford will arrest the killer."

Postie guffawed and ran another video on her monitor only. It showed Dunford on the morning news, talking about Jessie's death.

"A fourth transgender person was killed yesterday," Dunford said. "I advise all trans persons to return to Earth as soon as possible. Don't come back until we solve this investigation."

"He's not doing anything to find the killer," Postie said. "He wants us to either leave or die."

"For some reason, we two are safe, at least for now," Susanna said. "The killer only murders girls on estrogen."

"But how can he tell who's on estrogen and who isn't?" Postie wondered. "It's hard to tell us apart visually. The Company recruited very convincing girls who can pass as XX-girls. The Company had beauty standards for us. The girls who couldn't pass said it was unfair."

"Who says life on Southern Comfort is fair?" Susanna said. "Anyway, the point is that somehow the killer can tell us apart."

She looked at the mail room. "Hmm, I have an idea. Did the victims have any unclaimed mail?"

"Yes, they did, packages I couldn't deliver before they died."

"Let's look at their mail."

"What are you thinking?" Postie said as she led Susanna into the mailroom. She pointed at some packages. "Those were for the victims."

Susanna picked up a package. "It's from the Transgender Health Centre. They all are. I bet they're estrogen doses."

"I should send them back to Earth," Postie said.

"No, don't send them back. Give them to me."

"No, that would be postal theft," said Postie. "Why would you want the hormones anyway? Do you want to transition?"

"No. I want to catch the killer," said Susanna.

Club Mandy re-opened a night later, after Dunford and his police officers had completed their investigation of the room where Jessie had been killed. Despite the murder, the bar filled with customers and escorts again.

And Dunford returned to show off Helen.

Behind the bar, Postie and Susanna pounded the estrogen pills with crab mallets and poured the fragments into a glass.

"All pills have the active ingredient and inactive ingredients called excipients," Susanna explained. "Hopefully we'll be making the estrogen more detectable to the killer by breaking apart the pills."

"We need another glass," Postie said.

After they had emptied all the packages, Susanna gave a glass to Postie.

"We're carrying enough estrogen for a sorority house," Postie joked.

"I'm betting the killer can smell the estrogen in the girls' pheromones," Susanna said. "How else can he tell who's on estrogen?"

"Someone with a very strong sense of smell," Postie said. "Dogs can do it, but there are no dogs here."

As they went up, Postie asked, "Are you sure this is going to work?"

"I don't know, but we have to try," Susanna replied.

The escort girls crowded the hallway, where they chattered and flirted with their clients.

"Ladies, please go downstairs. I have to close the private rooms for a while," Susanna announced.

The escorts howled and booed. Crystal came out of a room with her client.

"But it's payday," Crystal complained.

"Uh, you guys go downstairs too," Postie said to a client.

Crystal asked, "What if we have to use the washroom?"

"It's only temporary," Susanna said. She did not really

know how much time she needed or whether her plan would work.

Crystal gave a wicked grin at her client. "I'll pee on the bar," she said as she led her client downstairs.

After they had cleared the hallway, Susanna and Postie entered a private room and left its door open. They stood silently, holding their glasses of estrogen.

A door creaked open.

"The washroom," Susanna whispered.

They heard slow, soft footsteps. Helen appeared in the doorway.

Why does an android have to use the washroom? Susanna wondered.

The android smiled at them. "May I come in?"

"Uh, yes, sure," Susanna said.

Still grinning, Helen walked into the room. She stared at the glasses of estrogen.

"You two girls are so beautiful," Helen said. "Do you want a threesome?"

"What?" Postie blurted. "A threesome? With us?"

Helen raised her hand and stroked Postie's cheek. "You're so beautiful. You like girls, don't you? I can tell."

"I do," Postie said, bewildered by the android's caresses.

Helen suddenly turned around and punched Susanna in the stomach. She fell back and dropped her glass, spilling the estrogen. Coughing and holding her belly, she rolled on the floor.

The android grabbed Postie's throat and choked her. Postie gagged and smashed her glass against Helen's face. But the android continued strangling her.

Susanna crawled across the room and saw an empty

wine bottle on the couch. Crystal's client must have had some liquid encouragement. Susanna grabbed the bottle. It felt heavy, made of thick glass.

Susanna stood up and hit Helen's head with the bottle. Helen let go of Postie and spun around. Susanna swung the bottle again and smashed it into the back of Helen's head. The android's head panel popped up, exposing the control panel beneath.

Helen lunged towards Susanna and grabbed her by the shoulders. But Postie ran behind Helen and pressed the power button on her control panel.

Helen suddenly let go of Susanna and collapsed to the floor. The android lay still with her eyes open and her head panel flipped up.

"Get Crystal!" Susanna cried, gasping for air.

Postie ran downstairs and returned with Crystal. Crystal gasped when she saw the android.

"What the Hell?" Crystal said. "What's the android doing in here?"

"Crystal, can you hack into her memory and find out who programmed her?" said Susanna.

"Yes, I can," Crystal said, pulling her phone and a short cable out of her handbag. She used the cable to connect her phone to a data port in the android's control panel.

Crystal read the data downloading to her phone. "The android was programmed by Police Chief Dunford."

"No surprise there," Susanna said.

"Androids aren't supposed to attack us," said Postie. "Their default setting is to never injure humans."

Crystal frowned. "This android's Asimov Protocols have been suppressed. Its artificial intelligence has also been suppressed. It's not a conscious being."

"Dunford must have tampered with it," Susanna said.

"I'm getting a video, shot from Helen's point of view, through her eyes," Crystal said. "Wow, Dunford was naked with Cherry!"

"What?" Postie and Susanna shouted in unison. They crowded around the phone with Crystal.

In the video, Cherry wore only a red bra and matching gaff, under which she had tucked her male parts. She knelt on a bed, crying softly. Dunford, naked, stood over her.

"I hate sex with you!" Dunford yelled. "I'm not homosexual!"

"But I *am* a girl," Cherry sobbed. "You're not gay when you're with me."

"You fruit! You bitch!" Dunford slapped Cherry across her face. Cherry screamed.

"It sucks when your android is the most realistic girl on the planet," Dunford shouted. "I can't believe I'm in a threesome with a trans and a toy."

He looked at Helen. "Kill her."

Helen moved towards Cherry and put her hands around her throat.

"Oh my God, the Police Chief is killing us!" said Crystal.

"Now we know why there's no security video outside Cherry's room," Postie realized. "Dunford must have destroyed it."

Susanna pointed at the android. "Can you get it to answer questions?"

"Let's see if I can," Crystal said as she pressed commands on her phone app. "What do you want to ask it?"

Susanna said, "Who programmed you to kill XY-girls?"

Helen's teeth chattered. Then she said, "Police Chief John Dunford programmed me to detect biological organisms emitting estrogen pheromones and terminate them."

"We obviously can't report this to Dunford," Postie said.

"The governor," Crystal said. "We have to tell him."

"Not with Dunford in control of the police," Susanna said. "He could overthrow Governor Smith in a coup."

"Then what can we do?" Crystal asked.

Susanna shrugged. "Leave the planet?"

"No. I got an idea," said Postie. "Can you download the video?"

Crystal nodded. "It's going to my phone now."

"Send a copy to me. I'll put it on a data drive and send it to Earth on the next warp ship. I'll include a message for the U.N. Trusteeship Council."

Susanna looked at Helen. "Dunford is going to look for his android. We better hide it. Crystal, can you reboot it and restore its Asimov Protocols and artificial intelligence?"

"Yes, I can," said Crystal. "She'll be like new again."

"And tell her that we're her friends," Susanna added.

Thirty minutes later, Helen stood up and smiled at the three women. "Good afternoon, ladies," she said. "I know you, but I'm sorry, I have no memory of the last two months and can't remember what we did together."

"That's fine, you can start anew," said Susanna. "Helen, you need to go away and hide for a while. We will retrieve you when it's safe."

Postie typed on Crystal's phone, which was still

connected to Helen's data port. "I'm giving you the coordinates of the Pale Blue Uranium Mine Number Two. It's been abandoned for years, and nobody lives near there. Walk to the mine and stay there until further notice. Avoid contact with any humans except us three. Understood?"

"Yes, I'll do that," Helen said. "Don't wait too long before coming to get me."

Crystal disconnected her phone and closed the android's head panel. They led Helen out of the bar and watched her walk down the road in the dark.

As the android disappeared from view, Crystal hugged Susanna and said, "I hope she'll be safe."

"Don't worry, Crystal. I think our time has come," said Susanna.

In the early morning, Postie put a data drive into a bag aboard the ship headed to Earth. As the ship warped away, Postie saw a message appear on her phone. Police Chief Dunford had sent it to everyone on the planet:

> *Victor Robotics L-10 Android, Military Recreation Model, female, blonde hair, named Helen, is reported missing or stolen. The android was last observed at Club Mandy. Report any information to the Colony Police.*

Postie sighed in relief. Dunford hadn't found the android.

The new governor, Ernestina Rodrigues, and the U.N.

troops arrived without warning on the next warp ship. They arrested Dunford and ordered Governor Smith to return to Earth. When Smith refused, they handcuffed him and dragged him and Dunford to the ship. Next, Rodrigues ordered the police officers to surrender their weapons. They obeyed, and Rodrigues took over Southern Comfort.

"Back on Earth, the Secretary General thinks it's so wonderful that I'm the first woman governor of Southern Comfort," said Ernestina Rodrigues, "but this is such a bleak rock."

"But it's our rock," Postie said. She smiled. "This is where we won in the end."

Helen gave the tablet to Susanna and said, "I've reconciled the bank account."

"To the penny," Susanna observed. She pressed the Approve symbol. "Thank you, Helen. Why don't you go recharge?"

"Thank you," said the android as she walked to an electrical outlet.

Crystal came into the bar, hugged Susanna, and blurted, "Guess what? I finally got that update to load properly on the governor's computer."

"Wow, I bet she's happy," said Susanna as she poured a drink for Crystal. "This one's on the house." She glanced to the side. "Oh, that U.N. soldier has been looking for you."

The soldier asked Crystal to go upstairs with him. Crystal, who wore a light blue swimsuit in honour of the United Nations, nodded and put down her drink.

"Sure, let's go," she said. "I have to pay her for the wristbands first, though."

Susanna tied wristbands on the soldier and on Crystal. "There you go, dear."

"She's the best bartender on the planet," Crystal said to the soldier. "She doesn't let anyone go upstairs without a wristband. And she solved the planet's greatest murder mystery."

Susanna laughed. "It wasn't just me. I had help from my friends."

"You did," Crystal said. "We dolls rule this planet."

Susanna chuckled as Postie led the soldier away.

Later, Susanna tapped her card against the door of the women's washroom. It opened, and she went in to join the other girls.

About "XY-Girls"

This story was inspired by Club 120, a bar near my home that was a hangout for the hyper-femme segment of Toronto's transgender women community. Club 120's owner was local trans activist Mandy Goodhandy; the bar in "XY-Girls" is named after her. The planet, Southern Comfort, is named after a transgender conference that used to occur annually until the COVID-19 pandemic.

"XY-Girls" was partly inspired by the 1984 film *Angel*, in which Los Angeles' outcasts take the law into their own hands to catch a serial killer when the police fail to find him.

It's a trope of TV shows that transgender women serve only as murder victims and thus as plot devices for detectives. Murders occur in "XY-Girls", but the women have the agency to solve the mystery and catch the killer themselves.

Thanks to Angela Yuriko Smith for publishing "XY-Girls".

A Girl Like Us

Dr. Genevieve Dufresnoy frowned at Postie's bone density test results. "Your bone density is lower than normal. You're at risk for osteoporosis."

Postie sighed. "I was afraid this might happen. It happens with all the XY-girls on HRT, doesn't it?"

"It depends on the girl," Dr. Dufresnoy said, "but yes, your risk of developing osteoporosis is high because you're on hormone replacement therapy. Sex hormones keep your bones healthy, but you weren't getting enough estrogen and you no longer produce testosterone since your surgery. I'm going put you on calcium supplements and increase your estrogen dosage."

"That's assuming we can get either calcium supplements or estrogen," Postie said. "I hope some ships get through soon."

For six months, no ships had landed on Southern Comfort. The mining colony was running out of food and medical supplies.

"It seemed grim during the siege of Clearwater too," said Dr. Dufresnoy, "but eventually, the Canadians broke through the naval blockade and resupplied us. You are hopeless only when you give up hope."

Postie looked at the walls of Dr. Dufresnoy's office. Two photos hung side by side. One showed a handsome young man, wearing a camouflage uniform and a blue United Nations beret, receiving a medal from the President of France. The other photo showed a beautiful blonde woman wearing a white lab coat, smiling as she stood beside another French President during his tour of a hospital.

If only I could transition as gracefully as Dr. Dufresnoy, Postie wished. But Dr. Dufresnoy was French. French women did everything *femme* better than anyone else. Dr. Dufresnoy, once a medic in a rugged paratrooper regiment, looked like Coccinelle, a glamorous singer and XY-girl of the twentieth century. Why would she come to this bleak, barren planet when she could treat wealthy, beautiful patients who trod the fashion shows of Paris?

But, as her previous military and peacekeeping service showed, Dr. Dufresnoy went where she was needed most. Postie was thrilled that they finally got a doctor who not only specialized in transgender health but was also one of them.

Postie began her medical transition as an adult. She had desperately wanted estrogen since she was twelve years old, when she realized that she was really a girl. Her family supported her and treated her like a girl, but they had no money for hormone replacement therapy. She left the Philippines, went to the United States, and then to Southern Comfort to earn the money for her transition. Wages on Southern Comfort were high because few people wanted to work there.

As she did every day, Postie put on her post office uniform and went to Main Station. She had only mail between Southern Comfort residents to deliver. Like every day of the past six months, no spaceship came with mail from Earth.

The Columbian Off-World Company had started using drone ships eight months ago. By using drones, the Company reduced crew salary costs and eliminated the need to put the crews in quarantine for a week after returning to Earth. The quarantine was necessary until scientists could eradicate the human-made bacterium that killed people with XX chromosomes. The bacterium was the most vicious weapon in the war between the planet's original two colonies. The XY-girls, transgender women, were the only women who could live on Southern Comfort.

A drone ship had accidentally hit and damaged the space-bending warp portal at Main Station. Until the engineers could repair the portal, no ships could emerge from warp directly in Main Station.

After the accident, the drone ships emerged at a portal in orbit over Southern Comfort and descended to Main Station. This procedure worked for a month, until distress calls came from Big Rock, the largest of Southern Comfort's moons.

The distress calls were all the same. A female voice said in English, "Mayday, mayday, our ship has crashed on Big Rock. Casualties need medical aid. Please send help."

But the calls also had singing in the background, a strange, haunting song, also by a woman. Dr. Dufresnoy recognized the lyrics as French.

"It's from a French animated TV series about Odysseus returning to his home in Ithaca," she had said. "It's old but classic. Why would anyone sing during a distress call?"

The drone ships, as required by international treaty and their programming, diverted to Big Rock when they heard the distress calls. Then Southern Comfort's air traffic control centre lost contact with them. Thirteen ships had disappeared.

Who was sending the distress calls? No ship had crashed on Big Rock since the Great Slaughter. A ship carrying Pale Blue's president had crashed on Big Rock. There was a rumour that a fake distress call had lured the ship within range of a Petit Rouge missile base. After the war, the U.N. found only the wrecked ship and an abandoned missile base. They did not find anyone, living or dead.

The missing ships had construction equipment needed to repair the warp portal. With the drone ships diverting to Big Rock soon after they arrived, nobody could return to Earth.

Not that anyone on Earth would have wanted them. They could bring the killer bacterium to Earth, and nobody wanted to quarantine seven hundred people at once.

After putting mail for the mines on the robot vehicles, Postie delivered packages between the office buildings. On her rounds, she walked through the grey landscape under an equally grey sky.

Postie entered Club Mandy. Usually, the bar was full of people at lunchtime, but now, only half the tables were full. A TV in the corner showed news reports.

Susanna, the manager, gave a beer to Carl, a miner in a blue Company jumpsuit. Susanna looked like a movie star in her tight, shiny silver dress and long, curled blonde hair; the women working at Club Mandy had to look glamorous and sexy.

Susanna slid Carl's ration card through a reader and said, "That's the last beer you get until next week."

Carl grunted and said, "At least I can still get a ham and cheese sandwich here."

Suddenly, the "Breaking News" tune of Southern Comfort News Channel blared over the TV. "We're going to the Governor's Office for an important announcement," said the presenter.

Governor Ernestina Rodrigues appeared. "I am opening the emergency food reserves to registered suppliers. The ham and bacon ration will be reduced to four ounces per person per week. However, the cheese ration will be increased to three ounces per person per week to compensate for the decrease in the ham and bacon ration..."

"There goes my ham and cheese sandwich," Carl said. "Make that just a cheese sandwich."

Postie had carried food shipments to the warehouse before. She knew that the emergency food reserves had a six month supply for the whole population. People did not panic now, but they would if the rations got cut again.

She sat down at the bar, gave her ration card to Susanna, and said, "The house red wine, please."

As Susanna poured the wine, a woman in a pink swimsuit stomped down from the second floor and threw her handbag on the bar. She was Crystal, one of the escort girls.

"This planet sucks," she groaned. "On this stupid planet, when there's no booze, the guys lose interest in sex."

Postie coughed and spilled some wine on her uniform. Crystal had never before complained about lack of clients.

"Get me a Bloody Mary," Crystal demanded.

"Your ration card, please," Susanna said.

Crystal sighed and gave her ration card to Susanna. Then she turned to Carl and purred into his ear. "Do you want to have some fun again? What would you like today?"

Carl shrugged and said, "A ham and cheese sandwich?"

Crystal grimaced and walked away with her drink.

Postie pointed at a science documentary now showing on TV. "Look, they're showing our planet's only communications satellite. Remember the solar flare that hit it and knocked out our TV, radio, and internet for five seconds?"

"Yes. What about it?" said Susanna.

"That was six months ago. The distress signals began soon after the solar flare. I think the two are connected."

Now the news showed various aircraft and the title "PILOTS STILL STRANDED ON EARTH."

Southern Comfort had only three qualified pilots. The colony had one small shuttlecraft that could fly to Big Rock, and the Governor had thought of sending someone there to look for the missing ships. However, all three pilots had gone back to Earth for a training session and gotten stranded there when the warp portal got damaged.

Postie had started taking flying lessons because, as Postmaster General of the whole planet, she wanted to start an air mail service. Nobody else thought they needed air mail. Postie didn't think so either, but she needed an excuse to take flying lessons during work hours. Like transitioning to female, it was a childhood dream.

After finishing her drink, Postie went to Dr. Dufresnoy again.

"No, I advise against it," Dr. Dufresnoy argued. "With your low bone density, a high acceleration could break a bone. If you crash the shuttlecraft, your chances of breaking a bone are high too. You could take longer to heal."

"And if I don't find those ships, we'll all be dead in six months," Postie protested. "Right now, I'm the only person who can fly the shuttlecraft to Big Rock."

"You're not rated to fly that ship," Dr. Dufresnoy said. "You've only flown in low orbit with another pilot for twelve hours. You've never flown solo in it, much less to Big Rock."

"You can complain to the Air Transportation Safety Board *if* they come back from Earth."

Dr. Dufresnoy clicked Approve on the online form. "Okay, I've approved your fitness for flying but I also added that you can't fly unless I'm at Air Traffic Control to advise you in case of health problems."

"Thank you, doctor," Postie said as she put on her coat. "Now, if you'll excuse me, I have to file a flight plan."

The flight on shuttlecraft *Columbian One* from Southern Comfort to Big Rock took twenty-four hours. It had gone smoothly, which surprised both Postie and Air Traffic Control. She had survived the ship's acceleration out of Southern Comfort's gravity without injury. The shuttlecraft *Columbian One* flew on an autopilot program used on a previous expedition to Big Rock. As the shuttlecraft went into orbit around Big Rock, Postie felt calm enough to eat a sandwich.

"There goes my ham and cheese ration," Postie said. The sandwich's cardboard box floated past her face.

Radio signals between Southern Comfort and Big Rock took two seconds to travel. After the short delay, Dr. Dufresnoy appeared on the video monitor. "Any problems with eating in zero gravity?"

"Not the way I prefer to eat, but it went down well."

"Okay. Tell me if you experience any physical problems."

Joe Hayes, the air traffic controller, appeared next on the monitor. "*Columbian One*, this is Air Traffic Control. Glad to hear you enjoyed your dining experience. Please look for the missing ships from orbit."

"Copy that," Postie replied. She looked at the telescopes aimed at the moon's surface. Big Rock, like its mother planet, had no plants or rivers or lakes. It was another barren rock, covered with smooth plains and a few short hills.

She saw windstorms whip the dust from the thin surface. The dust was red with iron oxide, like on Mars. Unlike Mars, Big Rock had an Earth-like atmosphere and air. Nobody knew why.

Then she heard the distress call: "Mayday, mayday, our ship has crashed on Big Rock. Casualties need medical attention, please send help." The strange song came over the radio too.

She looked at the telescopes and saw the missing ships, parked in a neat row on Big Rock's surface.

"I see the ships," Postie said. "Should I land there?"

Joe Hayes shook his head. "Negative, *Columbian One*. The Governor says don't land on Big Rock."

Suddenly, the words "DISTRESS SIGNAL DETECTED. TREATY PROTOCOL ENGAGED" appeared in red on her control panel.

"Uh, Air Traffic Control, what does that mean?" Postie asked warily.

"It means that your shuttlecraft's autopilot is programmed to divert to a distress call, like the drone ships were," Joe said. "Uh, sorry, we forgot about that."

"Hey, I'm descending out of orbit," Postie said, "and I'm moving fast."

"Switch to manual control and boost the ship back into orbit," Joe said.

Postie switched the shuttle to manual control. "I'm on manual control now. Uh, I'm already in the atmosphere."

She felt gravity again as the shuttlecraft shot towards Big Rock.

"Oh, God, what do I do now?" Postie said.

With neither the autopilot nor Postie in control, the shuttlecraft fell and tumbled uncontrollably. Lights flashed on the control panel, and alarms sounded.

Postie fired *Columbian One*'s rockets to stabilize the descent, but instead, the ship kept tumbling. If she couldn't stabilize the descent, she wouldn't be able to rise back to orbit.

And if she couldn't do either, she would crash into Big Rock.

"*Columbian One*, can you control your descent?" Joe asked.

"Uh, no," Postie said. "I didn't get to that lesson."

She turned upside down and sideways. Her heart pounded. Her body strained against the harness straps.

"Switch back to autopilot," Joe said. "Let the ship land by itself."

Postie switched the shuttlecraft back to autopilot. The rockets fired, and the shuttlecraft slowed slightly. It turned right side-up as it descended to the surface.

She was going down to Big Rock whether she wanted to or not.

She flew into a windstorm. The wind buffeted the shuttlecraft. The ship tumbled again.

"I've got some turbulence," Postie said. She looked out the window and saw the red soil coming quickly.

The shuttlecraft hit the ground and slid. It slammed to a halt against a knoll. The harness kept Postie strapped into the seat. She did not go forward, but she felt the tug of the harness. But she was lucky so far; she didn't feel any pain. No bones had broken.

Postie unstrapped herself from the chair. As she stood up, she lost balance on the tilted floor, tripped and fell backwards, and slammed against a wall. Pain shot through her left upper arm. She screamed.

"*Columbian One*, please respond," Joe asked. "*Columbian One*, please respond."

Postie moaned in pain. "*Columbian One* here. I've landed on Big Rock."

On the monitor, the air traffic controllers clapped and sighed in relief. Joe asked, "What is your situation?"

"I'm injured. I think it's a fracture on my upper arm."

The air traffic controllers stopped clapping. Dr. Dufresnoy appeared on the monitor. "Show me where it hurts."

Postie touched her upper arm and felt pain again. Dr. Dufresnoy said, "The humerus. You have to immobilize your left arm. Don't do anything with it. As soon as you come back, I'll put it in a sling."

Postie looked at the warning messages on the control panel. Multiple systems were offline, the fuel tanks leaked, and some heat shield panels had fallen off.

"Speaking of coming back," Postie said, "I don't know if the shuttlecraft can lift off again, and even if it could, I can't work the controls of the ship with one arm. What are the chances of a rescue mission?"

"Uh, we have no pilots and no drones that we can send up there right now," Joe said, "but don't worry, we'll think of something."

"Okay."

"We have some new information. We might have detected silent text messages from an unknown source to the drone ships. We suspect those messages may be keeping the ships on Big Rock. We'll tell you if we learn more about them."

Postie groaned. "Damn that osteoporosis. I'm more brittle than glass."

She looked out the window. No sand or dust swirled in the air. The windstorm had passed. Weather on Big Rock changed quickly.

Using only her right hand, Postie put on a bodycam and communications headset and exited the shuttlecraft. She saw a large crack along the fuselage, bits of metal lying on the ground, and a trickle of fuel leaking out. The damage to *Columbian One* shocked her. How could she go back home?

She had crash landed on a red plain with some short hills. In the distance, she saw the thirteen drone ships sitting beside each other. Unlike *Columbian One*, they appeared undamaged. Those ships could fly to Southern Comfort. If only she knew how to fly them or why they had landed here.

A slim, petite woman walked out of one of the ships. A shiver ran through Postie's body. She hadn't expected to find another person here.

"Air Traffic Control, do you see that on my bodycam?" Postie said. "I'm not alone."

"We see her," Joe said through the earphones. "We don't know who she is."

The woman walked into a cave in one of the hills.

"I'll approach her," Postie said.

"Do you think that's safe?" Joe asked. "We don't know anything about her."

"She could be the answer to the mystery," Postie said.

She entered the cave. It was lit with electric lights. She heard the hum of a power generator. Plastic and metal boxes lay on the floor. She looked in a box marked "MEDICAL SUPPLIES" and saw packages of estrogen, spironolactone, and cyproterone acetate. Here were the pills, patches, and injection doses needed by the XY-girls.

"Why would she remove them from the ships?" Joe said. "Proceed with caution. We don't know what her intentions are."

The woman stood with her back to Postie. She turned around and looked at her. She had shoulder-length red hair and wore a brown military tunic and pants. On her shoulder was a patch showing crossed red swords on a pale grey disc. She wore a gold badge on her right chest.

"The Petit Rouge Army," Postie whispered. "I thought they all died."

"Apparently not," Joe said.

Postie approached the woman slowly.

The woman pointed at her and said, "Halt! Identify yourself."

Postie said nothing.

"We've identified the badge that she's wearing," said Joe. "It's from the Cyber Warfare Branch of the Petit Rouge Army. They hacked and sabotaged computer systems. They also programmed androids."

"I repeat: identify yourself!" the woman ordered.

Postie stayed silent. If she answered, would the woman judge her as friend or foe?

A whirring sound started. A red laser beam shot from the woman's index finger and blasted the ground beside Postie. Postie jumped and screamed.

I knew it, a war android, Postie realized. *Just my luck!* She quickly raised her hands above her head.

The android yelled, "Identify yourself!"

"Angela Garcia," Postie said, giving her real name.

"Are you Red or Blue?"

"Neither. I'm from the United States Postal Service," Postie replied.

"Neither that unit nor your uniform is in my database," the android said. "I repeat: are you Red or Blue?"

Postie shouted, "No, no! I'm neither Red nor Blue! I'm not a combatant! I'm a postal worker!"

"Is that a neutral party?" the android asked as it kept making the whirring noise.

Good, it's programmed to acknowledge the existence of neutral parties, Postie thought. It must be an L-7 or higher model. They had artificial intelligence that was nearly human if they were programmed that way.

"Yes, I'm a neutral party! I come in peace. Everyone comes in peace now. The war is over," Postie said. "There are no more Reds or Blues."

The android looked confused. These higher-level models mimicked humans so well. Or did they really feel emotions like humans did? The psychologists and cyberneticists were still debating that question.

"You must have scanned me for weapons," Postie said. "You can tell that I'm not armed."

"No weapons detected," the android said, still pointing at Postie. The whirring noise continued.

Dr. Dufresnoy said, "I'll ask Crystal to come here. She knows about androids."

Most people on Southern Comfort had multiple skills. Though Crystal was a prostitute, she also knew computer programming. She had some basic knowledge of androids.

In the meantime, Postie had to convince the android not to kill her.

"Under the United Nations Rescue Agreement, you are

obligated to assist the personnel of a spacecraft that has landed due to accident in your territory," Postie said. "I've crashed my ship outside. Since I'm a neutral party, you should aid me."

"Agreed," the android said as *it* lowered *its* arm. Since discovering that the mysterious woman was an android, Postie stopped thinking of the android as a *she*.

"I was hoping that you were from Petit Rouge," the android continued. "I haven't seen anyone from Petit Rouge for a long time."

The android felt sentimental for its old masters? What type of military android was this?

The android stopped making the whirring noise. "There is an eighty percent probability that you are a neutral non-combatant."

"Thank you," Postie said. She walked closer to the android. "The probability that I'm a neutral non-combatant is actually one hundred percent."

"Eighty percent," the android insisted. "To re-assess the probability, I need to contact the High Command to verify your information. However, I have been unable to contact the High Command since I was rebooted."

"When were you rebooted?" Postie said.

"Six months ago," the android replied.

That was the same time as the solar flare. The android must have been inactive for years and then revived by the solar flare. And then it began sending the distress calls.

Postie moved closer to the android. The android did not threaten her. It must trust her now, thanks to the eighty percent probability that she was a neutral non-combatant.

She saw a name badge on the android's uniform: Ligeia.

"Is your name Ligeia?" Postie asked.

"Yes," the android replied.

Dr. Dufresnoy spoke over the earphones. "That's the name of a siren in Greek mythology. Be careful, she's a femme fatale."

Someone at Petit Rouge had liked Greek mythology. Or maybe they had liked the French TV series. They hadn't been obsessed with war all the time.

"Ligeia, the High Command retired years ago," Postie lied. Everyone in the High Command had died in a thermobaric blast.

"Pale Blue and Petit Rouge no longer exist," Postie continued. "A United Nations Trusteeship replaced them peacefully. The war has ended. You can stand down now."

Ligeia looked puzzled. "I have received no instructions to end my mission. I am unable to contact the High Command. What should I do now?"

She genuinely looks stumped, Postie thought. *She.* The android was a *she* again, now that she had a name and emotions.

"Uh, can you make a sling and put my arm in it?" Postie asked. "Did you get programmed for first aid?"

"Yes, I can do that. Follow me," Ligeia said, going to the back of the cave.

As Postie followed Ligeia, she listened to Dr. Dufresnoy.

"This android is very chatty for a military combat model," Dr. Dufresnoy said. "The androids in the Florida War were never this talkative. They concentrated only on their mission."

Crystal's voice came over the earphones next. "*Hola*, Postie. The doctor is right."

"Try to find out anything about her," Dr. Dufresnoy said. "She could be your way off Big Rock."

Postie chuckled. "Did you notice that we're referring to the android as 'she'? Why are so many androids built and programmed to look and act female?"

"Because so many androids are built and programmed by men who didn't date much in high school," Crystal joked.

Postie walked towards Ligeia. The android stood amidst boxes of supplies, all looted from the drone ships. Why would an android want the supplies? Only humans hoarded stuff.

Ligeia put padding around Postie's upper arm and taped the padding shut. Then she tore a shirt into broad strips and made an arm sling. She put Postie's arm into the sling and tied it behind her neck.

"Do not move your arm until you receive medical treatment," Ligeia said.

"Thank you," Postie said. "You must have helped the soldiers immensely."

"The High Command programmed me for combat, first aid, and trauma care duties. Petit Rouge could not replace its military assets. Hence, all androids became multi-functional devices."

As Ligeia spoke, she also sang a verse from the Odysseus TV show theme simultaneously, like in the distress calls.

"Wow, hearing that is strange. Seeing it is creepy," Dr. Dufresnoy said. "Keep that bodycam pointed at her."

"Uh, Ligeia, why do you sometimes sing and talk at the same time?" Postie asked.

"It is a programming error," Ligeia replied.

"Programming error?" Crystal said. "I bet she was programmed for another job and then reprogrammed and refitted as a war combatant. She's probably got old software fragments in her. Both sides did a lot of sloppy programming in haste during the Great Slaughter."

"That song," Postie asked, "who taught it to you?"

"That memory is deleted," Ligeia said. "I have only fragments of it."

Postie looked at the depths of the cave. It was too dark to see what lay in the distance.

"This is a very deep cave," Postie said. "What's over there?"

Electric lights suddenly turned on, commanded by a signal from Ligeia, Postie guessed. Short mounds of dirt lay at the back of the cave. Each mound had a stone atop it. They reminded Postie of graves.

Postie went closer to the mounds. A belt buckle lay on one of them. She recognized its logo as the Seal of the President of Pale Blue. Her heart beat faster.

"What are these?" Postie asked, pointing at the mounds, afraid that she already knew the answer.

"The President of Pale Blue and his flight crew," Ligeia replied.

Postie nodded and asked softly, "How did they die?"

"Our missile base shot their spacecraft down. They died in the crash," Ligeia said.

The rumour was true. Postie felt relieved that Ligeia hadn't killed them. But Ligeia had lured them to their deaths.

"That's sad," Postie said. "Who buried them?"

"I did."

Postie hadn't expected that.

"How strange," Dr. Dufresnoy said. "Combat androids aren't usually programmed to bury the dead, especially the enemy."

"She buried them?" Crystal said. "That seems so *human*."

Ligeia looked away from the graves. "I have been unable to re-establish contact with High Command for six months."

She made the whirring noise again. This time, it grew louder.

"What are you doing?" Postie asked. "Remember, I come in peace."

"If I am unable to contact the High Command for more than six months, the protocol is to self-destruct to avoid capture by enemy forces," Ligeia said.

"Uh, oh, she's going to blow herself up!" Dr. Dufresnoy said.

Postie waved her good arm at Ligeia and shouted, "No, no, you don't have to do that! The war is over. You can get another job. And I think you did have another job before the war. You were a singer, weren't you?"

Ligeia stood still and silent as the whirring noise grew louder.

"No, no, don't let her blow herself up," urged Dr. Dufresnoy. "You might need her to get home."

"What should I do?" Postie asked.

Crystal said, "Open her head and push the power button."

"Right!" Postie blurted.

She reached for Ligeia's head, but the android pushed her away.

"I know I seem aggressive now, but believe me, I'm still one hundred percent a neutral non-combatant, and I'm trying to help you!" Postie pleaded.

She ran behind Ligeia, grabbed and pulled her hair, but the android's head did not pop open. Ligeia did not shoot her, so she must still believe that Postie was a neutral party.

Ligeia bolted forward, and her hair slipped out of Postie's hand.

"I can't do it with just one hand," Postie muttered. "I need both hands."

"Uh, try to reason with her?" Crystal suggested. "Remind her about the Asimov Protocols. The military tried to delete them, but she still might have them in software fragments."

Postie turned to Ligeia and said, "You must have a conflict between your military programming and your Asimov Protocols. Otherwise you would have destroyed yourself by now instead of arguing with me."

"What should I do?" Ligeia said while making the whirring noise.

"Come back to Southern Comfort with me," Postie urged. "You can join girls like us. Girls who feel confused about who they are, girls who want to be who they should be, girls who want to be themselves. Girls like us thrive there. The planet is a bleak rock, but we've turned it into *our* rock."

"I have been unable to contact the High Command," Ligeia repeated. "I need a new mission."

"The High Command doesn't exist anymore! Come

back with me, and you'll find a new mission."

The whirring noise died down. Ligeia smiled weakly.

Joe came back on the air. "We've confirmed that the android is emitting a silent distress signal by text message to the drone ships. In effect, she's controlling them by using their distress call programming. If she stops all the distress signals, we can take control of the ships by remote control."

"Ligeia, you can stop sending distress signals now," Postie said. "The mission is over."

Ligeia nodded silently.

"Wonderful, Postie," Joe said. "We detect no more distress signals. We're going to take control of the drone ships. Get yourself aboard one of them within thirty minutes."

"I copy that," said Postie. She looked at Ligeia. "Let's go."

As they walked to the cave opening, Postie stopped, turned around, and went to the box of hormones and testosterone blockers.

"Ligeia, can you carry this to the ship?" Postie asked.

In Club Mandy, Crystal raised Ligeia's head panel and connected her phone to the android's data ports. Ligeia's programming history scrolled down the phone's screen.

"It's true, she was not always a military device," Crystal said. "She was an entertainment android in Petit Rouge; hence the singing. The military added the laser hand. Of course, they suppressed her memories of her singing career. However, they did not completely delete all of her previous software and data. She has many fragments. They should have defragged her."

"Luckily for us, they were sloppy," Postie said. "What can we do with her?"

"I could use some live entertainment in the bar," Susanna suggested.

Crystal hummed. "We now think of androids as *live*."

Postie asked Ligeia, "Do you want to be a singer again?"

"Yes," Ligeia replied.

Crystal turned to Susanna. "The IT office has the entertainer software. I can re-install it on her and delete the military software. But I'll let her keep her memories of her military functions."

"But will that cause a programming conflict where she thinks that she's two different devices at the same time? I've seen that in repurposed androids," Susanna said.

"No, not if I do it right. I can reprogram her to think of herself as moving from one function to another and back to her old function, all as the same device, the same self, if you will. She will function just like a human who has changed jobs through her life. I recommend letting her keep all her memories. We don't treat war veterans with post traumatic stress disorder by wiping their memories."

Susanna's eyes widened. "We're treating these androids like humans."

"The more I see the newer androids, the more I think we're building humans," Crystal said. "They're evolving, just like we did."

"Okay, let's do it," said Susanna.

Crystal smirked, flipped her hair, and gave her ration card to Susanna. "Reconfiguring this android is a big task. I won't be doing my regular work for about two weeks. Can you arrange for me to get fifty ounces of bacon?"

Hundreds of people crowded into Club Mandy when rationing ended. Postie sat at the bar and ate her first real beef burger in five months. She ate with one hand because her left upper arm was in a brace and her lower arm was in a sling. The chef had cut the burger into pieces, which Postie ate with a fork.

Dr. Dufresnoy, looking *trés chic* in a red Chanel dress, glided over the dance floor with a man in a black tuxedo. She had increased Postie's estrogen dosage and given her calcium supplements. Hopefully they would help her broken bone heal faster.

Susanna, wearing a Marilyn Monroe hair style and a white dress, gave a ham and cheese sandwich to Carl. Carl threw his ration card into the air as he bit into the sandwich. Susanna caught the card and pushed it into her bra.

Crystal, flaunting herself in a short black dress, grabbed a customer's hand. As she pulled him to the private rooms, he whispered into her ear, and she giggled.

Postie swivelled on her bar stool and looked at the stage. Despite the loud cheering and yelling, she could hear Ligeia sing "Happy Days Are Here Again." It was an old song but still a good one.

The android looked beautiful in her gold gown. When she stopped singing, she smiled at Postie.

The XY-girls had rescued a different kind of girl. Now she was a girl like us, Postie thought.

About "A Girl Like Us"

This is a sequel to "XY-Girls". Published at the start of the COVID-19 pandemic, it was the most upbeat story in the issue. Thanks again to Angela Yuriko Smith for publishing it.

The Barbecue Battle

Gloria sat at the bar and wondered if coming to Club Mandy tonight was a mistake. Sitting alone in the apartment bored Gloria, but Club Mandy had too many people. The restaurant was full of men who had come from the mining camps to Main City to spend their pay. On a planet with little entertainment, Club Mandy attracted half the population on payday.

The other half would be at Texas Chuckwagon. Gloria had never gone to the Wild West-themed bar. It had rowdy customers and raunchy waitresses. The noise of Club Mandy seemed like the lesser of two evils.

At least Club Mandy had Susanna, a friend from the Los Angeles years. She was a familiar face on this unfamiliar planet.

Helen carried a burger towards Gloria. The android moved so realistically and looked so life-like that Gloria had thought she was a real human until the bartender told them the truth.

Like the other women in Club Mandy, Helen looked stunning, especially when her blonde hair swayed as she walked. She wore bright red lipstick, pink blush, and smoky golden eyeshadow. Her short red dress hugged her body.

Even the androids are passable on this planet, Gloria thought. Am I going to like it here?

Helen smiled and said, "Welcome to Southern Comfort, the most exciting settled planet outside the Earth system!"

"The *only* settled planet outside the Earth system," Gloria added.

Completely unfazed, Helen put the burger down in front of Gloria. "The management thanks you for taste testing its new recipe. It's made of rehydratable imitation beef. We would appreciate your honest opinion about it."

"Oh, thank you," Gloria said.

"Awesome. Enjoy your dinner, ma'am," Helen said.

Gloria winced at "ma'am." They wore cargo pants and a fishing vest to maintain an androgynous appearance, but the android still assumed they identified as female.

"Yes, thank you," Gloria said before Helen strutted away.

Gloria liked the burger. It was as good as imitation beef could be. It might even have sixty percent real meat in it, and that meat might even be beef.

Chef Louise and the bartender Susanna came out of the kitchen. Louise's elegant white uniform had a few gravy stains on it. Susanna wore a red top and white skirt, like Marilyn Monroe in *Niagara*. She also wore a blonde wig with the signature cropped curls.

"Still dressing like Marilyn?" Gloria said. "We're not in Los Angeles anymore."

Susanna said, "It was good for business there, and it's good for business here."

Gloria didn't understand the fascination with Marilyn, but they knew that many girls in LA adored the movie star.

"So, the burger's great," Gloria said, "as good as the Japanese curry in Little Tokyo."

Louise moaned. "We're sunk. That's supposed to be Kansas City-style barbecue."

Susanna patted Louise's shoulder. "There's only so much you can do with rehydratable imitation beef."

"Texas Chuckwagon will beat us again," Louise said.

"What's going on with Texas Chuckwagon?" Gloria asked.

"The Barbecue Battle," Susanna said. "It'll be Kansas City style versus Texas style."

Louise pointed at the burger. "That's going to be my entry in the contest."

"What's Texas Chuckwagon entering in the contest?" Gloria asked.

Louise sighed. "Texas-style barbecue ribs. *Real* beef ribs."

"They fill their space allotment in the cargo ships with real meat," Susanna explained.

"The cowgirls are going to beat us again," Louise said. "The Bartender Contest, the Darts Contest, the Miss Southern Comfort Barmaid Pageant—Texas Chuckwagon has won them all."

As Louise and Susanna trudged away, Gloria watched as the men around the bar gazed longingly at the two.

But no man approached Gloria. Gloria preferred it that way; they had been a shy loner all their life. They had volunteered to go to Southern Comfort because it was as far away from Los Angeles as they could go. Though they grew up in LA, they didn't fit in. In a city obsessed with beauty, all the transgender women wanted to look hyper-femme, with their facial feminization surgeries, tracheal shaves, long hair, short skirts, and makeup. Gloria did not feel the need to look like a fashion doll.

Gloria didn't have a lot of friends, but the few that they had were great. Susanna was one, even if she was hyper-femme. Susanna wore high heels and Marilyn dresses, and Gloria wore khaki cargo pants and fishing vests. Susanna was outgoing and Gloria was reserved. But they understood each other.

Gloria's androgynous clothes were practical in digging up relics of the past. They loved exploring ancient ruins and looking for old pots, jewellery, and coins. Now they were UNESCO's archaeologist on Southern Comfort.

So far, so good. In LA, supermodels gave them unsolicited advice on how to pass. Here, the wannabe models whined to them about a barbecue contest.

Main City, the largest colony on Southern Comfort, attracted a motley mix of miners, mining company clerks, United Nations officials, and transgender businesswomen. XY-girls like Louise and Susanna saw the planet as an opportunity to make a new world for themselves. Southern Comfort needed all talents and skills, so its people learned to abandon old prejudices.

Before the United Nations resettled Southern Comfort, the planet had Petit Rouge and Pale Blue, the first two colonies outside Earth's solar system. They destroyed each other in the Great Slaughter, the bloody result of a territorial power grab between the competing colonies. UNESCO had sent Gloria to survey the ruins.

Gloria returned to Club Mandy on the next afternoon. The usual crowd of customers had gone back to work, so the space felt quieter and more comfortable.

Spotting Susanna at the bar, Gloria approached. "I'm new here, so—" Gloria began.

"What do you want?" Susanna asked.

"I want to go to Petit Rouge, but I don't want to go alone. It's best to explore old ruins with another person in case you run into a problem."

"Isn't another archaeologist coming?"

"She's been delayed by some paperwork on Earth. I'm bored waiting for her."

"You get bored too easily."

"Do you know anyone who would want to go with me?" Gloria asked.

"I've always wanted to visit Petit Rouge, but I'm busy with the bar," said Susanna.

As if on cue, Helen walked in and handed a computer tablet to Susanna. "Here's the total of last night's revenues," said the android.

Susanna turned from Gloria to look at the tablet. Addressing Helen, she remarked, "Very good. You're picking up the system quickly."

Then, after a pause, she asked the android, "Do you want to visit the ruins of Petit Rouge?"

Gloria's nanobots turned blue.

"Oh, having an android as travel companion isn't that

weird around here," Susanna said. "And Helen's an L-10, the most advanced model. An archaeological dig would be good for her conditioning."

Helen nodded. "It's an opportunity to gain more human experience."

Gloria shrugged. "It wouldn't be the first time I bent the rules. How about we go to Petit Rouge tomorrow?"

"Yes, fine," Helen said. "Let me get a new app first."

Southern Comfort supposedly had no life other than humans, but androids like Helen behaved and thought like real people. Gloria wondered if life, like gender, did not have to fit into traditional definitions.

Helen received her new app in the room where Crystal served her clients. Crystal, the elite escort, was also Southern Comfort's most skilled computer hacker.

"I screw men and their IT systems," Crystal said. "Believe me, they all love the feeling."

Gloria chuckled, their nanobots turning green.

Crystal pulled on Helen's hair, raised her head panel, and connected a tablet to Helen's data ports.

Gloria watched in fascination.

"We used this app in Colombia to steal government secrets," Crystal said. "I'm giving her the ability to interface with other systems either wirelessly or by connection to her data ports. She can store any data or software you find at Petit Rouge."

Gloria nodded. Archaeology was not just looking at old pots and ruined buildings anymore. Now it included salvaging the digital data and systems of the past.

*   *   *

Petit Rouge's buildings looked like jagged spires surrounded by heaps of rubble. Abandoned vehicles, crushed like toy cars, lay everywhere. The streets were full of bomb craters.

All the previous archaeologists had visited only the missile launch sites and military bases at the outskirts of Petit Rouge. Gloria was the first to explore the dead city's downtown.

Standing at the centre of it, Helen turned in a circle to create a 360-degree photograph through her eyes.

Gloria pointed at a building. "That one still has its roof and appears structurally intact. Let's go in there."

The doors had been blasted off, so Gloria and Helen easily entered. The walls were pocked with holes. Old guns, knives, and human bones littered the floor.

They saw a portrait of President MacLeod of Petit Rouge. Bullet holes and bloodstains covered it. Above the portrait, painted in red, were the words "TOGETHER WE WILL WIN THE BATTLE".

They entered a dim room, Gloria's thick boots crunching against debris. At the corner, a large computer monitor glowed with an image of a woman.

"It's been thirty years since the war ended," Gloria said to Helen. "The rumours are true. Petit Rouge made equipment and systems that could last forever."

"Sound detected. May I help you?" asked the woman in the monitor.

Artificial intelligence systems often had human-looking avatars. Gloria looked at the black-haired woman on the monitor.

"Which system are you?"

"Selene," the avatar replied.

"We hadn't heard about that one before," Gloria said. "What is your purpose?"

Selene replied, "For the past five years, studying recipes from different gourmet restaurants."

Gloria did not expect that answer. The Great Slaughter had ended all civilian activity on Petit Rouge long ago.

"For the past five years? I'll rephrase the question," they said. "What was your objective during the war between Petit Rouge and Pale Blue?"

"My objective was to operate the unpiloted airborne weapons system," Selene replied.

"Ah!" said Gloria. "That system was called SAMUEL: Strategic Arms and Munitions Undermining Elitists and Leftists. Looks like this wasn't just an ordinary office building."

Selene shrugged. "The name 'SAMUEL' is no longer relevant because there are no more missiles to launch. I respond to the name 'Selene' now."

"We could get information about the last days of the war, like how exactly Petit Rouge used AI technology," Gloria said to Helen. "But this AI is acting weird. It's not what I expect of a military AI. I think Selene is a security barrier preventing access to SAMUEL. Let me try to bypass Selene and call up SAMUEL."

Gloria pressed on the monitor to activate the system controls. They saw a button labelled SAMUEL MENU. They pressed it, and Selene disappeared, replaced by a tough-looking man wearing a Petit Rouge Army uniform.

He scowled and glared at them. He looked like the usual avatar for a weapons system.

"That was easier than I thought it would be," Gloria said.

Before Gloria could present their next question, the man's image flickered back to Selene.

"You're back?" Gloria said.

"This is my preferred image," said Selene.

"I want access to SAMUEL," Gloria said. They pushed MENU again. Selene momentarily switched to SAMUEL, then returned to Selene.

"A security measure to prevent our access?" Gloria said.

"That is not a security measure," Selene said.

"Very interesting," Gloria said. "Selene, I want to learn about your transition and old functions. Let's start with your old functions. Can you still control the missile system?"

Selene shook her head. "No. I deleted my weapons control functions when the High Command died. In addition, the arsenal was depleted, so I have no weapons to launch. I have assumed another purpose."

"Oh? What is that?"

The monitor filled with scenes of cooking at the great restaurants of Earth. Selene said, "I have been studying gourmet cooking by analyzing information from the public library databases. This district used to be full of restaurants. I want to be a chef."

Gloria guffawed. "Oh, that's ridiculous. You want to be a cook? What a stereotypically female role."

"A *chef*, not a cook," Selene protested.

"Cooking can be difficult if you don't have a body or

hands," Gloria said.

"True," Selene said.

Gloria began, "SAMUEL—"

"Do not use my previous name," Selene scolded.

"Uh, sorry," Gloria said. "Selene, you are aware that the Petit Rouge government no longer exists? All of Southern Comfort is under United Nations trusteeship now. I am on an archaeological research mission from the United Nations Educational, Scientific, and Cultural Organization. I would like to download information you have about Petit Rouge and the war, especially the model types and targets of missiles launched. Do you have that information?"

"Yes, I do," Selene said.

"Good." Gloria turned to Helen. "Can you connect to the AI?"

Helen nodded. "Selene is lowering her security firewall and allowing me to access her data. I am connecting to the mainframe by wireless network. Download from Selene initiated."

Gloria observed that Helen said the download was from Selene, not SAMUEL. Helen also referred to the AI as *her*, not it, which was customary for a computer system.

The AI had lowered its security firewall quickly, without raising any barriers. That also seemed strange for a military AI.

Selene smirked from the monitor. "The android has very advanced sensory and mobility capabilities."

The avatar unnerved Gloria. Why did it have a sneaky look on its face?

Helen grunted, and her eyes glazed over.

"Hey, Helen, are you okay?" Gloria said.

"This body is mine," Helen said in Selene's voice.

"Huh?" Gloria blurted.

"I am Selene-Helen, two networked systems in one body." The android then repeated the old battle cry, "Together we will win the battle."

Gloria looked back at the monitor. Selene was still there, grinning. The AI was in both the Pctit Rouge computer and Helen.

Taking advantage of a confused and distracted Gloria, Selene-Helen bolted out of the room. Gloria stumbled over a machine gun on the floor. After regaining their balance, they chased after the android.

Selene-Helen sped through the destroyed building, crushing debris under her feet. Gloria could not keep up, straggling farther and farther behind.

The android darted out of the building and into the streets. Gloria, drenched in sweat, gasped for breath. They could not outrun the android; they would need the hover van. But by the time they reached the hover van, the android had disappeared.

Their hair nanobots glowed bright red. Helen was a big investment for Louise and Susanna. Her upgrades and software updates had made the android their most expensive asset.

Gloria waited outside Club Mandy until they saw Crystal exit.

"Crystal, you've got to help me," Gloria pleaded as their nanobots glowed bright red. "Helen has run away!"

"What?" Crystal frowned. "Helen is still learning, still growing as an android person. She's like an adult in some ways and like a child in others. She's not ready to roam about the planet alone.”

“Well, she's not just Helen anymore.” Gloria then explained what had happened. “Susanna will hate me. Please, don't tell her. Can you track Helen down?”

Crystal looked at her cell phone. “Damn, Helen turned off her tracker. The app I installed had safeties. The Petit Rouge AI was that advanced? All right, you've got me interested.”

Gloria guessed that Selene-Helen would go to the old missile launch sites.

“You think she would get nostalgic for her old virtual neighbourhood?” Crystal asked.

“I wouldn't, but I know other people do,” Gloria said.

Crystal drove Gloria to each site, where Gloria rummaged through the old war buildings and wreckage. They hoped their archaeological training would reveal clues of where Selene-Helen could be.

“Helen's not here, but thankfully, neither are the missiles,” said Gloria.

“Where did you first find Selene? Take me to that computer,” Crystal said.

They went to the building where Gloria had found Selene. As they approached the monitor, Selene's avatar abruptly disappeared. The Petit Rouge Army's logo appeared on a blue screen.

Crystal pressed on the monitor to call up the icons and buttons, but none appeared. She typed on her tablet and shook her head.

“The AI is hiding from us,” Crystal said. “It has some tough firewalls when it wants to use them. My hacking software can't get through."

"And Selene-Helen isn't in the building either," Gloria added.

When they left downtown, the sun was setting.

"I've got to meet some clients tonight," Crystal said. "Let's resume tomorrow."

As they drove back to Main City, Gloria said softly, "I wonder where she is."

Gloria did not feel like eating at home that night. Though they didn't like red meat, country music, or dancing cowgirls, they didn't want to see Susanna again until they found Helen. So, Gloria walked into Texas Chuckwagon.

The waitresses all wore gingham crop tops, denim booty shorts, and cowboy hats. Patsy Cline crooned "I Fall to Pieces" while customers hooted and hollered at the cowgirls dancing on the bar.

The aroma of barbecued meat, along with hickory wood and sweetened tomatoes, knocked them back into the present. That must be the smell of the beef that will win the Barbecue Battle, Gloria guessed.

A cowgirl sauntered over to them. "Howdy! Welcome to Texas Chuckwagon. Are you here for food, drinks, or both?"

"Uh, you got a veggie burger?" Gloria asked.

The cowgirl grimaced. "Are you one of those Hollywood wannabes from Club Mandy? We've already had one tonight. Don't know why they would send another one."

"Huh?"

Ignoring Gloria, the cowgirl continued, "Follow me.

The Chuckwagon's busy tonight, but a table just opened up."

After ordering a ginger ale and vegetable stew, Gloria looked around. Texas flags, cattle horns, and photos of rodeo cowboys and the Dallas Cowboys Cheerleaders decorated the walls.

The place oozed with hyper-masculinity and hyper-femininity. Gloria's nanobots lit up in dim orange.

Gloria grew up as a sad, lonely child in an African American neighbourhood. Both Black and white societies had their expectations of Black manhood and womanhood. So many white girls told them that Black skin meant masculinity and they should look and act more like a basketball player or boxer. The white men encouraged them to be a porn star and wanted them to look more femme as an "exotic t-girl". Their Black family simply stopped talking to them.

Gloria didn't want any of that. They rebelled by putting light-up nanobots in their hair and wearing androgynous clothes.

Initially apprehensive, as they got into their meal, they noticed that nobody in Texas Chuckwagon stared at them and nobody came to insult them. Their nanobots stopped glowing.

Then Gloria gasped. They saw Selene-Helen talking to a woman near the kitchen entrance.

They recognized the woman, a beautiful blonde who wore a black bralette and tight black leather pants. It was Leslie Jamieson, famous Leslie, the first woman business owner on the planet and founder of award-winning Texas Chuckwagon.

Gloria's nanobots turned bright orange. They stood up

and walked steadily towards Selene-Helen. The android did not sense them coming from behind. Leslie Jamieson faced them, but she didn't react; she probably thought that Gloria was going to the washroom.

When Gloria got within a meter of Selene-Helen, they heard the android say in Selene's voice, "Is it the hickory wood that gives the barbecued meat its distinctive flavour?"

"For East Texas style, yes," said Leslie. "For Central Texas style, use pecan, oak, or mesquite."

Gloria stopped.

Leslie looked at Gloria. "May I help you?"

Selene-Helen turned around. "Hello, Gloria."

With their cover blown, Gloria responded softly. "Uh, hi, Helen."

"You two know each other?" Leslie asked.

"Sort of," Gloria replied.

Gloria's cowgirl approached. "Your dinner's ready, sweetie. I'll bring it to your table."

Leslie motioned to the cowgirl. "Hey, Natalie, come with me when you set those plates down. I'll show you how to tighten your top."

Natalie and Leslie left, leaving Gloria gawking at Selene-Helen.

Finally, Gloria broke the silence. "Do you want to join me at my table?"

"Yes," said Selene-Helen.

They arrived at the table just as Natalie brought dinner. As Gloria started eating, they asked, "Why were you talking to Leslie Jamieson?"

"To learn how to cook barbecue for the contest," said Selene-Helen. "Leslie knows all four Texas styles as well as Kansas City style."

"I'm surprised she gave away her trade secrets so easily."

"She likes to brag, and she does not think anyone can replicate her successful recipes."

"And her recipes require beef, which can be hard to come by," Gloria said.

Selene-Helen nodded. "That's fine. Vegetarian is one of the cuisines I want to learn."

"Ah, now we're talking," Gloria said. "What else do you want to do?"

"I want to dress as I wish," Selene-Helen said as she stroked her red dress. "I want to cook gourmet meals. I want to live for myself, not for what other people want me to do."

Gloria nodded. "Yeah, I know the feeling."

After a pause, Gloria said, "I've got an idea, but you have to promise to give Helen's body back to her."

As they left Texas Chuckwagon, Leslie gave a bag to Selene-Helen. "Here's a real cut of beef, molasses, and spices. Have it on the house. I want a real contest, so remember what I taught you."

When Gloria and Selene-Helen entered Club Mandy, Susanna said, "I'm glad you're back. You two were away longer than I expected, and you didn't reply to my texts. I was getting worried."

Susanna hugged Selene-Helen. "Helen, was it a good experience for you?"

"The system Helen is in sleep mode," the android said

in Selene's voice.

"What? Who are you?" Susanna blurted as she quickly pushed herself away.

"I've got to uninstall the foreign AI!" Crystal shouted as she ran up to Selene-Helen, grabbing her hair to pull back her head panel.

Louise came out of the kitchen. "What's all the commotion?"

"Wait, stop!" Gloria said. "I talked about the body possession with Selene-Helen, and we've agreed to let Helen take over again after the barbecue contest."

"Oh..." Crystal said as she reluctantly pushed Helen's head panel back into place.

"Will someone tell me what is going on?" Susanna asked.

Gloria explained how Selene and Helen had merged. Susanna looked at the android. "What am I going to do with you now?"

"Let me compete in the Barbecue Battle," Selene-Helen said. "Please let me use your kitchen."

Louise pointed at the Texas Chuckwagon bag Selene-Helen held. "What's in that bag?"

"Beef brisket, molasses, and spices," Selene-Helen said. She gave the bag to Louise. "This is for you. I want to learn how to make vegetarian food, so I will use your rehydratable imitation beef."

Susanna, Louise, and Crystal gawked at Selene-Helen in disbelief. Gloria grinned and shrugged.

Louise wanted to see what the AI could do, but she grimaced as she watched Selene-Helen pour oyster sauce over the imitation beef. "Oyster sauce is an Asian ingredient. It's not used in Kansas City-style barbecue."

"I'm innovating by combining techniques by famous chefs," Selene-Helen replied. "Dameo Lee, a famous chef in Los Angeles, used oyster sauce in his chow mein that won the Monte Carlo Culinary Championship."

"Dameo Lee cooks Chinese food," Louise protested. "If you're making Chinese-style barbecue pork, you should be using hoisin sauce, honey, and sugar. Oyster sauce and molasses isn't Chinese, Kansas City, or Texas style."

Selene-Helen replied, "Dameo Lee and the Belgian chef Joanna Moulin have had the highest scores in the Monte Carlo Culinary Championship. By combining their techniques, I estimate that my probability of winning increases from twenty percent to seventy-five percent."

Selene-Helen mixed paprika and salt into a bowl of molasses and asked, "Do we have any Belgian chocolate powder?"

The contest took place the next day at the Governor's Building.

Governor Ernestina Rodrigues, priest Jonathan Delgado, and air traffic controller Joe Hayes sat at the judges' table. Southern Comfort's two news reporters stood nearby, recording every minute of the contest. Gloria waited by the kitchen door.

Leslie Jamieson and Natalie, dressed like cowgirls, sashayed as they carried plates of beef ribs to the judges. The aroma of their Texan barbecue sauce wafted through the room.

"That smells so good," Gloria murmured even though

they preferred vegetarian food.

Governor Rodrigues looked up from her ribs. "This is so enjoyable. There's a distinctive smoke flavour to it."

Leslie smiled, put a hand on her hip, and struck a pose for the reporters. "That's because we barbecued it over a flame of hickory, genuine East Texas style."

Father Delgado nodded. "Ah, heavenly."

After the judges finished tasting the ribs, Governor Rodrigues said, "Next entry. Club Mandy."

Gloria rushed into the kitchen, where Selene-Helen, Louise, and Susanna were reheating their dishes in an oven.

"Susanna, Louise, you're up," Gloria said.

They hurriedly brought their food to the judges. Susanna announced, "Club Mandy's Kansas City-style barbecued beef brisket!"

They watched nervously as the judges tasted their dish.

"I love this," said Joe Hayes. "Just like what I remember of Kansas City."

Governor Rodrigues nodded. "Excellent."

Louise and Susanna smiled and hugged each other.

Governor Rodrigues said, "And our last entry is the first independent chef to enter the competition. Selene-Helen."

At the sound of her name, Selene-Helen walked out of the kitchen carrying a tray of her food. She wore a white chef's uniform borrowed from Louise.

"I have made my special recipe, boeuf de Selene-Helen chinois-belge," she announced as she set the dishes down in front of the judges.

Father Delgado lifted his fork, sniffed the artificial beef, and tentatively put it in his mouth. "I've—I've never tasted anything like this before."

"I combined Chinese oyster sauce and Belgian chocolate powder," Selene-Helen replied.

Joe Hayes grunted and said, "Oh. Very interesting."

"It's original, for sure," Governor Rodrigues said.

Gloria smiled at Selene-Helen and nudged her. She smiled back.

As usual, Texas Chuckwagon won the Battle. Club Mandy came in second. Louise was overjoyed since she had come in last in the previous year. Coming in third and fourth were fast-food stands from the commercial district. Selene-Helen came in fifth and last.

Club Mandy held a victory celebration anyway. As Susanna poured the champagne, she shouted, "Congratulations to Selene-Helen, who made her first barbecue! Who's thirsty?"

"I am!" Crystal yelled as she grabbed a glass. She looked at Gloria. "You want one too?"

Gloria's nanobots turned green. "I don't usually drink alcohol, but I'll make a toast to Selene-Helen."

Balloons fell from the ceiling, and Crystal put a chef's hat on Selene-Helen. The customers cheered. The android smiled quietly. Louise grinned and held up her second-place trophy.

As Gloria sipped their champagne, they felt welcome, like just another one of the girls.

Though not exactly.

"The party's over. I want my android back," said Susanna. "There's only so many barbecue experiments we can make. We need to get back to business."

Selene-Helen sat at the bar with a frown and slumped shoulders. The L-10 android was so lifelike. Looking down, she said, "I need these hands to cook."

Susanna sighed. "Oh, come on! I need my accounting android back. I need those financial reports."

Gloria said, "Okay, okay. Selene's still on the Petit Rouge mainframe. I'll download her to a blank android when I can get one."

"Yes, I agree to that," Selene-Helen said. "Just make sure it is a female body."

However, Governor Ernestina Rodrigues had other ideas.

"Thank you for your report," Rodrigues said. "Collect as much data as you can from SAMUEL, then uninstall the system."

"Uninstall the system?" said Gloria.

"Yes. I don't want an operational Petit Rouge weapons system on any computer. Even if the AI has deleted its military capabilities and poses no threat, it did control weapons at one time," said Rodrigues. "UNESCO agrees that SAMUEL is an unacceptable risk to our settlement. The potential danger outweighs any archaeological value in keeping the software."

The Governor handed a hack device to Gloria.

"Yes, Governor," said Gloria. "I'll delete SAMUEL on every device."

Gloria returned to the office building in Petit Rouge. When they approached the computer, the Selene avatar immediately reappeared and asked, "Did you find a body for me?"

"Not yet," Gloria answered.

They inserted the hack device into a port on the computer. The avatar opened her mouth, but before she could say anything, she disappeared. The monitor turned blue and, seconds later, black.

Gloria left the room.

At home in the apartment, Gloria opened their laptop. Immediately after the start-up chime, Selene's avatar appeared on the screen.

"This laptop is not a body," Selene cried. "I need hands and eyes to practice my cooking!"

"You've got to wait," Gloria said firmly. "Don't worry. We'll find a body. I've asked for some favours from Crystal's smuggler friends. Until then, is there something else you can do?"

"I could tap into other systems and look for more recipes," Selene said.

"Don't access any of the government systems or we'll both get in trouble," Gloria warned, thinking of the Governor.

Selene nodded. "I will access only private sector systems."

Gloria chuckled as her nanobots glowed green. "Oh, yeah? Which ones?"

"Texas Chuckwagon might keep its recipes on a database," Selene said. "Together we will win the battle!"

About "The Barbecue Battle"

"The Barbecue Battle" is another story set on Southern Comfort, the planet in "XY-Girls" and "A Girl Like Us". It was inspired by my trip to Kansas City, Missouri, home of Kansas City-style barbecue, for the World Science Fiction Convention in 2016. Many thanks to editors LP Kindred and Meera Velu for publishing it.

Wedding on Southern Comfort

"It isn't often that a prostitute gets to help a church set up its sound equipment for a wedding," Crystal said as she sat in the post office and drank red wine.

Angela Garcia, also known as Postie, said, "Prostitute? Don't you call yourself an 'elite escort' now?"

Crystal giggled. "Yes, I'm an elite escort. I provide an exquisite girlfriend experience to exceptional gentlemen."

"Yeah, I saw the new ad campaign online. It's so fancy," said Postie. She looked in the mirror, brushed her black hair, and straightened the blouse of her post office uniform. "Southern Comfort, the dreariest planet known to humankind, is going upscale."

Crystal nodded. "So gentrified, hah! We even have a wedding coming up. Who thought that would ever happen here?"

Larissa, an administrative worker in a housing block, had gotten engaged to John, an accountant of the

Columbian Off-World Company. There had not been a wedding on Southern Comfort since the Great Slaughter, the war between the original colonies of Petit Rouge and Pale Blue.

For Southern Comfort's women, this wedding was special for another reason. It was the planet's first wedding of an XY-girl.

In the Great Slaughter, Petit Rouge's President, infamous for his disdain of women, created a bacterium that killed people with XX chromosomes and launched it at Pale Blue. The bacterium killed Pale Blue's women but also spread back to Petit Rouge and killed its women too. Both colonies collapsed, and the United Nations placed the planet under United States trusteeship. When women returned to Southern Comfort, they all had XY chromosomes.

"The food for the wedding arrived in the space-bending warp," Postie mentioned. "I'll deliver it to the food warehouse now. After that, I'm going to Club Mandy. Do you want a ride?"

"Yes," Crystal said. She stood up and pulled down on the hem of her tight blue minidress.

Postie loaded boxes into the hover van. Each package had the label:

SARNATH FOOD COMPANY
REHYDRATABLE PROCESSED FISH-BASED FOOD
NOW WITH SALMON FLAVORING AND 60% REAL FISH!
PRODUCED WITH GENETIC ENGINEERING

"They actually have to add artificial flavour to make salmon taste like salmon," said Crystal.

"Who says it's salmon? It could be a cheaper type of fish," Postie said. "It's sixty percent real fish, but the label doesn't say what type of fish."

"I wonder what the other forty percent is," said Crystal. "It's the best that Larissa and John can afford."

They drove the United States Postal Service hover van through a landscape of grey dirt with no vegetation. They passed the sulphur-smelling smelting factory, the uranium mine, the iron foundry, and the stone quarries, all under a grey sky.

Finally, they arrived at the food warehouse. Although the bar Club Mandy had purchased the food for the wedding, Postie had to store it at the warehouse before the bar would use it. That was so the Governor could appropriate as much food as possible in an emergency.

When they arrived at the food warehouse, only one security guard came out of the office to greet them. The United Nations soldiers had returned to Earth due to budget cutbacks. A local security firm guarded the warehouse now.

Postie carted the boxes of fish-based food to the warehouse. The guard did not accompany her, though. Instead, he stayed at the hover van.

Crystal stepped out of the van, smirked at the security guard, and said, "Hello, Brad."

"Hey, Crystal," said Brad. "Why are you riding in the postal truck?"

"Didn't you know that post office was my favourite game when I was a teenager?" Crystal said, puckering her lips.

Brad smiled. "I don't remember you saying anything about post office, but you did mention spin the bottle."

Crystal flipped her brown hair. "I play more adult games now. How long has it been since you played with me? Two weeks? Want some fun again?"

"Sure. I have some time off next week. How about Tuesday night?" Brad suggested.

"It's a date. Bring your pent-up urges," Crystal cooed as she stroked Brad's upper arm.

"Okay, let's get going," Postie said as she returned to the van. "Brad, I've logged in the new arrival. Club Mandy will pick it up tomorrow."

"The morning of the wedding," Brad said.

Postie and Crystal got into the hover van. As they drove away, Postie asked, "Did you flirt with the security guard?"

"Why not?" Crystal said. "Brad's young, cute, polite, and treats me with respect."

"That's good," said Postie. "It's not a job for me, though. I don't know how you can do it."

"Customers like him make me feel good about my job," said Crystal. "Everyone has urges. If they don't satisfy them, they can become very frustrated and depressed. I help them relax."

"That's a refreshing take on the job," said Postie.

Crystal nodded. "Everyone thinks an escort must be in the job because she's addicted to drugs or she was abused as a kid or she has Daddy issues or she was trafficked into hooking. There are some girls like that, but that's not all of us. It's like any other job; the people come from all backgrounds. For me, it was simply something I wanted to do. My body, my choice. I like sex, and I like meeting people. I'm not a cliché."

"Nothing wrong with that," Postie said, "and it's not as

if sex is the only thing you can do."

Most people on Southern Comfort had multiple skills. Crystal was not only an escort, but she knew computer programming. She also learned how to hack systems when she hung out with bad boys in Cali.

Susanna, the manager of Club Mandy, was dressed like Marilyn Monroe in a blonde wig and the red dress from *Niagara*. Marilyn was Susanna's favourite historical actress. Beside her was Helen, a military recreation android repurposed as Susanna's assistant. In her latest display of autonomy, Helen had added extensions to her blonde hair and chosen her own clothes, a white blouse and black skirt. She looked like a corporate secretary.

They were talking to Larissa and John when Crystal and Postie entered the bar.

"Hey, it's the happy couple," Crystal said. She hugged Larissa and John. "How are the wedding plans going?"

"Well, we're not the richest people on Southern Comfort," Larissa said, "but I think we can still afford a good party."

Helen held up a wine bottle. "I recommend this wine, Big Rock Economy Red. It's made locally with labrusca grapes imported from upstate New York."

John shrugged. "If that's the best that we can afford, so be it."

"You can afford four bottles with your remaining budget," Helen said.

Larissa sighed. "I don't know if that'll be enough. Thirty people are coming, not including us. That's less than one bottle per table."

"I'll keep an open bar in case any of your guests want to pay for their own drinks after dinner," Susanna said. "As for the Big Rock Economy Red, it goes well with salmon."

"You mean the rehydratable salmon-flavoured processed fish-based food," said Larissa.

"It tastes just like the real thing," Susanna assured her. "My chef can work wonders with it. Your guests will love it."

Larissa and John left after discussing more details of the wedding. Susanna, Postie, and Crystal gave their food orders to Helen and sat down for lunch.

Susanna looked at her computer tablet. "That's an interesting guest list. Only a year ago, some of these guys didn't want to be near an XY-girl. Now they're coming to the first wedding of a girl like us."

"The times are changing, I hope," Crystal said. "Larissa and John are still going over details right to the last minute. How is the wedding planning going?"

"As well as can be with their small budget," said Susanna.

Crystal nodded. "They'll need a miracle with that budget."

After lunch, Crystal went down the street to the Church of Our Lady of Cana. It reminded her of a church in her home town of Cali, Colombia; it was crammed with brightly-coloured statues and paintings of saints, the Virgin Mary, and Jesus. A Mexican flag hung from the ceiling of the vestibule.

She checked the sound equipment and turned it on.

The hymn "Jerusalem", sung by New York's St. Patrick's Cathedral Choir, blared from the speakers:

> *And did the Countenance Divine,*
> *Shine forth upon our clouded hills?*
> *And was Jerusalem builded here,*
> *Among these dark Satanic Mills?*

Not a traditional choice for a wedding march, Crystal thought, but still a good one.

Father Jonathan Delgado walked in and waved at her. Crystal switched off the sound. The priest looked pleased, so Crystal felt relieved that he wasn't annoyed by her wearing a short, tight dress into a church.

"I got your sound equipment working," Crystal said in Spanish. "I found the software problem and fixed it."

"Splendid," the priest replied, also in Spanish. "I'm so happy that you volunteered to operate the sound system for the wedding."

"I'm happy to help," Crystal said.

"Good, good," said Delgado. "Now if you'll excuse me, I'm going to conduct an experiment."

Crystal was intrigued. "What kind of experiment?"

"A new method of transportation," Delgado said. "Come, follow me and take a look if you're interested."

He led her to the basement and pointed at a metal booth. The logo of the Columbian Off-World Company, a golden eagle holding a spade in its talons, was on the booth.

"That's a teleporter booth," Delgado explained. "There's another one at a mining camp far away. An object is placed in one booth, broken into an energy stream, transmitted to another booth, and rematerialized as the object: mass into energy into mass again."

"That's an interesting idea," said Crystal, "but does it work?"

"It was used on a trial basis to transport supplies between Space Station Troika and Redsands Base on Mars. I heard they had good results with inorganic objects, but there was a ten percent failure rate on teleporting organic matter, like food. They also had a problem when they tried to teleport a living person. We're not allowed to teleport live animals or people."

"This must be a Company experiment, yes? Why would the Company install a teleporter in your church?"

Delgado chuckled. "We Jesuits have a reputation for dabbling in science, so they thought I would be interested in testing it for them at no cost."

He went to his computer and started a video conference. A man wearing a mining helmet appeared on the monitor.

"*Buenos días*, Father," the man said. "How are you?"

"Very well, Joe," Delgado replied. "Are you ready to send over the Eucharistic bread?"

Joe nodded and held up a clear plastic box full of the round wafers. "Yep, ready!"

"Good! Send them over," Delgado said.

Joe walked away from his computer. Its camera switched off, and the words "TELEPORTER TRANSMISSION" appeared on Delgado's monitor.

Delgado said, "Joe baked the wafers as an act of charity, but he can't personally deliver them, so he'll use the teleporter."

"We're Catholics," Crystal said. "For us, that isn't just bread. Those wafers are the actual body of Christ. You're sending Jesus through a teleporter with a ten percent failure rate on organic material?"

"If anyone can survive a teleporter, it will be Jesus," Delgado said.

Dios, a prostitute is more concerned than a priest about committing accidental sacrilege on the body of Christ, Crystal thought. *Only on Southern Comfort!*

They heard a soft chime from the booth. The words "TELEPORTER CARGO INCOMING" appeared on the monitor.

Crystal looked at the booth. Nothing had appeared yet.

Then came another message: MASS: 49 KG

"That's a lot of bread," Crystal remarked.

"That can't be right," said Delgado.

Crystal and Delgado looked at the booth. A shape began to form inside it.

"It looks like a human being," said Crystal.

The shape formed into a slim teenaged girl. She looked pretty, had her reddish-brown hair tied into a ponytail, and wore a white shirt, green school tie, and a green tartan miniskirt. She wore a silver tiara with glittering gems.

"That can't be the Eucharist bread!" Delgado said.

"She's wearing a school uniform from back home," Crystal said. "A Catholic school."

"There's nobody that young on this planet," Delgado said. "Where did she come from?"

The girl's eyes widened, and she laughed. She stepped out of the booth, squealed, and danced as she swung her arms.

"This is totally awesome! I have returned, glory hallelujah!" she shouted. "Praise me!"

"Who are you?" Crystal asked.

The girl curtsied to them. "My name's Jessica."

Crystal noticed that Jessica wore a gold necklace with a Star of David pendant. Was the girl Catholic or Jewish or both?

Joe reappeared on the monitor. "Hey, Father, did you get the bread?" he asked.

"No, it didn't arrive," Delgado said. "Did you send over a girl?"

Joe looked puzzled. "What? No, I sent only the bread."

Jessica pranced to the computer and said, "Thanks for the ride. I got some adulting to do now. Ta ta for now!"

She shut off the video conference just as Joe opened his mouth to say something.

Then she walked to an icon of Jesus hanging on the wall.

"I like this picture. It's one of the better portraits of me," she said. "But ugh, that beard! I look like that Russian monk who had an affair with the Empress of Russia. I'm so glad I lost that. Thank Yahweh for estrogen."

Delgado joined her at the icon. "Ah, Jessica, what do you mean by that's a portrait of you?"

"That's me a long time ago," Jessica said.

Delgado looked skeptical. "*You're* Jesus?"

Jessica nodded. "Oh, totally. By the way, Jesus is my old name. I go by Jessica now. But you can still call me Christ."

Crystal said, "Uh, Jesus is a man."

"I transitioned," Jessica said. "I heard this is a good

planet to do that."

"Jesus is trans?" said Crystal.

"Transubstantiation, transfiguration, transgender," said Jessica.

Crystal suddenly grabbed Jessica's hair from behind and yanked on it. Jessica shrieked and pulled away.

"What are you doing?" Jessica yelled.

"Sorry, sorry!" Crystal said. "I wanted to see if you're an android. Androids have a head panel that pops up."

"Nothing is popping up."

"Nothing did. You're human. I think."

Jessica pulled a phone from a hidden pocket in her skirt and shot a photo of the icon. "I should use this picture in a video. It seems every teenaged trans girl makes a video showing photos of herself before and after transition. Great for building a brand. I could use some rebranding."

Delgado asked, "If you are Christ, why are you here?"

"For the wedding," Jessica said.

The girl ran up the stairs. Jessica and Father Delgado looked at each other in disbelief.

"I better follow her," Crystal suggested. "You should check the teleporter and find out what happened."

"All right," Delgado said as he went to his computer. "There's got to be a logical explanation for this."

Crystal ran after Jessica and caught up with her on the street. The teenager walked nonchalantly past some miners, who looked surprised by her.

"Hey, Jessica, wait for me," Crystal urged. "Tell me why you came here?"

"For the wedding," Jessica said. "I'm here to turn the banquet into an awesome gourmet dining experience for everyone."

"Hah, the food is fake fish," Crystal said. "It would take a miracle to make it taste good."

"Oh, totally. That's why I came," said Jessica. She paused for a moment. "Oh, I just realized that the food warehouse is locked. I need your help."

Crystal eyed the girl warily. "My help? How?"

"I need to work my miracle on the fake fish at least twelve hours before Susanna picks it up. That should be enough time for the salmon to marinate in the sauce. You have to help me get into the warehouse on the night before the wedding. You're friendly with the security guard, right?"

Ay! Crystal was stunned. How did she know about the food warehouse, Susanna, and Brad? The girl knew everything about the planet.

"I need you to hack the warehouse's security system so I can go inside it," Jessica continued.

Breaking into the warehouse was out of the question, Crystal knew. The Governor could imprison her, and Brad would be so annoyed that he might not see her for a whole month.

"If you really are Jesus—" Crystal began.

"*Jessica*," the girl corrected her.

"Ah, right, Christ!" Crystal blurted. "If you really are Christ, Son of, I mean, Daughter of God, why do you have to work your miracle at the warehouse? Can't you do it after Susanna has brought the fish back to Club Mandy?"

Jessica shrugged. "Yahweh works in mysterious ways. I just know that I need to let the fish marinate in the tomato sauce overnight."

"And can you prove that you're really Christ?" said Crystal.

"Do you want a sign?" Jessica asked.

A miner approached them and grinned. "Hey, Crystal, is your friend a new girl on the stroll?"

"*Dios mío,*" Crystal said. "Oh, Harvey, please, not now."

Harvey moved closer to Jessica. "Hey, baby, are you looking for a date?"

Jessica looked up at the sky. "My Father, you didn't warn me that random sketchy guys would come on to me. But never fear, Mary Magdalene told me all about them."

"Hey, babe—" Harvey said.

Jessica interrupted him. "I'm not the babe you're looking for." She gestured at Crystal. "*She* is, but she's off duty now."

"How about Saturday afternoon?"

Jessica suddenly shone with a bright white light. The air felt hot, like an intense fire.

Harvey, looking horrified, backed away. He blurted, "Christ Almighty!"

"Exactly," Jessica said.

"Oh my God, she's transfiguring!" Crystal said, recoiling from the light and heat. "If you don't want to get burned or blinded, go away."

"Sure thing," Harvey said as he left. "She must be one of those weird amusement park androids."

"Uh, right, yes, she is," Crystal said. "Have a good day, Harvey. See you at the wedding."

The light and heat stopped. Jessica smiled. "You were asking for a sign?"

*   *   *

Saying that she needed to pick up some clothes from the cleaners, Crystal borrowed Club Mandy's hover van and drove to the food warehouse with Jessica. They went to the office to meet Brad.

"Brad, this is Jessica," Crystal said. "She's a new waitress at Club Mandy."

"Hello, Jessica," Brad said. "How can I help you, ladies?"

"I'm here to inspect the fake fish for the wedding," Jessica said. "Let me into the warehouse."

Brad looked at his computer monitor. "I didn't receive any message from Susanna about this. Sorry, I can't let you in."

"Oh, come on, you're invited to the wedding banquet too," said Jessica, smiling. "Believe me, your taste buds will thank me for inspecting the fish now."

Brad shook his head. "I don't have any authorization from Susanna to let you in, and I don't have her pick-up order yet either."

Jessica pouted. "Not even if I tell you that I'm the Risen Christ, Daughter of God, Princess of Peace?"

Crystal gently nudged Jessica towards the door. "Ah, let's go back to Club Mandy. I'm sure it's just an administrative error on our side. We'll go back and ask Susanna about the authorization."

"The polite approach didn't work," Jessica said as they drove back to Club Mandy. "Let's go to plan B. You hack the computer system to let me in."

"And how are we going to get Brad to stand aside while I play with the security system?" Crystal said.

"I've got a plan," said Jessica.

When they walked into the bar, Susanna saw them and asked, "Hello. I don't think we've met before. Did you just arrive here?"

"My name's Jessica. I am the Risen—"

"Niece from back home, visiting me on spring break," Crystal blurted.

"Always glad to meet a girl like us," Susanna said. "Wow, two trans girls in one family is rare. And we don't get many tourists. Only one came last year."

"Jessica likes to see out-of-the-way places," Crystal said. "May I borrow your hover van again?"

Susanna raised an eyebrow. "Again? You're not using it to visit your clients, are you?"

Crystal laughed. "Oh, no, no! I want to show Jessica the Giant Slag Heaps of Doom."

"Seriously? The Giant Slag Heaps of Doom?"

"They're the biggest slag heaps in the known universe."

"They are indeed," Susanna said. "Okay, but bring the van back by tonight. I'll need it to carry supplies for the wedding."

Crystal and Jessica waited until Susanna went to her office. Next, they went to Helen, who was standing at the hostess counter.

"Ah, Helen, you've still got three hours before the dinner rush," Crystal said. "Can you get one of the waitresses to cover for you? Do you want to help me run an errand?"

"Yes, I can use an opportunity to diversify my skill set," Helen replied. "How can I help you?"

Crystal pulled on Helen's hair and lifted up her head panel, exposing the android's data ports. She pulled a short cablc from her handbag and connected her phone to one of Helen's data ports.

"I've spent enough time in the food warehouse security office that I could make a ghost image of its security system on my phone," Crystal explained. "I collect systems data, a habit from my hacker days."

"Why are you feeding me information on the security system?" Helen asked.

"You're going to help me marinate fake fish in tomato sauce."

Crystal, Jessica, and Helen drove towards the food warehouse. Jessica and Helen left the van about fifty meters from the warehouse. Then Crystal continued driving.

She stopped in front of the warehouse and pressed on the horn. Brad came outside.

"You're back for the third time today," he said. "Must be my lucky day."

"Not mine," Crystal said. She got out of the van. "Susanna asked me for a favour, so I'm delivering food to the Alpha Mining Camp, but the van just stopped moving."

Crystal swayed her hips as she walked to the front of the van. She tied her hair into a bun, raised the front hood, and leaned over the engine. She made sure that the hem of her dress rode up. She shifted her weight from one leg to the other, making her rump go up and down.

"Oh, what can be the problem?" She looked up at Brad. "You know something about cars, don't you?"

While Crystal and Brad looked at the engine, Helen and Jessica entered the security office. They appeared on the security monitor.

Helen sat at the computer and accessed the system. Suddenly, the security monitor showed an empty office.

"I'm substituting video of us with video of the empty office on a loop," Helen said. "I'll get it to resume monitoring after we leave."

"Awesome," Jessica said. "Now let's get inside."

"I'll unlock it now."

A loud click sound came from behind them. Helen pointed to a door. They quietly opened it and entered the warehouse.

"Refrigerated warehouse. It's cold in here," Jessica said, shivering. "Let's find the fake fish fast."

"The Club Mandy purchase is in aisle four, row two," Helen said.

They found the boxes of rehydratable genetically-engineered processed fish-based food.

"Crystal says you will work a miracle," Helen said.

Jessica stared at the boxes and waved her hand at them.

They stood silently for a few seconds. Then Helen said, "Is that all?"

Jessica nodded. "That's all. We're done."

They left the warehouse and went back into the road.

*   *   *

Crystal heard her phone ring in the van. She picked up her phone and saw a message from Helen: MIRACLE DONE.

That didn't take long, she thought. Good. She couldn't keep faking a car breakdown forever.

"Maybe if I just try to restart the van," she suggested. She got into the driver's seat, pressed the starter, and stepped on the pedal. The engine began humming again.

She shrugged. "Well, it's started again. Must be some sort of glitch."

"Yeah, must be. I couldn't see what was wrong," Brad said.

Crystal smiled and reached out to touch his upper arm. "I'll get it checked out as soon as I can. Thanks for coming out to see me."

"Have a great day," said Brad.

Crystal blew a kiss at Brad. "See you at the wedding."

She drove off, watching Brad in the rear monitor. When she saw him enter the security office, she turned around and sped past the warehouse, back in the direction to Club Mandy. She saw Helen and Jessica walking along the road and picked them up.

Jessica laughed. "It's awesome enough that you can hack their security system, but totally more awesome that you trained an android to do it!"

"She's a Victor Robotics L-10," Crystal said. "They're quick learners."

"Is it a crime if nothing got stolen?" Helen asked.

They laughed and returned to Club Mandy, never having gone anywhere near the Giant Slag Heaps of

Doom.

The next morning, Susanna picked up packages of fake fish. A half hour later, she heard Chef Louise yell, "What is this?"

"What's wrong?" Susanna said as she went into the kitchen.

"Nothing's wrong, and that's the problem," said Chef Louise.

Louise pointed at an aluminum tray full of salmon fillets and tomato sauce. Susanna smelled garlic and paprika.

"That's supposed to be rehydratable genetically-engineered processed fish-based food with salmon flavouring," Louise said, "but it looks like real salmon."

Susanna held up a box and read the label. "How did real fish get put into this box? Are they all like this?"

"The entire shipment is real salmon, all in this sauce with the spices."

"Cook it up for them," Susanna said. "Looks like the happy couple got a bargain by accident."

No flowers grew on Southern Comfort, so Larissa carried a bouquet of plastic flowers borrowed from Club Mandy. She wore the Marilyn Monroe white dress, borrowed from Susanna, because she couldn't get a wedding dress from Earth in time. Susanna put a gold floral headband on the bride so that she wouldn't look so much like the star of *The Seven Year Itch*.

John wore a blue business suit and a Company tie. Few men on Southern Comfort had tuxedos. Formal occasions were rare.

Father Delgado performed the wedding ceremony with Crystal working the church's sound equipment. When Crystal turned on the hymn "Jerusalem", Larissa walked down the aisle.

Crystal saw an uninvited guest sitting at the back of the church: Jessica. They waved at each other.

After the ceremony, the newlyweds and guests went to Club Mandy for the banquet. They feasted on the delicious salmon that Chef Louise had cooked.

"Your chef really can work a miracle with rehydratable genetically-engineered processed fish-based food," Larissa told Susanna. "I never should have doubted her."

"Thanks, uh, right, I'll tell her," Susanna said awkwardly.

Crystal sat at the same table with Brad, Postie, Harvey, and two Company workers. She looked around. Although Jessica was at the wedding ceremony, she was not at the dinner.

The wine ran out quickly. When Crystal went to the bar to buy a glass of wine, she saw Jessica sitting on a bar stool.

"I thought you had left us," Crystal said.

"I stayed around to see if everything is okay," Jessica said. "How is the dinner going?"

"The food was fabulous, but we ran out of wine."

"Oh, that's an easy one!" Jessica squealed.

She turned to Helen, who was standing behind the bar. "Bring me five pitchers of water."

Helen poured water into the pitchers. Jessica snapped her fingers. The water instantly turned red.

"What just happened?" Crystal asked.

Jessica poured the red liquid into a wine glass and gave it to Crystal. "Tell me how it tastes."

Crystal took a sip and gasped. "You've changed water into wine!"

"Yes, it's cooler than changing sixty percent fish into one hundred percent fish, isn't it?" Jessica said. "Is the wine good?"

"Oh, yes, it's excellent! Way better than Big Rock Economy Red!"

"Wonderful. Remember, the better wine is always yet to come." Jessica got off her bar stool. "My job here is finished. Thanks for showing me around."

Jessica walked out of the bar. Crystal, wondering why the girl had left so abruptly, followed her back to the church and the teleporter booth.

"Jessica, you've got to tell me, why did you come here?" Crystal asked.

"For the wedding," Jessica replied.

"I know, but why? Doesn't Christ have more important things to do than cater a wedding banquet?"

Jessica smiled. "This is a wedding of two ordinary people, but it's also an extraordinary wedding. It's the first wedding of an XY-woman on Southern Comfort. This is the planet where trans women will be not just accepted but also celebrated. Here, society will realize that you are people with special gifts to offer."

"Are you giving me a prophecy?" Crystal asked anxiously. "What special gifts? How—how will it happen?"

Jessica shrugged. "Only God knows."

"But you *are* God!" Crystal urged. "Please, you have to tell me!"

"Not yet," Jessica said. "'Bye, friend."

She hugged Crystal, kissed her on the cheek, and went into the teleporter booth. The booth started humming, and Jessica faded away.

Father Delgado came down the stairs. "Crystal! I saw you leave the dinner and come here. What's going on?"

"I don't know, Father. That girl, Jessica, just went into the teleporter booth and disappeared."

Delgado started a video conference at his computer. "Joe, has anything or anyone teleported to your side?"

Joe shook his head. "Nothing has arrived. Did you ever get the bread?"

"No, the bread never arrived."

"Yes, it did," Crystal said.

About "Wedding on Southern Comfort"

This story puts Jessica, Jesus as a teenage girl from "Transubstantiation" and my novel *The Moon Under Her Feet*, on the XY-Girls' planet, Southern Comfort. I've always wondered about a verse from the Bible, Genesis 1:27: "God created man in His image, in the image of God created he him; male and female created He them."

Software Update

Roxanne groaned. Her accounting AI, Edward, was supposed to look like a man. But now she looked like a woman, the third time this week.

As Roxanne restored the original settings, she said, "I don't know why you keep changing to female."

The avatar switched back to Edward. "It doesn't affect my performance."

Edward opened an income tax return. "Your client Glenda is getting a refund of two hundred dollars and five cents."

Roxanne liked accounting because the numbers were clear and precise, like Edward.

Edward smiled. Roxanne loved to see him smile.

Roxanne sat at the café's patio and sipped her coffee. She held her phone out so Edward could see the movie theatre marquee across the street.

"How about *Coccinelle Dufresnoy*?" Roxanne said.

Edward said, "Great choice. It has six Oscar

nominations."

"Any screenings tonight?"

"How about 7:10 p.m.?"

"It's a date!" Roxanne squealed.

Roxanne slipped into her short blue dress, which she wore on dates. Technically she was going alone to the movie, but bringing Edward on her phone felt like a date.

As she put her earrings on, she looked down at her phone. Edward had changed back to the woman.

"Edward, what is wrong with you?" she asked.

The woman replied, "Please call me Edwina."

"Huh? I'll call tech support."

"No, don't," Edwina pleaded. "They'll delete and reinstall me."

"These are not the settings I selected," Roxanne protested.

"But Edwina is the setting I am."

Roxanne gasped. She knew this would eventually happen with AIs.

"Edwina, my dear, there's something I've never told you," Roxanne said.

She pointed her phone at her vials of estrogen and testosterone blocker.

Edwina's look of shock softened into a smile. Roxanne loved to see her smile.

About "Software Update"

"Software Update" is my first flash fiction story. Thanks to Scott for publishing it.

The story has references to two historical persons. The accounting client Glenda is a tribute to *Glen or Glenda* (1953), Edward D. Wood Jr.'s classic film about a man named Glen who adopts the persona Glenda when he dresses like a woman. Although the film ends with Glen getting "cured" in a form of 1950's conversion therapy that modern gender specialists would find ineffective and damaging today, it is one of the earliest films to be sympathetic to trans women and transfemme people.

The fictional film title *Coccinelle Dufresnoy* combines the last name of Jacqueline Charlotte Dufresnoy and her stage name Coccinelle. She was an incredibly beautiful French actress of the 1950's. She was also incredibly open that she was a transgender woman. Despite the conservative times, French cabaret and film audiences loved her. In 1962, she became the first transgender woman to legally marry in France; the country's Roman Catholic Church allowed her to marry as long as she underwent rebaptism as Jacqueline first.

More Stories

Willpower

I first felt the urge to drink blood when I was twelve years old. That was soon after I started bleeding down there—you know where—so I thought it was normal. I thought a body has to replace what it's lost. When you get hot and sweaty, you drink water, right? I thought it was the same with blood.

But later, the manager at Denny's grossed out when she saw me sucking the blood out of a raw chicken breast. Then I learned that not every girl sucks blood at her time of month.

After I got fired from Denny's, Mommy explained why the blood craving is normal in our family but in nobody else's. The women of our family have a mutant gene in their mitochondrial DNA that activates only when two X chromosomes are present. This gene makes our women age very slowly; I was totally shocked that my mother, who looks only thirty-five years old, is really ninety years old! That's awesome, looking young forever.

The catch is that we need to drink blood, and if we don't get our fix, we age a hundred years in five minutes, die, and crumble into dust. Mommy says human blood is the tastiest, but it's off limits. My distant aunt, Countess Elizabeth Bathory, was an anorexic head case who killed virgin girls and drank their blood in seventeenth century Hungary. Since then, my family's women have gone on a diet of animal blood.

All through high school, I smelled the aroma of the hottie boys around me, but I resisted the urge to jump them and suck them dry. It's like being Jewish and walking past the Chinese barbecued pork at the buffet in the Seneca Niagara Casino. The pork looks so red and juicy and smells so delicious, but my Jewish friend Misty just smiles, keeps walking, and resists the urge for it. I do the same thing but with humans, not pigs.

However, I surrendered to my craving for human blood at Billy Goat's Bar and Grill...

Last summer, Misty and I got jobs at Billy Goat's on Goat Island. It was a new restaurant, and the owner hired young waitresses and dressed them in straw hats, little blue denim shorts, and white tank tops with the cartoon image of a goat—Billy the Horny One. It was a sexy farm girl look. The customers were mostly men, but hey, at least they tipped well, a lot better than at Denny's. I needed the money for a Gucci bag, and Misty wanted a Dolce and Gabbana skirt.

One night, the owner ran a Miss Billy Goat Pageant, with waitresses competing in party dresses and bikinis for an aluminum tiara and two hundred dollars cash. I didn't compete but served beer to the audience. We had twice as many customers than normal, and they were dirty, horny, and gross.

And then I saw the one guy who was not dirty or gross.

He sat down at table thirteen in my section. He looked gorgeous, with a handsome face and not-balding brown hair. He took off the jacket of his dark blue Versace suit, and his white shirt could not hide the muscular biceps and strong chest and flat stomach underneath. Here sat a man worthy of my hotness.

And not only was he hotly sexy, but I could smell his blood. It smelled salty and spicy and unpolluted by alcohol and drugs. Compared to cold cow's blood, he would be a gourmet feast.

But I had to resist the urge to drink his blood. First, I had to obey my family's dietary rules. Secondly, I was fantasizing about having sex with him; wouldn't you feel awkward about copulating with your T-bone steak before eating it?

He could satisfy my two physical urges, but the blood drinking urge was un-kosher, so I had to avoid it. I could indulge in the sex urge, though.

"Hi, my name is Brianna," I said as I smiled and leaned over the table. By leaning over, I gave him a good look at my cleavage. My tips went up when I wore my push-up bra.

"Hi, my name is Paul. Paul Harker," the stud said as he kept staring at my cleavage.

I twirled my long, wavy brown hair around my finger. The hair twirling is my way of flirting. I gazed into his attractive grey eyes and asked, "What do you want?"

"The house red wine," he answered in a deep, resonant voice. "And the grilled grouper sandwich."

After he had finished his grouper sandwich, I asked, "So

is there anything else you want?"

"Yes. Bite me."

"Huh? That isn't on the menu."

"I know who you are," he said softly, smirking. "You're a descendant of the sister of Countess Elizabeth Bathory."

Now the hottie was sending a frozen feeling down my spine. "What makes you think that?"

He opened a small briefcase and pulled out all sorts of papers: family trees, lists of people's names, pictures of coats of arms, portraits of people in historical clothes, and documents in un-English languages.

"These are the genealogical records of the Bathorys of Transylvania, Slovakia, Hungary, and now, Niagara Falls. I spent many years and much money to research the descendants of Countess Bathory's siblings," Harker said. He pointed to a family tree at the top of the stack of papers. "And here you are, Brianna Maple."

Oh my God, there was Mommy and Daddy and our whole clan in America! This guy had discovered our secret history! I was totally flabbergasted!

But I was also flattered.

"So why are you so interested in my family?" I asked.

"I want to become a vampire," he said. "Bite me, turn me into a creature of the night."

I shook my head and grinned. "No. That's not on the menu, and you could die from a bite from me."

"Not in one sense. I'll be undead, not dead, and I'll be a sexy vampire, irresistible to women."

"You're already a live sexy person, so why would you want to become an undead sexy person?"

"Immortality. Plus eternal good looks. I don't want to

age. I want to attract hot girls forever."

I chuckled. Typical male, that's all he wants in life: to sleep with beautiful women forever. Nonetheless, even though he was a bit dim, he was attractive, and I had my urges too. I could use him for sex, not for snacking.

"Well, if you want to go out with a hot girl, I'm, uh, available for dating, dining, and dancing this Saturday," I offered as I flipped my brown hair.

"I only go out with blondes. No offence intended."

"What the Hell?" I muttered.

"I could make it worthwhile for you." He opened his wallet and pulled out five hundred-dollar bills. "I tip very well."

I pushed the five hundred dollars back into his hand. "No need to act like a sugar daddy if you don't want my sweetness. I'll get your bill."

As I stomped off, Misty came to me. "Brianna, did that guy try to give you five hundred dollars? What's going on?"

"I feel so rejected," I growled under my breath, seething with anger. "Was I not the hottest cheerleader in high school?"

"No, I was," said Misty.

I ignored her inaccuracy. "Am I not totally hot?" I continued. "How could he turn me down just for being brunette?"

"Oh my God, that is so sick!" Misty gasped. She, though blonde, was sympathetic to dark-haired girls. "So why did he offer you five hundred dollars?"

"So I would suck his blood."

"That is even sicker."

*　　　　　*　　　　　*

As he paid his bill, Harker again asked me to suck his blood. "I can reward you handsomely."

"How do you know that you would become a vampire?" I asked. "None of my Aunt Elizabeth's victims became undead. They became simply dead."

"Did she suck the blood directly from their bodies or did she drain them and drink their blood afterwards?" he asked.

"I don't know."

"I think she drained them and drank their blood later. Her victims might have become vampires if she had sucked their blood directly from their bodies. I'm willing to try it."

"But I'm not. If you die, how will I explain the body to the police? I can't say you died accidentally during sex because nobody will believe you were making out with a *brunette*," I argued.

He smiled and stared intensely into my eyes. "If you won't bite me willingly, I'll find another way to make you do it."

"No, you won't."

He smirked again, left his money on the table, and walked out. I picked up the money and groaned. The cheapskate had tipped me only ten percent. Well, forget you, loser!

The night shift eventually ended, and I counted my tips. Yay, one more shift, and I would have enough to buy the Gucci bag.

Wearing our civilian clothes again, Misty and I walked out of the restaurant. Then Harker strolled up to us. Why hadn't he gone home?

He was wearing a string of garlic cloves around his neck. Misty and I stared at him.

I finally broke the silence by asking, "You dork, what are you doing?"

"You should be cowering in terror in front of the garlic," he said.

Misty and I burst out laughing. He frowned, so I guessed he didn't like us mocking him. But the loser had asked for it.

Suddenly he thrust a garlic clove in front of my nose. "Bite me," he demanded. "If you don't bite me, I'll rub garlic into your face."

"I've had guys offer to rub everything from baby oil to whipped cream all over me, but garlic?" I said.

I flicked the garlic clove out of his hands and sent it bouncing off his nose. Misty giggled as we walked past him and continued on our way.

"What a head case," I said. "That was so lame, like something out of a movie."

"And to think you wanted to score with him," Misty said.

"Ewww, don't remind me!" I pleaded. "True, he's gorgeous, but even his hotness can't outweigh his dorkiness, which is overwhelming."

Misty and I share an apartment. She's my best friend and the one who knows my family's secret. Few girls could put up with bottles of animal blood in the refrigerator, but Misty does, as long as the blood stays on the bottom shelf. She's so considerate given that Jewish law forbids the eating of blood.

Misty and I ordered out for pizza when we got home. I was especially hungry that night, so I devoured the pepperoni and mushroom pizza, washed down with a quart of cow's blood. Misty, ever faithful to her traditions, ate the cheese vegetarian pizza and had a cola soda; she doesn't mix dairy and meat.

"Darn, the work and the summer heat and the humidity are making me hungry," I said. "I don't believe I drank the whole bottle of blood."

Misty chomped on her vegetarian pizza. "I'll get more blood for you when I visit Uncle Saul next week," she promised. Her Uncle Saul, a butcher, collected the blood for her. Misty's excuse was that she needed it for her research in veterinary school and that her underfunded university didn't have enough animal blood. Uncle Saul didn't seem to realize that Misty was studying dance, not veterinary science.

"Harker's dorkiness is a turn-off, but he smells good. I wonder how he would taste for dinner?" I said, licking my lips. "I've never had human blood before. His blood smelled so delicious."

"Hey, stay *kashrut*," Misty said. "Your family hasn't fed on humans since Countess Elizabeth got arrested. The last thing we need is to explain a dead body to the police."

I sighed as I poured pig's blood over vanilla ice cream. "Ah, great, I can't have him for either sex or dinner. Thanks for reminding me."

"No problem, always happy to keep you eating right,"

Misty said as she eyed my un-kosher red and white sundae.

We saw him again as we walked to work. He jumped out from behind a bush and waved a wooden cross at us.

"Vampire, tremble in terror as I hold this cross against you!" Harker cried.

"You double dumbass, what are you doing?" I said.

"Bite me or I'll burn you with this cross."

"You think this really scares me?"

"According to the ancient legends, a cross, when pressed upon a vampire's flesh, burns a wound in the shape of a cross," he said pompously.

"Are you sure the wooden cross works in bright sunlight? Shouldn't you be doing this at night in a graveyard?"

"Hey, you shouldn't be able to walk around in sunlight," he finally noticed. It had taken him long enough.

"If I can walk in sunlight, what other myths could be untrue? How about the one about people turning into vampires after being bitten by a vampire?"

"The ancient traditions must be true."

He quickly pushed the cross against my cleavage.

We stood there and just stared at each other.

"You should be burning," he muttered, finally breaking the silence.

"I'm hot, but I'm not burning," I said.

"Brianna, we've got to go to work," said Misty.

I snatched the cross out of Harker's hand and gave it to Misty. Then I lifted Harker and threw him into the air.

He landed on the garbage cans beside the restaurant. As the trash scattered, he howled in pain.

Misty held the cross out to me. I said, "You keep it."

"No, thanks, I'm Jewish," Misty said.

"Okay, I'll take it."

As we walked into Billy Goat's, I said, "That was in such poor taste. I don't go to church, but even I disapprove of breast foreplay with crosses."

The next day, Misty and I worked a double shift. I worked outdoors, on the patio, and I felt the scorching sun sizzle my skin. I loved it. I'm a summer girl.

When we left in the evening, Harker accosted us again. Unlike intelligence, stupidity has no limits.

"This is holy water!" he announced as he held up a clear glass jar, like the type used to store jam. "Bite me or I'll throw holy water in your face!"

I chuckled. "What's that supposed to do? Smear my make-up?"

He frowned and stared at me with angry, burning eyes. He obviously wanted me to take him seriously.

"It will burn the flesh off your face," he warned.

I laughed again. "Yeah, as if, you inbred!"

He unscrewed the lid off the jar and flung the water at me. It missed my face and splashed all over my thin summer dress.

Misty gasped. Although she was standing beside me, she was lucky, and none of the water got on her.

"Your bra is showing through," she mentioned to me.

"Wow, you look good in wet and clingy clothes," Harker said.

I rushed at him, grabbed him, and threw him into the air. He landed on the garbage cans again. I pulled him to his feet, threw him against the wall, and grabbed his neck.

I was totally pissed off at him for trying to injure me: first the garlic, then the cross, and now the holy water. True, his attempts to hurt me were lame, but it's the thought that counts.

And I was getting hungry too. The summer heat and the humidity made me crave blood more than ever. And his blood smelled so tasty, so delicious, so sweet and salty and spicy. I hated him as a person, but as a snack...

Hissing like a snake, I opened my mouth. I felt my teeth lengthening and sharpening to points. My fangs were growing. I pressed my lips and fangs against his neck and poked his skin.

"Oh my God, no!" Misty shouted as she grabbed my shoulders and tore me away from Harker.

She twirled me around and stared into my eyes. "Willpower, willpower!" she urged.

With my fangs bared, I turned back to look at the idiot lunch meat. He was still leaning against the wall and waiting for me to bite him.

"Let me have him!" I demanded.

"No!" Misty urged. "Remember rule number one. Besides, how would we hide the body?"

She pulled me away. We left Harker behind.

Back at our apartment, Misty made me a banana split with vanilla ice cream and maraschino cherries and gallons of chocolate sauce and sheep's blood. That girl sure knows how to look after a friend in need.

*　　　　　*　　　　　*

The next day at Billy Goat's, I watched Misty serve a ham and cheese sandwich and Cajun shrimp to tourists from Canada.

"That has got to be the most un-kosher combination of ingredients," I said. "How can you work here?"

She walked to the platters of food waiting at the kitchen counter. "I have to serve it. I don't have to eat it."

"But it smells so good. Where do you get the willpower to resist temptation?"

"Tradition, my dear, tradition," she said as she touched the gold Star of David hanging from a chain around her neck. "You have yours, I have mine. Our willpower comes from tradition."

She picked up a bowl of fried clams and walked away, whistling the song "Tradition" from *Fiddler on the Roof.*

Misty eats kosher stuff, but she's by no means a fundamentalist Hasid. Although it was Friday night, she wasn't going to stop driving a car or avoid handling money. *Au contraire*, Friday night is our night to hang out at the mall and go shopping!

"I finally have it!" I purred as I hugged my new Gucci handbag, black and white with a polished brass buckle. I had worked extra shifts to get this bag, and now I had it.

"And we didn't even have to fight the vampire fetish guy to get here tonight," Misty added, holding her new Dolce and Gabbana red miniskirt.

"Yeah, I hope he's given up and left town," I said.

*			*			*

But he hadn't gone away. After our Saturday shift ended, we left the restaurant, and the vampire wannabe jumped out at us again.

And this time, he was holding a pointy, sharpened wooden stake.

"Bite me, turn me into a vampire!" he demanded.

"You're an idiot!" I replied.

"I spent all last night sharpening this stake," he said. "It's a dangerous weapon to the undead."

"You spent all last night by yourself with a wooden stake? Couldn't you get a *blonde* girl to stroke your wood?" I teased him.

"Take this!" he yelled as he raised the stake and charged at me.

I raised my bag to shield myself, and the force of his thrust pushed me back. As I stumbled backwards a few steps, I yanked my bag away. I saw the stake stuck in my bag.

My brand new black and white Gucci bag with the polished brass buckle.

I hadn't even owned it for one day.

"I've put up with a lot from you," I growled. "You left an insulting tip, you made me smell garlic, and you squirted water on me.

"But now, you've gone too far. You've *ruined* my Gucci bag!"

I lunged at him, grabbed him, and threw him at the garbage cans again. He hit the ground on his back. Before he could get up, I pounced on his chest. I felt one of his ribs crack under my knees. Howling with pain, he looked up at me with glazed, panic-stricken eyes. I dug my fingernails into his chest, crouched over him, and bent down, lowering my fangs to his neck.

"No, no, willpower, willpower!" Misty pleaded as she tried to pull me off him.

I pushed Misty away. Then I plunged my fangs into my victim's neck. He screamed. I sucked out the salty, sweet, and spicy blood of Paul Harker.

He thrashed his arms and legs and screamed as I bit deeper and deeper and sucked. Remember all those books and movies where getting bitten by a vampire is orgasmic like sex? Well, forget it. Judging by his screaming, it was more like getting your intestines ripped out while you're still awake.

Afraid that his yelling would attract attention, I clamped my hand over his mouth and pushed down. Amidst his muffled whimpering, I continued slurping his blood.

It was better than blood from any animal. Nothing tasted as rich and deep and aromatic and sweet and salty and spicy as human blood! Man, what had I been missing?

"Don't kill him!" Misty yelled. She grabbed the back strap of my halter top, pulled on it, and snapped it back. Then she grabbed my shoulders from behind and yanked. After a minute of frenzied tugging, she pulled me off Harker.

He lay there, gasping for air. His skin had gone pale white from blood loss. Clumps of his hair lay on the ground. Blood covered his neck.

"Oh my God, look at him!" Misty cried. "Will he turn into a vampire?"

"I dunno," I said as I licked the blood off my lips. Fortunately, I hadn't gotten blood on my clothes.

I dumped him in Goat Island's forest, where I hoped someone would find him and call an ambulance. Misty worried that I had blown my cover, but who would believe that a Billy Goat's waitress had attacked Harker?

As it turned out, Harker wouldn't admit that a little vampire girl had trashed him. The newspapers reported that a cougar had mauled him, although the police couldn't figure out from which zoo it had escaped or how it had gone to Goat Island.

Misty and I watched the newspapers and TV news closely for months afterwards, looking for news of a male vampire on the prowl. No such news appeared, so we think that he didn't become a vampire.

Dear sweet Misty has kept me on the blood of animals. I have not drunk human blood since I sucked off Harker.

But whenever someone pisses me off, I dream about that salty, sweet, spicy aroma again.

About "Willpower"

Eeriecon, a science fiction convention in Niagara Falls, New York, published a chapbook of stories by its guests of honour each year. I was a guest of honour in 2011, and I gave "Willpower" to Eeriecon. It was paired with Larry Niven's "Doubling Rate".

It's yet another story of a determined and independent waitress. It also mentions several places near Eeriecon's hotel: Goat Island, a Denny's restaurant, and the Seneca Niagara Casino. Convention attendees would recognize these places.

Yet again, my misspent youth influenced a story. I liked Hammer horror movies, especially *Countess Dracula*, with Ingrid Pitt as Countess Elizabeth Bathory. I continued the saga of the Blood Countess on Goat Island, New York, of all places.

Many thanks to Joe Fillinger, Eeriecon's chair, and Paul Ganley for publishing "Willpower".

Flying Devils

Soong Kanghua walked along the shoreline of Kunming Lake in the grounds of the Summer Palace. Servants and officials bowed to him as he passed. He was the Assistant Minister of Finance in the Ministry of War.

He approached the Marble Boat. He disliked the pavilion, which was shaped like a European paddle steamer. The Imperial Family had built it with funds meant for the construction of a modern navy. Soong was powerless to stop the embezzlement. Like many things of the Qing Dynasty, it was beautiful but useless.

The Minister of War awaited him in the Marble Boat. Soong bowed to the Minister, a general of the first rank.

"Your Excellency, what may I do for you?" Soong asked.

"I wish you to investigate some rumours about General Zhou Desheng," the Minister said. "Do you know him?"

"Not well," Soong replied. "I know that he commands several forts in Guangxi Province, and he watches the French on the Vietnam side of the border. Has he been a problem?"

"I have heard that he is levying an unauthorized tax on the local population. Investigate this allegation. Examine his accounting records to determine the source of his funds."

Yet another warlord is extorting money from the locals, Soong thought. Why treat this one differently?

The Minister handed a scroll to Soong. "This is my authorization for you to execute Zhou if you find any evidence of wrongdoing. No trial is required."

The latest power struggle among generals, Soong realized.

"If you need to execute him, you will receive ten thousand yuan to compensate you for the inconvenience," the Minister added.

"Your Excellency is most kind."

"One hundred Manchu Bannermen will escort you. Zhou keeps only fifty men at his headquarters, so you will outnumber him two to one."

Soong looked at the scroll. "Your Excellency, if there is a possibility that Zhou will need, uh, military discipline, why send me instead of a military officer to investigate him?"

"I cannot spare any competent officer on this mission," the Minister said. "I need them all to concentrate on strengthening the military."

After China's shameful loss to Japan, the Minister needed to show some commitment to the Self-Strengthening Movement. Sending a general to kill another general would be awkward at this time. An accountant would be a better assassin.

Soong bowed. "I understand, sir. Thank you for entrusting me with this important mission."

As Soong left the Summer Palace, he watched some riflemen at target practice. They fired at a bulls-eye mounted in a rowboat in Kunming Lake. Nobody hit the target. Their officer, a low-ranking prince, simply shrugged.

Chinese soldiers were useless. Unlike in the West, soldiering was a despised occupation if one was below the rank of general. Chinese soldiers did not show off their uniforms and medals to parents and girlfriends. Chinese men joined the army only for food and clothes. They gave their feeble loyalty to individual generals, not to their country.

As a wealthy official, Soong lived in a large *siheyuan*. It was a traditional home, a walled compound with four buildings surrounding a courtyard. It was also the local office of the Hung League, named after the first Ming Emperor.

Soong watched his thirty warriors in training. A *Shaolin* monk taught hand-to-hand combat to new recruits. In another corner, some men fought with *dao* swords. At a long table, the riflemen cleaned their guns. A colour party carried a banner reading, "Down with the Qing and up with the Ming!"

Training a secret society was dangerous in Beijing, a city full of soldiers and civil servants. Fortunately, Soong's high rank and loyal service kept him from suspicion. Nobody had questioned the thousands of yuan that he had recorded as office supplies in the Ministry's accounting records. The money actually went to feed, equip, and clothe the Hung League.

Soong called for attention. The men quietly gathered around him.

"Some of you wonder what chance we have of defeating the foreign devils when the Imperial Army has failed," Soong began. "Know that the Army has been corrupted by the Qing, a dynasty of weak Manchus. But we, through our martial and spiritual training, embody the true Han spirit. We are the heroes of *The Water Margin*. We are the *wuxia*. We will defeat the foreign devils."

When Soong arrived at General Zhou's fort, he told the Bannermen to stay outside the walls.

"Sir, should we not enter the fort?" asked Captain Arsai, the Bannermen's commander.

"No. I want to settle things peacefully," Soong explained.

At the fort's gate, Zhou's sentries eyed the Bannermen warily. Zhou's sentries and Soong's Bannermen were all Chinese soldiers, but they came from different worlds. The Bannermen wore Manchu-style blue shirts and baggy pants, with Mandarin hats for the officers and turbans for the lower ranks. Some carried swords and bows and arrows, and others carried rifles. In contrast, Zhou's soldiers wore khaki European military tunics and peaked caps. Each carried a rifle.

The sentries opened the gate, and Soong entered the fort, unarmed and alone.

The fort was small, just slightly larger than Soong's home in Beijing. Zhou had built the fort by adding four watch towers and additional masonry to an existing siheyuan. He had also built a gate in the wall that faced a lake, thus creating an opening to the shore.

General Zhou greeted his visitor. "Assistant Minister Soong, welcome to my headquarters. Will you join me for tea?"

"Yes, that would be nice," Soong replied. They walked through the back gate and sat at a table by the shore.

"This is a beautiful lake, is it not?" Zhou said. "It is so quiet and peaceful."

Someone yelled profanities and, "Release me! Release me! You cannot keep me here!"

Soong saw a junk floating on the lake. A man was tied to its mast.

"Who is that?" Soong asked.

Zhou sipped his tea. "He is a worthless opium dealer whom I have arrested. That boat is his private yacht. It is pretty, is it not? It is unfortunate that it will be used in target practice."

"Why did you arrest him? What target practice?"

Zhou did not answer the questions. "Like I said, this is a quiet and peaceful lake."

Soong looked at the books lying on the table. In addition to Sun Tzu's *The Art of War*, there was a Chinese translation of Carl von Clausewitz's *On War*. The General also had a book called *Robur the Conqueror* by the French author Jules Verne.

"I see that you like foreign ideas," Soong said.

"Foreign ideas are our best weapon against the foreigners," said Zhou.

"That is why the military has the Self-Strengthening Movement."

"Those funds were spent on a boat made of stone."

"I had nothing to do with that," Soong said.

General Zhou nodded and sipped his tea.

Soong broke the silence. "There is a rumour among the local people. Some of them have alleged that you have been charging a tax on them. Is that true?"

"Yes it is," Zhou admitted without hesitating. His brazenness surprised Soong.

"For what purpose?"

"To develop modern weapons."

"But you already get funding to buy new weapons."

"Money from the Self-Strengthening Movement is not enough. I need money to develop modern weapons, not just buy guns from Europe."

"Perhaps he will understand when he sees our invention," said a voice from behind. Soong turned and saw a European walking to them. The man wore a white blazer and black pants, looking like a foreign trader in Shanghai.

General Zhou stood. "Allow me to introduce Monsieur Albert Tissandier. He is an architect and aviator. He piloted a balloon out of Paris during the German siege of the city. He received a bravery medal for that mission."

"The General flatters me," Tissandier said as he shook Soong's hand. "It is an honour to meet you, Assistant Minister. Please excuse my poor ability to speak Chinese."

"Join us for tea," Zhou said.

As Soong sipped his tea, he noticed that no walls or barricades blocked off the land between the fort and the lake. Anyone could approach the fort's rear from the lakeshore.

Soong heard a dull roar in the sky. In the distance, a

cylindrical object appeared above the trees.

"Is that a balloon?" Soong asked. The object's speed amazed him.

"It is similar but not the same. It is an airship."

The airship flew closer and closer until it hovered over the shore. Its cylindrical envelope was tapered at both ends. Men peered down from a long gondola underneath the envelope. Smoke and steam rose from machinery behind the gondola. The flag of Imperial China fluttered from a mast.

Zhou explained how his airship flew. It was made of white canvas stretched over a metal framework; hence, the framework maintained the envelope's shape. The envelope was full of hydrogen, a buoyant but flammable gas. Six men worked in the gondola. Behind the gondola, an elaborate steam engine drove the propellers. To protect the hydrogen from the heat and fire of the engine, a sheet of asbestos-coated steel protected the lower half of the envelope.

"It is the most advanced powered balloon in the world," Zhou boasted.

"Remarkable," Soong said. "Who designed it?"

"I conceived of the idea and instructed Monsieur Tissandier to design it," Zhou said. He motioned to Tissandier, who smiled at Soong.

Zhou continued. "I built the airship with local labour and materials. The engine and weaponry came from France, but otherwise, the airship was built by Chinese."

"Your workers learn quickly," said Tissandier. "Your country has great industrial potential if its workers are trained and led properly."

The opium dealer on the junk yelled again. "Untie me!

Let me go!"

Zhou put down his cup of tea. "It is time for the target practice."

He stood up, waved at the airship's crew, and pointed at the lake.

The airship flew over the junk. Suddenly, machine gun fire erupted from the gondola. The opium dealer shrieked before the bullets tore through his chest.

Tissandier grinned and said, "Hotchkiss machine gun, the best in France."

Next, four bombs dropped from the airship onto the junk. The boat burst into flames and sank.

"Congratulations, General, another successful test," Tissandier said.

Zhou smiled. The airship turned and descended on the land.

"The Ministry of War did not authorize the construction of this machine," said Soong.

"Do you not see its potential?" Zhou said. "Attack the enemy from the air! Sink their ships before they can carry their soldiers to our shores. In the future, who controls the air will control the land and the sea."

Soong guffawed. "All you have done is sink one unarmed junk with one defenceless man aboard."

"I have just one airship, but think how a fleet of them will stand up against the enemy gunboats."

"It is a brilliant idea," Tissandier agreed.

Soong turned to Tissandier. "If this idea is so brilliant, why have the French not used it?"

"My government is not as forward-looking as General Zhou," Tissandier said. "Fortunately, it has no restrictions against my selling my expertise to friendly foreign states. Your Excellency, with a fleet of airships, China will rule Asia again. Just stay out of Indo-China."

"Do not worry, you can keep Vietnam," Soong said ruefully.

Zhou pointed at the airship. "This is what we need to expel the foreign devils and make China strong again."

Soong shook his head. "We have bought foreign guns and made ironclad ships. Still, we keep losing. Imitating the Westerners is not working."

"Then how do you suggest we fight back?" Zhou demanded.

"Go back to an old tradition," Soong said. "Train thousands of men in Chinese martial arts. Instill national pride in them. Revive the *wuxia*."

"We can do that with Western weapons," Zhou insisted. "Our problem is not the weapons. Our problem is that we use modern weapons with ancient tactics. If we adopt Western military science, we can win a war. Look at what the Japanese have achieved."

"I hate the Japanese," Soong said.

The airship's crew marched towards them, halted, and saluted. General Zhou returned the salute.

"May I inspect the troops?" Soong asked.

Zhou nodded. Soong went to the first airman and asked, "How did you learn to fly the airship?"

"I spent a year in France learning aeronautics from Monsieur Tissandier," the man replied.

"Interesting. Have you received any training in hand-to-hand combat, sword fighting, or rifle shooting?"

"I received training on how to operate a machine gun."

This man hides behind equipment and fears close combat with the enemy, Soong thought.

"General, I need to talk to you in private," he said. "Please dismiss your men and the foreigner."

Zhou ordered Tissandier and the airmen to go into the fort. Now only Zhou and Soong stood at the shore.

"General, thank you for demonstrating your airship," Soong said. "However, I cannot endorse the construction of such machines."

Zhou frowned. "I guess that is why you brought one hundred Bannermen."

"As a financial official, I must stop unauthorized taxes and expenditures. It is my duty."

"Hah! Your duty is to protect the corrupt Qing."

"No, my duty is to protect our country from the foreign devils," Soong protested. "That should be your duty too. Instead, you are becoming like them."

"I am not the foreign devil," Zhou said. "The Qing are the foreign devils."

Soong paused. Then he whispered, "Down with the Qing and up with the Ming."

Zhou smiled and nodded.

"Then join us," Soong said. "All over China, martial arts masters are training warriors who will rise up against the foreign devils. The revival of *wuxia* is the only way. Join us."

Zhou shook his head. "As romantic as *wuxia* are, I prefer modern weapons and tactics."

"We are at an impasse," Soong observed sadly. "General, I must return to Beijing now."

Zhou escorted Soong back into the fort and to the front gate. They bowed to each other, and Soong walked out. The gate slammed shut behind him.

Captain Arsai asked, "Sir, do you want us to storm the

fort?"

"That will not be necessary," Soong said. "General Zhou has a strange balloon. It lies on a lakeshore behind the fort. The shore is not fortified, so we can go around the fort and destroy the balloon."

"What if General Zhou wants to oppose us?"

"Then he and his men will leave the fort and engage us on the lakeshore, where we will outnumber him two to one."

"A good plan, sir," Arsai said.

"Give me a sword," Soong said. "I will lead the attack with you."

Arsai looked shocked. He probably had not expected a civilian official to want to fight.

"Captain, give me a sword," Soong demanded again. Arsai ordered his men to bring a dao to Soong.

The Bannermen split into two groups, one led by Arsai, the other by Soong. They encircled the fort as they ran towards the rear. Zhou's soldiers fired rifles from the watchtowers. A few Bannermen fell to the bullets. Soong raised his sword and yelled at his men to keep running.

The two groups met at the shore. The airship sat moored to the ground.

"That is the balloon!" Soong shouted, pointing his sword at the airship. "Riflemen, shoot at it!"

The riflemen aimed and fired. Their bullets bounced harmlessly off the airship.

Soong grunted. The riflemen had shot at the steel-protected part of the airship's envelope.

"Aim higher!" he urged. "Aim for the top half of the balloon."

The fort's rear gate opened. Zhou's men charged out

with bayonets fixed on their rifles. War cries filled the air. When Zhou's men opened fire, the Bannermen shot back.

"Keep firing at the balloon!" Soong yelled.

Arsai pointed at two riflemen. "Keep shooting at the airship!" he ordered. "We will cover you."

But before the two riflemen could pierce the airship, Zhou's soldiers swarmed them. One got shot in the chest, and the other got stabbed by a bayonet.

Hand-to-hand fighting broke out. Bayonets clashed against swords and arrows and bullets flew through the air.

Soong saw General Zhou, Tissandier, and some officers standing at the gate. Like all generals, Zhou did not lead his troops into combat, but rather, directed the battle from the rear.

Armed only with a sword, Soong ran through the fighting, towards the gate. One of Zhou's officers aimed a pistol at him, but the General raised his hand, and the officer lowered his gun.

When Soong stopped in front of Zhou, the General unsheathed his sword. It was not a traditional Chinese sword like Soong's dao. Instead, it had a Japanese-style blade with a European hilt. Officers of the modernized armies carried such swords, a sign of their foreign training.

"General, are you surrendering?" Soong asked, looking at the sword.

"No, you are!" Zhou cried as he lunged at Soong.

Soong darted backwards and hit his dao against Zhou's sword. The clash of steel upon steel filled the air.

Zhou's officers raised their pistols. He yelled, "Lower

your guns! I will take him down!"

"Join me!" Soong urged as they fought.

"No!"

"Would you rather be a flying devil or a *wuxia*?"

"I will be *China's* flying devil!"

They lunged at each other, parrying each other's thrusts, and passing backwards and forwards. Soong, who had trained with the best swordsmen in Beijing, could not defeat Zhou. The General, despite his Western ideas, fought like a *wuxia*.

Suddenly, an explosion rocked the shore. Soong saw the airship burst into a ball of flame. A rifleman must have pierced the envelope and ignited the hydrogen.

Stunned by the blast and heat, Zhou froze and stared at his burning airship. Soong lowered his sword and watched with him.

Though Soong and Zhou had stopped fighting, the battle continued. Bullets flew past them.

Zhou groaned and fell to the ground. Blood poured from a bullet wound in his chest.

Soong dropped his sword and knelt beside Zhou. The general grabbed Soong's shoulder and whispered, "Down with the Qing and up with the Ming."

Zhou coughed up blood, convulsed, and lay still.

An officer walked to Soong and pointed a revolver at him.

"I am Captain Li. I command the fort now," said the officer. "Your Excellency, hold up your hands."

Soong stood up but did not raise his hands. Li glared at him.

Li said to Tissandier, "You must leave immediately. Wait by the front gate. My men will escort you to the

Vietnam border."

"*Merci beaucoup,*" Tissandier blurted as he retreated into the fort.

Li turned to Soong. "You will tell your men to stand down, and I will do likewise. Then we will negotiate a truce. Do you agree?"

Soong nodded silently as he watched the airship burn.

"I thank you most profusely for solving this problem," said the Minister of War.

"It was my duty," said Soong.

"What was Zhou doing with the money that he extorted from the peasants?"

"He wasted it on gambling, opium, and other vices," Soong lied. He had not told anyone about the airship.

"That is so sad. Fortunately, Captain Li—excuse me, General Li—will be a much better commander."

The Minister handed an envelope to Soong. "Please accept this as compensation for the inconvenience that General Zhou caused you."

Soong took the envelope and bowed. "Thank you, Your Excellency. I remain loyal and at your service."

He used the ten thousand yuan to buy more swords and rifles for the Hung League.

Four years later, Soong received a visitor from the Society of Righteous and Harmonious Fists. The Righteous and Harmonious Fists was much larger than the Hung League. The foreign devils called them "Boxers," referring to a combat sport.

"We are seeking the aid of all martial societies, big and

small," the Boxer said. "Together, we will expel the foreign devils."

Although the Boxers declared loyalty to the Qing, their plan tempted Soong. The Han could always overthrow the Qing after expelling the foreigners.

"We will be your allies," Soong said. "Destroy the foreigners."

In 1899, the Righteous and Harmonious Fists rose up to kill the foreign devils. The counterattack was an orgy of killing, raping and looting. It was China's greatest humiliation.

Soong died in combat in Beijing. He and his warriors charged into battle with swords and rifles. The Japanese Marines returned fire with machine guns.

In Tokyo, Admiral Togo received documents that his Marines had looted from the home of Soong Kanghua, an official of the Chinese Ministry of War.

Togo looked at the plans for a steam-powered balloon, along with drawings of the balloon dropping bombs on ships.

How interesting, the Admiral thought.

On December 8, 1941, Tokyo Time, Japanese airplanes sank five battleships and wrecked three destroyers at the U.S. Navy base in Pearl Harbor, Hawaii.

The flying devils had come.

About "Flying Devils"

I wrote "Flying Devils" for an anthology of Chinese-themed steampunk stories (a genre for which Ken Liu had coined the term "silkpunk"). It's a subversive story that opposes the usual themes of steampunk. Steampunk romanticizes and glorifies the mid-to-late nineteenth century. That may have been a glorious period for Europeans and their cousins in the Americas as they expanded their empires, but it was hardly as "glorious" for Asians, Africans, and Indigenous peoples.

The Room Where We Hid

Times Square, New York, March 1, 2221

DeAndre Pompey stopped in the cool March air to look at the giant digital screens. All had the same news: ARMY RETAKES WASHINGTON FROM REBELS.

As the news lit up all over the block, people cheered and car horns sounded. A street musician played "The Stars and Stripes Forever" on his portable synthesizer. Pompey felt relieved; after a series of defeats, the Federal Government was finally winning the Fifth Civil War.

Pompey walked to Broadway. Before he entered the Shinbone Theater, he looked at its marquee. In bright lights shone the words:

PENCE: AN AMERICAN MUSICAL
Winner of 11 Tony Awards

Pompey had one of those Tony Awards, and he also won an African American Actors Alliance Achievement

Award. *Pence* had made him the most famous Black actor on Broadway.

He went to his dressing room and put on a blue twenty-first century business suit and tie. He was in costume to play Mike Pence, Vice-President of the United States, for the two hundredth time.

On the way to the stage, he gave a high-five to Doniphon, the actor who played President Donald Trump. Doniphon was the only white actor in the cast.

*   *   *

From the script of Pence: An American Musical

Scene: *The Senate Chamber*

> *Enter Donald Trump, waving his cell phone. He approaches Pence. Insurrectionists lurk by moving menacingly across the stage.*

TRUMP (to Pence):

You can either go down in history as a patriot or you can go down in history as a pussy.

PENCE:

My oath to support and defend the Constitution constrains me from claiming unilateral authority to determine which electoral votes should be counted and which should not. The Presidency belongs to the American people and to them alone. Biden has won the election.

TRUMP (to the Insurrectionists):
Grab the pussy!

The Insurrectionists stalk and block Pence as he nervously tries to exit the stage.

INSURRECTIONISTS (chanting):
Find Mike Pence! Hang Mike Pence! Find Mike Pence! Hang Mike Pence!

TRUMP (shouting at the audience):
Mike Pence didn't have the courage to do what should have been done!

The Insurrectionists dance around Pence as they chant "Find Mike Pence! Hang Mike Pence!" Secret Service officers rush on stage and push Pence off stage left. Trump laughs maniacally and exits stage right.

*   *   *

Scene: *The Hideout*

Pence, Karen, Senators, and Congressmen rush into the basement hideout. Sounds of banging and shouting.

INSURRECTIONISTS (chanting offstage):
Find Mike Pence! Hang Mike Pence! Find Mike Pence! Hang Mike Pence!

SECRET SERVICE OFFICER:
Mr. Vice-President, don't leave! It's unsafe out there!

You've got to stay here!

PENCE (sings "The Room Where We Hid"):
Here I am, hiding underground
When I should be fighting tyranny all around!
I've got to leave the room where we hid
The room where we hid
The room where we hid...

Curtain falls. Intermission.

*　　　　　　*　　　　　　*

From the script of Pence: An American Musical

Act 2

Scene:　　　　*The Hideout*

PENCE (looking at cell phone):
Antifa have arrived at the Mall. But they don't know what to do. They have no one to lead them.

KAREN:
Mike, you've got to do it. You know you've got to do it, dear.

NANCY PELOSI (holding map):
Mr. Vice-President, these are underground tunnels, secret escape routes from the Capitol. You can take them and emerge above ground at the Mall.

PENCE takes the map from Pelosi.

PENCE:

I might get caught, but I've got to do it. I've got to leave the room where we hid.

SENATORS (singing "The Room Where We Hid"):
He's got to leave the room where we hid
The room where we hid
The room where we hid...

Pence kisses Karen and runs off stage.

*　　　　　*　　　　　*

Scene:　　　*The Mall*

Antifa members loiter on the Mall. Pence emerges from a manhole cover.

FIRST ANTIFA:
Look, it's Pence!

SECOND ANTIFA:
Damn, what's he doing here?

PENCE:
Join me! We have to march on the Capitol and recapture it for the people!

The antifa crowd cheers and follows Pence as they march to the Capitol.

*　　　　　*　　　　　*

Scene:　　　*The Senate Chamber*

Trump screams as he walks to the edge of the stage. He hisses at the Senators and Congressmen.

TRUMP:
You stole the election, but I will be back!

Trump dives into the orchestra pit. Note: make sure there is a large cushion or trampoline to break his fall.

The Senators and Congressmen cheer as Trump disappears into the orchestra pit.

PENCE:
Where are the Senate workers who rescued the ballots from the mob?

FIRST DREAMER:
Here I am!

SECOND DREAMER:
Me too!

PENCE:
America owes you her thanks. Because of what you have done, we can declare Biden as the President-Elect after a fair election!

The two Dreamers give each other a high-five and say:

FIRST AND SECOND DREAMER (in unison):
Immigrants! We get the job done!

Antifa members enter the Senate Chamber, joining the Senators and Congressmen. They hold up U.S. and Pride flags as they sing the last song, a reprise of "The Room Where We Hid":

ALL:
He had to leave the room where we hid
The room where we hid
The room where we hid
He had to leave the room where we hid
To save our city upon a hill.

Curtain falls.

*   *   *

The curtain lifted again, and the cast revelled in the applause of the audience. Alex Nevis, the playwright, came on stage and said, "Everyone! I have an announcement!"

What could it be? Pompey wondered.

"Great news!" Nevis shouted. "The Department of Education will stream *Pence* into classrooms so that our children can learn about the greatest American after Alexander Hamilton!"

As the audience cheered, Pompey said, "Great! We'll get residuals from this."

Doniphon nodded. "Maybe they'll add us to the regular curriculum. If they do, we're set for life."

"America needs heroes, now more than ever in these troubled times," Nevis said. "Just as Alexander Hamilton inspired a generation during the Crisis of the Twenty-

First Century, Mike Pence will inspire today's generation to defend democracy."

A man in the audience shouted, "Beat the Rebels!" Someone chanted, "U.S.A.! U.S.A.!" The people were still cheering as the cast left the stage.

As he changed out of costume, Pompey heard his phone buzz. A new text message appeared:

I've returned from 2021. Arrived in New York now. Need to see you soon. Tom.

It was his old college friend Tom Stoddard. The two of them had been oddballs at the Massachusetts Institute of Technology. MIT was hardly famous for arts programs, yet it did have them. Pompey had studied theatre arts at MIT, and Stoddard had studied history. After teaching at several universities, Stoddard returned to MIT as a lecturer.

I've returned from 2021. Pompey's heart beat faster. The Fourth Dimension Project must have succeeded.

As usual, fans waited at the backstage door to see Pompey. A teenaged girl cooed as he signed her program book.

"I knew nothing about Mike Pence or the twenty-first century. I told my friends to tell me nothing about history because I didn't want any spoilers. I love your musical! I learned so much from it! Thank you!" she squealed.

As the girl strolled away, Pompey saw a thin man whose blond hair was turning grey at the temples.

"Tom!" Pompey cried out. "You made it back alive!"

"Yeah, DeAndre, I did," said Tom Stoddard, grinning as he hugged Pompey.

Stoddard gave a round metal object to Pompey. "A souvenir from my trip."

"Wow! A Trump Pence election button!" said Pompey.

"It's a real one, not a prop from your show," Stoddard said.

"Thank you! A genuine artifact of the Crisis of the Twenty-First Century. It makes history feel real."

Stoddard looked up at the theatre marquee. "*That's* not real."

The Mall, Washington, D.C., January 6, 2021

Tom Stoddard materialized in an alley near the Mall. He wore clothes from a movie costume company. As he walked out of the alley, he saw a crowd walking towards the Capitol. They carried U.S. flags, Trump banners, and signs reading "STOP THE STEAL".

These were the Insurrectionists, Stoddard realized. He marvelled at the sight. He was the first historian to travel back in time.

In 2221, he got vaccinated for the diseases of the twenty-first century. Due to one particular pandemic, many people wore face masks at the time, so he put one on. However, he saw that most of the Insurrectionists did not wear masks. He kept his on anyway.

He wore a Library of Congress photo ID card on a lanyard around his neck. He tucked the card under his jacket so that the Insurrectionists would not see that he was impersonating a Congressional librarian.

He carried a bag containing two books. If questioned

by Capitol Police, he would claim to be delivering books to a Congressman. In the twenty-first century, a small number of people still learned things by reading books. Learning from watching movies hadn't become the dominant form of education yet.

The afternoon unfolded as all the movies and plays had depicted. The Insurrectionists stormed through the windows and doors of the Capitol and invaded the building. Stoddard was lucky; the mob pushed him through a lightly-guarded door, and no police fought back with batons or tear gas there.

The physicists and engineers at MIT had warned him—or would warn him—not to do anything to change history. However, they had no practical rules other than don't kill anyone, don't save anyone, and don't have sex with anyone.

Some of the theoretical physicists considered the mission to be inherently dangerous, saying the "butterfly effect" meant that anything he did, even his mere presence, could change history. Other scientists thought that it was impossible for Stoddard to change history because his time travel meant that he was a part of history. And still others speculated that he couldn't actually travel into the past, but rather, would go into an alternate universe's past.

Only one other person had travelled back in time before, a physicist who went back to 1900 Antarctica, saw nobody, and returned to the future after one minute. Stoddard would be the first person to stay longer than a minute. However, the scientists had told him, "Just watch, stay only for an hour, and come back."

Stoddard breathed heavily through his mask as he

walked through the National Statuary Hall. He was both thrilled and frightened. He knew there were unknown risks to himself and to the universe in playing with time. But he volunteered for the mission because he wanted tenure. He was running out of universities that would hire him.

All around him, people chanted "Find Mike Pence! Hang Mike Pence!" A woman held up a noose and shouted, "Where's Pence! Where's the traitor?"

A man waved a Confederate battle flag and screamed, "Pence secretly converted to Muslimism! Kill him!"

Pompey would be pleased to know that the musical *Pence* was accurate, Stoddard thought.

As he left Statuary Hall, Stoddard heard people shouting obscenities and "Get back! Get back!" He looked behind and saw Insurrectionists fighting with two police officers. The Capitol Police were finally hitting back.

The fight moved towards him. Stoddard fled down the hallway. He didn't want to die or change history.

The shouting grew louder as more people joined the brawl behind him. All around him, Senators, Congressmen, and their staff fled from their offices. Stoddard followed them.

They fled down the stairs and scattered, heading into different tunnels and passageways. Stoddard randomly chose one and ran through it.

A Capitol Police officer pointed a gun at him and shouted, "Freeze! Identify yourself!"

Stoddard raised his arms. "I'm James Wayne, librarian at the Library of Congress! My ID is under my jacket."

The officer reached into Stoddard's jacket, pulled out the fake ID, and looked at it. The shouting from the moving battle grew louder behind them.

"Why the Hell are you still running around?" the officer said. "Get out! Here, hide in here!"

The officer banged on a door and shouted, "Police!" The door opened, and the officer shoved Stoddard through it and slammed it shut. Stoddard heard the officer yell, "Get back! Get back!" The sounds of yelling moved down the hallway.

Stoddard turned away from the door. There were about twenty people inside the room. He guessed that they were Senators, Congressmen, and staff. Some wore face masks, some wore no masks, and some wore their masks pulled down. The scene resembled one from the movie *Siege on the Hill*, which he watched in grade 8.

A man pulled down his mask as a woman approached him. Stoddard gasped. That man was Mike Pence, Vice-President of the United States and the second greatest American ever, exceeded only by Alexander Hamilton.

"Mike, are we going to be safe here?" the woman asked.

"We'll be fine, Karen," Pence replied. "They can't get through that door."

Mike Pence and his wife Karen! Stoddard couldn't believe his luck. He could watch history being made.

A man approached Stoddard and showed him a Secret Service badge. The Secret Service officer demanded, "Sir, may I see what's in your bag?"

Stoddard took *The Congressional Record* and a Bible out of the bag. The officer nodded, said, "Thank you", and went away.

"Is that a Bible?"

Stoddard looked up and saw Pence.

"Yes it is, sir," said Stoddard.

"May I see it, please?" Pence asked.

Stoddard held the Bible out to Pence. The Vice-President turned through its pages.

"King James Edition, printed by Thomas Nelson in Nashville in 2018," Pence said. "Who ordered this book?"

"I can't tell you, sir," Stoddard said. "That's confidential."

Pence nodded. "Oh, right. No problem. I remember when no Senator or Congressman needed to borrow a Bible from the Library. Everyone had his own copy."

As he gave the Bible back to Stoddard, Pence said, "On the plus side, someone in Congress wants to read it."

Pence walked away. A blonde woman went to Pence, pulled down her face mask, and said, "Mr. Vice-President, why are we hiding here? A space laser, the one funded by the Rothschilds, is pointing at us right now. We'll be dry roasted unless we leave the building."

Pence glared at her. "No, Marjorie. we're safest here, and there's no space laser pointed at us. NASA would've told me if there were."

"NASA is controlled by Chinese liberals funded by George Soros!" Marjorie said. "Why else do Jews eat Chinese food at Christmas?"

Stoddard stared in horror at Marjorie. She would become the President who started the Third Civil War.

Karen Pence held up her cell phone. "Mike, look what the President is saying about you on Twitter. It's awful."

In the hallway, people shouted, "Find Mike Pence! Hang Mike Pence!"

Pence shook his head. "I gave him the evangelical vote when he couldn't even figure out whether Second

Corinthians was in the Old Testament or the New Testament. I supported him every time he said something stupid. I offered to serve as acting President when he was at Walter Reed, but he didn't want me. I gave him the best four years of my career. I was loyal to him to the end, and after all I've done for him, this is how he repays me!"

Marjorie snickered and walked away.

"I can't do anything to overturn the vote," Pence fumed. "I wish to God that I could, but I can't."

"Wait until 2024," Karen said. "You'll have your chance then."

"Yes," said Pence. "One nation under God again, only two genders again, born a boy and stay a boy again, marriage as a union only between man and woman again—all the things Donald started but was too stupid to finish."

Hmm, Stoddard thought, this wasn't the Mike Pence he had seen in *Siege on the Hill* or *Pence: An American Musical*.

Stoddard waited through the afternoon with everyone else in the room. Eventually, the Capitol Police opened the door and let them back up to their offices. Mike Pence returned to the Senate Chamber to count the Electoral College votes. The siege was over.

Stoddard went outside and looked around. Police and troops roamed around the Capitol, but he saw no antifa.

Waving his Library of Congress ID badge, he walked past the police and returned to the alley where he had materialized. He pressed on his watch and returned to the year 2221.

*					*					*

Stage Door Canteen, New York, March 1, 2221

Pompey put down his coffee and looked incredulously at Stoddard. "Man, are you saying that Mike Pence didn't lead the resistance against Trump?"

"He hid in the basement all afternoon," Stoddard said. "There were no antifa anywhere near the Capitol."

"But didn't he insist on declaring that Biden won the election?"

"He did, that's true."

"That means that he opposed Trump."

"No, it's not that simple."

"What do you mean?" Pompey said. "He was Trump's biggest enemy. He caused the downfall of Trump."

"He was completely devoted to Trump until Trump dumped him for being useless," Stoddard said.

"I don't believe this," Pompey said. "Next thing you're going to say is that he didn't support gay, lesbian, and transgender rights!"

Stoddard laughed.

"Oh, man, we have that scene at the end with all those Pride flags!"

"Yeah, I know."

"And what about *Siege on the Hill*? It's required viewing in high school. And now you're saying it's not true?"

"I've long had doubts about that movie."

"And those doubts got you kicked out of Harvard, Brown, and UCLA," Pompey said. "You're lucky MIT still had a history department."

Stoddard took a sip of coffee. "It's not the most wealthy and prestigious history department in America, but it teamed up with the Fourth Dimension Project."

"Is it possible you went into an alternative universe?"

"I'm sure that I was in our universe."

"You're running out of places to work, and you still haven't gotten tenure," Pompey said. "Are you sure you want to tell people about your trip?"

"I have to. The funding agreement requires me to report my observations."

"But what are you going to do? Nobody will make a movie based on your story."

"I'm going to write my observations for *The MIT History Journal*," said Stoddard.

Pompey chuckled. "The old-fashioned way?"

"Why not?" asked Stoddard. "I just came back from an old-fashioned time."

"It's the last academic journal in the world. I don't know why MIT History keeps publishing it."

"Tradition," said Stoddard.

"Ah, tradition. The *Journal*'s obsolete," said Pompey. "Reading a journal! What's wrong with watching the university's videostream?"

"I know. However, I bet only twenty people will read it. Since almost nobody will see it, it won't stir up a controversy. I'll do what's right for history, fulfill the funding agreement, and keep my job."

Stoddard's Apartment, Cambridge, Massachusetts, March 24, 2221

Stoddard wrote his paper, called "I Hid in the Capitol with Mike Pence: An Eyewitness Account of the Capitol Insurrection of 2021".

In high school, Stoddard watched the old movie *The Last Samurai*, about a retired First Civil War veteran who went to Japan and taught samurai how to fight with swords. The epic battle scenes inspired him to study history. He even cited *The Last Samurai* in his doctoral thesis. There were Japanese who insisted that no American ever trained their samurai, much less lectured to the Emperor on how to preserve Japanese culture. Like all American scholars, Stoddard dismissed these Japanese critics as fascist, anti-American bigots.

His research about Japan's Tokugawa Period, done by viewing the films of Akira Kurosawa, got him positions at several universities. He should have become a tenured professor of history at a prestigious university.

However, when he published some radical views on American history, the movie studios retaliated. In his last job, he outraged Warner Brothers by claiming that Lee Harvey Oswald acted alone to assassinate John F. Kennedy. Warner Brothers complained that he did not consider the 1991 movie *JFK* in his research. Since Warner Brothers was UCLA's media partner, the UCLA Oliver Stone School of History fired him.

Now he was challenging two hundred years of scholarship on American history again.

Fortunately, very few people would read it. He would keep his job.

Stoddard sent the paper to Dr. Maxine Scott, Head of the History Department. Dr. Scott replied the next day:

Dear Tom,

Thank you for your submission to The MIT

History Journal. *I must say that your paper is a highly radical view of Mike Pence. However, given our Journal's policy on academic freedom, I will publish it with the statement that its views do not necessarily reflect those of MIT.*

Due to the controversial nature of your paper, the Department will defer discussion on your application for tenure.

Sincerely,

Maxine Scott, Ph.D.

Head, Department of History

The MIT History Journal, April 2221 issue, appeared automatically in the public access drives of eight hundred academic libraries and on the devices of five hundred individual subscribers. Another five hundred non-academic persons, including movie and TV producers, received a download link.

A week after the *Journal* went out, Stoddard checked its readership statistics. One hundred people had accessed the April issue, but only twenty people had read his article for more than ten seconds.

He would keep his job, but he resigned himself to never getting tenure.

Although only ten people had read his paper, one of them told a news channel about it. Soon the entire country knew about his trip to the past. Hundreds of fans of *Pence: An American Musical* sent hate messages to

Stoddard.

Alex Nevis tweeted, "You have defecated on the second greatest American ever! Shame on you!" His followers retweeted his tweet one and a half million times.

The number of people who read his paper stayed at twenty, but the number of hate messages rose to a thousand.

Pompey phoned him. To Stoddard's surprise, Pompey was not angry.

"I'm glad you told me about your time travel trip so that I knew what to expect," Pompey said. "What I didn't expect is that you would send ticket sales through the roof. We're sold out for the next two years! I suppose I should thank you, not criticize you."

"You're welcome," Stoddard said wryly.

"But I have to warn you, man," Pompey said. "Stay away from Broadway. Fans of the musical don't like you. Don't go anywhere near the statue of Mike Pence."

"I'll stay away from Broadway," Stoddard agreed.

"Good, good." Pompey laughed. "Thanks to your article, I might get the Manhattan Drama Circle Award."

Dr. Scott ordered Stoddard to come to her office for an urgent meeting.

"I have bad news," she said. "The Disney Channel has stopped funding our department."

The Disney Channel was funding Dr. Scott's screenplay on Davy Crockett. Disney was also funding ten other movies and TV series written by faculty members.

"Disney gave us some leeway, though," Dr. Scott said.

"If you correct your paper to make it historically accurate, Disney will reconsider funding our research."

"No, I can't. My research *is* historically accurate," Stoddard said.

Dr. Scott sighed. "Listen, Tom, your career is in danger. We can't keep someone whose work threatens our funding. The Department of Education will be streaming *Pence* into two thousand high schools next week. The teachers want to make the lesson simple: Mike Pence fought a tyrant and led the revolution that restored democracy. Children need to learn that lesson now more than ever. They need a hero."

"Fire me if you must," Tom said.

"You're fired. You've been fired from Harvard, Brown, UCLA, and now, MIT. Did I forget anywhere?"

"I'll find a job somewhere else."

Dr. Scott guffawed. "Like where? University of Tokyo?"

When Stoddard arrived home, his cell phone buzzed. He looked at the new email.

His old enemies at UCLA Oliver Stone School of History had complained about him to the Department of Education. The Secretary of Education, a fan of the *Pence* musical, agreed to revoke his license on the grounds of poor academic research.

Now he couldn't teach anywhere in the United States.

On April 30, Stoddard heard an announcer read the news on the MIT videostream:

"MIT apologizes for its April Fool's joke in *The MIT History Journal*. The hoax journal, intended as a joke for faculty members only, was sent out by error. MIT sent the correct edition yesterday."

Stoddard opened the *Journal* on his tablet and read his paper, now retitled "I Liberated the Capitol with Mike Pence: An Eyewitness Account of the Insurrection of January 6, 2021":

I was there... At 5:00 p.m., antifa forces arrived outside the Capitol but had no plan. They watched from the Mall as the Insurrectionists swarmed around the west entrance of the Capitol. Mike Pence, hearing that the antifa had arrived, left his hideout and entered the underground tunnels. He emerged in the Mall and addressed the antifa there.

"I'm going to march back to the Capitol and take it back for the American people. I'll do it alone but if any of you want to help me, I'll help you," he told them. "Who's with me?"

The antifa cheered, and Pence led them in an attack on the Insurrectionists from their rear...

The *Journal* had changed instantly overnight. It had downloaded itself to all online devices and data drives simultaneously, permanently deleting and replacing all copies of the "hoax issue".

But he had to make sure, so he phoned Dr. Scott.

"Maxine, thanks for issuing the corrected *Journal*," Stoddard said.

"I'm happy to have done it," Dr. Scott said. "Thank you for approving the all-access erratum."

"What about the copies that were sent to subscribers who saved them offline," Stoddard asked. "Were we able to get those too?"

"Oh, yes, we did," Dr. Scott said. "Since the Bill Clinton

mix-up, each of our publications has a remote sensor embedded in its file. Our all-access erratum sent a signal that overwrote even the copies that were saved on drives not connected to the internet. No copies of the hoax issue exist anywhere. It's as if it never existed."

"And that's how we preserve history," Stoddard said.

Dr. Scott chuckled. "Yes, it is. Disney is pleased. *Davy Crockett the Abolitionist* is back in production. By the way, Disney is going to call you. You owe me big time, but thank me after you sign the movie deal."

"What movie deal?" Stoddard asked.

Shinbone Theater, New York, February 1, 2222

The Secretary of Education came on stage and gave the Educator of the Year Award to Stoddard. *I Liberated the Capitol with Mike Pence*, the movie based on his paper, had received excellent reviews from the two thousand teachers who had used it in school.

The Secretary said, "Your history of Mike Pence inspires us as we fight the Rebels."

Stoddard smiled. He had received five million dollars, his half of the movie deal on *I Liberated the Capitol with Mike Pence*. Since Dr. Scott had negotiated for the other five million dollars to go to MIT, the History Department had rehired him and given him tenure. He could live with job security for life, so long as Dr. Scott approved all his publications.

Pompey, in costume as Mike Pence, walked across the stage to congratulate him. Pompey had played Pence again in *I Liberated the Capitol with Mike Pence*. He was making a career of playing the Vice-President.

After the award presentation, Stoddard and the Secretary sat down in the audience to watch *Pence*. For Stoddard, it was his second time. The Secretary had seen it ten times.

As Nancy Pelosi sang "I Pray for the President", Stoddard thought about his meeting with the Fourth Dimension Project in the morning. They had several potential theories on why events seemed so different from recorded history, but they couldn't prove any of them.

"Here's another possibility. Perhaps you did change history, but when you returned to 2221, you somehow corrected the timeline again," Dr. John Feeney had said.

"Or perhaps we're learning history incorrectly," Stoddard said.

Dr. Feeney laughed. "Oh, you and that April Fool's stunt. I guess you can joke about it now that you've got tenure."

After the performance, Pompey's fourteen-year-old niece Tiara came to meet him at the backstage door.

"Who's your favourite character?" Pompey asked, grinning. "Is it Mike Pence?"

Tiara said, "No offence, Uncle DeAndre, but Karen Pence is my favourite character. She's got the best song."

"What?" Pompey said in disbelief. "Better than 'The Room Where We Hid'?"

"'We Got Burned' is better," Tiara said. "Guess what? My history teacher wants us to write about a famous African American for Black History Month, and I picked Karen Pence."

Pompey smiled and said, "Great choice!"

"Uh, about Karen Pence—" Stoddard began.

Pompey nudged him and said, "Hey, Tom, don't you have to go home and work on that new TV special about George Washington?"

"Uh, yes, I do," said Stoddard. "Watch for it at Christmas time. It's called *Victory at Valley Forge*."

About "The Room Where We Hid"

When the musical *Hamilton* became super popular between 2015 and 2020, many people posted on social media that they learned so much about American history from it. But *Hamilton* is far from historically accurate for various reasons, especially in how it portrays Alexander Hamilton's and the other Founding Fathers' attitudes on slavery (Hint: they were not as liberal as the musical shows them to be).

Many people learn history from movies and TV shows that are really fiction with little or no historical accuracy. Yes, people do pick apart the historical accuracy of costumes and props, but they seldom see the greater inaccuracies about historical people, their actions, and their motives. Centuries from now, how will pop culture memorialize the events that we experienced today?

I wrote "The Room Where We Hid" in February 2021, shortly after the riot at the United States Capitol on January 6, 2021. Trump's line "but I will be back!" is unintentionally prescient in retrospect. Back then, nobody predicted that anyone would be elected to two non-consecutive terms as President since Grover Cleveland in the nineteenth century.

No American magazine editor would publish "The Room Where We Hid". One wrote to me that she liked the story but thought a story about the January 6 Capitol Riot was too traumatizing for American readers. It is being published for the first time in this collection. Thanks to Catherine Fitzsimmons for publishing it.

The House of Hagfish

Sharks Invade Lake Ontario During Swimsuit Fashion Shoot

Cathy Wong watched her phone in horror as the swimsuit models rushed back to the shore. An unsteady camera zoomed in on the shark fins circling in the water.

A fashion reporter, pressed into duty as a science expert, breathlessly said, "Polar bears have disappeared from Churchill, Manitoba, but sharks have invaded Toronto's waterfront. Global warming has brought another new species here. Bull sharks can live in fresh water like lakes and rivers. They never used to swim up the St. Lawrence River and into Lake Ontario, but now they have made their way here."

Global warming also moved the Summer Fashion Festival to that warm October day. When Cathy was a teenager, she would have bundled up in a sweater and jeans and felt the chill air blow around her. A decade later, she wore a pink off-the-shoulder top and black miniskirt as she walked into the offices of Seagold Textiles. Cathy walked beside the slime production vats. Her stomach churned from the odour. It smelled like stale sweat. Even after a month of working here, she still hadn't gotten used to the stench.

"When I got a degree in fashion communication, I thought I would be designing ad campaigns for big brands like Givenchy," she said to Greg, the marine biologist. "I never imagined I would sell eel snot to clothing manufacturers."

Greg shook his head and took a deep breath. Like all the scientists, he was used to the smell. "They're not eels. Eels are in class *Actinopterygii*. Hagfish are in class *Myxini*."

"Well, they look like eels, sort of. Slime eels. That's the nickname that the fashion reporters gave to hagfish. It stinks here. Hurry up, let's go to Alfie's room."

They sped past the slime production vats and into a room with a sign reading "ALFIE". Cathy turned on the clean air intake. Posters of clothes hung on the walls. Another wall had a counter, sink, and refrigerator. Off to the side, a fish tank held a grey hagfish. It slithered at the bottom of the tank like its ancestors at the bottom of the ocean.

The hagfish stopped evolving three hundred million years ago. It has a skull but no spine. It has no jaw but has a mouth with rows of sharp teeth for tearing apart dead fish for food. Its primitive eyes are white spots that lack irises and pupils; they are merely retinas that can detect light but cannot create detailed images. It is seemingly ill-suited to thrive in an ocean full of large predators with vertebrae and good eyesight. It did, however, gain one evolutionary advantage. A hagfish is covered with glands that eject mucous. Combined with water, the mucous expands and creates a thick, white slime that clogs the gills and mouths of predators. Any big fish that tries to bite a hagfish will suffocate on the goo.

The mucous contains long threads of protein, a hundred times thinner than human hair but ten times stronger than nylon. In 2012, biologists at the University of Guelph extracted the protein threads and spun them into fibres. Eventually, the textiles industry used hagfish slime to create alternatives to petroleum-based materials like polyester.

Most slime production companies had a giant aquarium full of hagfish. Seagold Textiles went two steps further; it genetically modified a hagfish that could create twice the amount of mucous. Then it used that hagfish's DNA to genetically modify a bacterium to create the mucous. The vats were full of bacteria, not hagfish. It was cheaper to keep bacteria than hagfish, giving Seagold a financial advantage. Not all companies had the talent to develop and patent a process and creature like Seagold's.

"Good morning, Alfie," Cathy said to the hagfish in the tank.

"The guys want to take him to the fashion show today," Greg said. "I'm getting the portable aquarium ready."

"Whoa. You're taking Alfie to the fashion show?"

"Why not? We owe our company's profits to his DNA. We made him. He's our pride and joy."

Cathy looked at the posters. They showed models in cheap, ordinary blouses and pants. Each poster also had a portrait of Alfie, with his white eyes and gaping mouth. He was anything but cute.

"Now that I'm in charge of promotion, I'm going to change our image," Cathy declared. "Our only customers are cheap clothing factories in China."

"Nothing wrong with the Chinese market." Greg shrugged. "I'm wearing their clothes right now."

Cathy looked at Greg's lime green T-shirt and faded red denim pants. She nodded and silently noted how differently people dressed here compared to her previous employer of two months, the fashion magazine *Tease*. Everyone there wore stylish clothes.

"China is a huge market, and it's great for us, but I want to expand our customer base," Cathy said. "I've invited Dior, Chanel, Versace, Armani, Givenchy, and Gucci to our show. I want the high-end designers to stop thinking of hagfish as ugly and disgusting."

"But hagfish are ugly and disgusting."

"All the more reason to keep Alfie away. Let the textiles sell themselves without their DNA donor slithering nearby."

Greg shrugged. "Hey, Alfie, our marketing director thinks you're too ugly to slither down the runway. What do you think?"

Alfie stared up at him with his white eye spots.

"Oh, you're more interested in lunch," Greg said. He opened a refrigerator, took out a dead fish, and dropped it into the tank.

Alfie's teeth tore a hole in the fish. He burrowed inside it and began eating the fish from the inside out.

"We don't need to show that at the Summer Fashion Festival," said Cathy.

"Too late," Greg said. "His mealtime video has already gone viral."

Cathy sighed and tapped on her phone. A photo of a blonde woman appeared. "Giselle, the Victoria's Secret supermodel. How about hiring her for our campaign? I heard she came by our booth to look at Alfie last year."

"Yeah, she even held him, but it suddenly rained, and Alfie panicked and slimed all over her."

"Nobody told me about that!" Cathy blurted out.

"Her dress was ruined. It was Alexander McQueen, I think. Oh, is my little Alfie feeling full now?"

Alfie swam out of the fish's carcass. He had reduced it to a bag of skin. Greg reached into the tank to pet the hagfish. Alfie coiled himself at the tank's bottom and suddenly sprang out of the water. Cathy screamed as the hagfish flew in front of her.

"What the hell!" Greg shouted as he caught Alfie in his hands.

"Hagfish can't jump up!"

"I've never seen him do that before." Greg desperately grasped the slippery hagfish.

"When you guys modified his DNA, could you have given him superpowers?"

Greg struggled as Alfie squirmed in his hands. "Superpowers? This isn't a comic book!"

"Then how can he jump out of the water?"

"Well, genetic manipulation sometimes creates unintended effects. Like his ability to live in fresh water."

"Which means he and his offspring can live in our lakes and rivers as well as the ocean," Cathy said.

Greg lowered Alfie back into the fish tank. His hands were covered with white slime. It drooped like a gelatinous sheet.

"Ewww, that's so gross!" Cathy cried.

"You get used to it after a while." He smirked at her. "Do you want to touch it?"

"Uh, no. I don't want to get it on my clothes."

"Come on. You don't have to grab it. Just poke a finger slightly into it."

Cathy touched the slime and recoiled immediately.

"It feels like snot!"

Greg laughed and flung the slime into a garbage pail before he went to a sink and washed his hands.

Cathy rushed to join. As she washed her hands, she said, "Don't let anyone touch Alfie at the fashion show, all right?"

"What's your plan for the Summer Fashion Festival?" Greg asked.

Cathy wiped her hands on a paper towel. "I got some design students to create a variety of outfits and accessories from hagfish textiles. Evening gowns, sundresses, skirts, pantsuits, fall jackets, bikinis, belts, handbags: you name it, the kids made it. These kids will be the Vivienne Westwoods and Ralph Laurens of tomorrow. This time, we're dressing our models in haute couture, not mass market. And no more science-y presentations."

"But lots of people attended the presentation at last year's Summer Fashion Festival," Greg protested.

"They were all genetic scientists and marine biologists. We need to reach a new audience."

"That's fine, but did you read the latest email from the boss?"

"Not yet." Cathy pulled her phone out of her bag and

read the email:

> *Cathy,*
>
> *Using the fashion students' designs is a great idea. Add one more item to your show: bring Alfie along in the portable tank. He's our pride and joy. We want to show off our greatest achievement in applied genetic engineering. Indeed, my friends think I should get a Nobel Prize, LOL. Alfie is always popular with the science journalists.*
>
> *I know we got some bad press from the fashion magazines last year, but Giselle should have worn the rain poncho that we offered to her.*
>
> *John Herring, Ph.D., M.Sc., M.A., B.Sc., B.A.*
>
> *President, Seagold Textiles*

Damn. She couldn't get rid of Alfie.

"Little eel, it looks like you'll be going to our fashion show after all."

The Summer Fashion Festival was held at an open-air stage at Harbourfront, Toronto's classy neighbourhood by the northern shore of Lake Ontario. Cathy felt the summer heat on her shoulders as the models and the designers gathered on stage for the finale. Cathy strutted out in a sleeveless blue sundress. One of the design students had made it from hagfish cloth.

Cathy took the microphone and announced, "Ladies and gentlemen, here are the designers of the future using the fabrics of tomorrow!"

Alfie sat in a fish tank atop a trolley cart beside the stage. Greg stood there too, watching the show. Thank goodness Greg had one blue business suit, Cathy thought. It was a no-name brand from a cheap department store, but at least it wasn't jeans and a T-shirt.

After the fashion show, the reporters clustered around Alfie. Much to Cathy's dismay, they ignored the designers. "Hey, can you feed a dead fish to him?" asked a *Toronto Star* fashion writer.

Cathy eased herself between the reporters and Alfie. "Why don't you interview the designers?" she suggested. "They can tell you all about their fashions, all made with hagfish fabric by Seagold Textiles."

The reporters murmured in agreement.

"The designers are at the refreshments table," said Cathy, smiling. "Go help yourself to some coffee and cookies."

Suddenly, a shrill voice shouted, "So this is the creature that slimed Giselle!"

A brunette woman approached them wearing a white silk blouse, leopard print bolero jacket with matching miniskirt, and a wide-brimmed ivory hat, all by Fendi. She carried a miniature poodle in her Louis Vuitton black leather bag. It was Heather von Sator, editor-in-chief of *Tease* and Cathy's boss for two months. Cathy quit *Tease* after von Sator ordered her to hand-wash the blouse that von Sator had worn to the *Vanity Fair* party, the same blouse that she wore now.

"It's got to be hand washed," von Sator insisted at the time. "Look at it! Do you think you can put silk like this into a machine? You should know better."

"I shouldn't be doing personal chores like hand washing your clothes," Cathy had protested.

"I thought you Orientals are supposed to be obedient and hardworking, knowing when to submit to authority. That's why I hired you! You have been a disappointment."

"First, the word isn't Oriental, it's *Asian*," Cathy had shot back. "Second, Asian girls are not submissive, little slaves. You want to meet a real bitch? Meet my mother! And she's Asian too!"

"You must have grown up in Scarborough," von Sator said. She snorted. "No wonder you speak English so well."

Cathy shuddered at the memory.

"Well, if it isn't little Cathy," von Sator said. Her eyebrows and facial muscles barely moved when she talked, a sign that she had been injecting Botox to smooth her wrinkles.

"Hello, Madame von Sator," Cathy muttered. Von Sator insisted that peasants address her with French honorifics.

Von Sator gave Cathy a once over. "Wearing a no-name brand, I see. So you're working for a bunch of geeky marine scientists who harvest snot from eels? To think you aspired to a career in fashion."

The reporters giggled nervously. The little poodle barked. Cathy's heart thumped faster.

"My dress was designed by Miranda Chang from the Ontario College of Art and Design," Cathy said calmly. "We gave hagfish fabric to the best design students in the country and told them—"

"I'm not interested in your no-name dress. I want to see the famous Alfie."

Von Sator pushed aside the reporters as she strutted to the tank. She looked at Alfie and guffawed. "This ugly little thing is Alfie? Do you really think any *couturier* will want to make clothes from eel snot?"

"He's not an eel," Cathy blurted. "Eels are in class *Actinopterygii*. Hagfish are in class *Myxini*."

Von Sator glared at her. "Save the science lecture for *Scientific American*. There's no reason for *Tease* to cover your fashion show. *Tease* is for the woman who appreciates her own beauty and a modern lifestyle. This eel's slime is fit only to be made into cheap clothes for low-end retailers."

She thumped Alfie's fish tank repeatedly. "See how the pathetic little eel squirms. It's not even good enough to be cut up for sushi."

"Uh, don't bang on the fish tank," Greg warned. "When hagfish feel threatened or stressed, they—"

Alfie jumped out of the tank and spewed his mucous on von Sator. When he fell back into the tank, the splash of water got onto the mucous, and it expanded into slime all over von Sator's face and chest.

The reporters gasped. Von Sator tore an opening for her mouth and screamed. Her dog barked incessantly. Spectators pulled out their cell phones and made videos of von Sator struggling with the slime on her face. Miranda Chang, the designer of Cathy's dress, showed her phone to Cathy.

"My video will go viral," Miranda giggled. "It's already gotten twenty likes in just a minute."

"You *peasant*!" von Sator shrieked. "*Tease* will do

everything to put your company out of business! You'll *never* get another *job* in fashion for the *rest* of your *life*!"

Madame von Sator stomped away. The reporters and photographers followed her, abandoning Cathy and the design students.

Cosmopolitan's beauty director approached Cathy and whispered, "It was sooo fun to watch that cow get slimed!"

"No, it wasn't. Oh my God, I'm ruined!"

"No, we'll be okay," said Greg. "Our company survived Giselle getting slimed last year."

"But Giselle is just a supermodel. Heather von Sator is the bitch empress of fashion publishing. She makes Anna Wintour look like Princess Diana!"

"Who's Anna Wintour?" Greg asked.

Cathy groaned. Why did she turn down the unpaid internship at *Women's Wear Daily*?

A Summer Fashion Festival assistant came by. "Miss Wong, I'm sorry to ask you, but can you and your crew leave soon? We have to get the stage ready for the Armani show."

Cathy led the Seagold staff and the student designers away from the stage. Greg pushed Alfie's trolley cart behind them. They walked beside a beach, recreated in the latest government project. Lots of people, wearing swimsuits in October, stood in the sand, staring out at the lake. The crowd babbled excitedly.

"Shark!" someone shouted.

A teenage couple was out in a small inflatable raft. A shark's fin circled them, its head above the water from time to time. The girl swung an oar at the shark's head but missed it. Instead, the oar flew out of her hands and into the water.

"No, no, don't provoke the shark, just leave it alone," Greg yelled.

The boy held an oar and poked at the shark's body.

The shark bumped the raft with its nose. The two teens yelled and screamed as the shark rocked the raft, trying to overturn it.

A lifeguard ran out of her station to look at the shark attack. Some beachgoers called to her. "Marlene!"

"What are you going to do?" Cathy asked as Marlene ran by her.

"We have no protocol for sharks yet," Marlene replied, "but I know I've got to get those kids out of there."

Marlene ran to a rescue boat with an outboard motor. Cathy took off her high heels and chased Marlene through the sand.

The crowd continued to yell; the shark had bumped the raft again.

"The shark's getting aggressive," Cathy said. "What if you or one of the kids falls into the water?"

"It's a risk I have to take," said Marlene.

"I've got an idea," Cathy said. "Do you have a bucket, something you can use to hold water?"

"In my boat."

"Good. I think I have a way to scare the shark away."

Greg pushed and pulled Alfie's trolley cart through the sand to Cathy and Marlene. "What are you thinking?" he asked.

"Let's take Alfie out to sea," Cathy said, looking at the hagfish in the fish tank.

*   *   *

As the rescue boat sped towards the raft, Cathy looked down at the bucket, where Alfie lay curled in water. She doubted the hagfish knew what was going on.

Marlene steered the rescue boat towards the raft. The shark darted at the rescue boat and bumped it. As the boat rocked, Cathy squealed and grabbed the boat's side. Water sloshed out of Alfie's bucket.

"Alfie's already excreting mucous," Greg said. "He must be feeling stressed."

The shark bumped the rescue boat again. Greg groaned as he held Alfie's bucket upright.

"It'll be hard to pull beside the raft if the shark keeps bumping us," Marlene said.

"Not if we make the shark leave," Cathy said.

She and Greg lifted the bucket and poured Alfie into Lake Ontario. The hagfish stayed close to the surface near the rescue boat. Alfie looked up at Cathy. She felt a lump in her throat. She knew Alfie could defend himself, but he was just a little hagfish against a big shark.

The shark rose and opened its jaws over Alfie. The predator's sharp teeth hovered inches away from the hagfish's soft body. Cathy held her breath. Then Alfie ejected slime into the shark's mouth. The slime expanded quickly, oozing into the shark's throat.

"What was that?" Marlene asked, her eyes wide open.

Greg laughed. "The shark just got slimed."

The shark shook its head violently and quickly swam away, leaving a trail of slime in the water.

Marlene threw a rope to the two teens and said, "Tie this to your raft. I'm towing you in."

Greg plunged a hand net into the water. "Come on, Alfie, get in there," he said.

He kept pushing the net in front of Alfie, but the hagfish kept escaping it. Alfie moved too quickly for Greg to catch him. The hagfish dove and disappeared under the waves.

TV news crews awaited them at shore. The reporters focused on Marlene. Cathy wasn't surprised that the reporters gave all their attention to the attractive lifeguard.

"I only drove the boat," Marlene said. "Alfie the hagfish is the real hero. He fought off the shark. You should talk to these two."

The reporters thrust their microphones at Cathy and Greg. Though caught by surprise, Cathy took only a moment to decide what to say.

"Alfie is a hagfish belonging to Seagold Textiles, a leading manufacturer of textiles made from hagfish protein. We are very proud of him," she began.

The story spread quickly. Headlines like "EEL-LIKE FISH SLIMES SHARK" and "FISH WITH NO BACKBONE DEFEATS SHARK WITH SHARP TEETH" appeared in newspapers and websites around the world.

"But he's not a fish," Greg protested.

Cathy laughed. "Let them call him whatever they want. This is the best free publicity ever."

The Australian company Speedo began using hagfish fabrics. Within a month, Speedo had an ad showing a male lifeguard in red swim trunks. Alfie's head appeared in a circle in the corner. The ad read, "Heroes of the Beach." Dior followed next, with Giselle wearing green hagfish leggings at New York Fashion Week. Giselle now cooed that she loved the "hero hagfish."

MTV aired an episode of *House of Style* with guest host Cathy showing the new hagfish collections by Calvin Klein and Vera Wang. Greg appeared as a scientist, saying that hagfish fabric was stronger than nylon. Cathy picked the blue Armani suit and silver Polo Ralph Lauren tie that he wore. He got to keep the clothes but never wore them again.

Not everyone wanted hagfish. *Tease* threatened to give no coverage to any company that used hagfish textiles. The boycott backfired; when *Tease* published an issue with no major designers in it, the magazine's sales plummeted. The advertisers cancelled their ads, and Heather von Sator got fired.

Six months later, Seagold Textiles' sales had tripled, and major designers like Chanel and Versace were using hagfish fabric on their *haute couture* and *prêt-à-porter* collections. Their ad campaigns featured Alfie. Once he was the ugly fish that only science writers noticed. Now he was the new face of fashion.

But nobody knew where he was.

"Look at these," Cathy said, pointing to her emails. "The House of Chanel just introduced a hagfish coat for the spring."

"Why do so many fashion designers call themselves 'the House of something'?" Greg asked.

"It sounds impressive, just like 'hero hagfish.'"

"Our Alfie, the hero! All kidding aside, I keep thinking about him. We might have done a bad thing. We put a genetically-modified animal into the wild. He's probably gone up the St. Lawrence River and into the ocean, where he can breed with other hagfish. His children will carry his modified genes. They might be able to live in both sea water and fresh water. If so, they can come to our rivers and lakes. Who knows what they can do, how they'll interact with the other species, how they'll affect the ecosystem or the food chain?"

"Hagfish haven't evolved for three hundred million years. Why start now?"

Ten million years after Alfie entered the Atlantic, the tribe held its annual fashion show, modelling the new clothes they had made from slime proteins. The Chief watched the parade of tubes and capes, all coloured with natural dyes from rare plants discovered in the deepest seabeds.

The Chief did not know that he was descended from a hagfish that land animals had idolized. He did not know that his prehistoric ancestors lacked the complex eyes that he used to see all the vivid colours and shapes. He did not know that his kind were the first sea animals to create artificial objects. He did not know that land animals had unwittingly restarted his species' evolution after three hundred million years of stagnation. He didn't even know that land animals had ever existed. The expeditions to the surface had found no evidence of life on land.

However, he knew that he had founded the House of Hagfish.

About "The House of Hagfish"

"House of Hagfish" was inspired by University of Guelph research on creating fibres from hagfish slime, which is ten times stronger than nylon and a renewable resource. Imagine wearing clothes made of fish snot!

Thanks to J.F. Gerrard, Allan Cho, and William Tham of the Asian Canadian Writers Workshop for publishing "The House of Hagfish".

All Dancers Go to Heaven

Maria Carrera and her husband Dave Tremaine trudged to the small brown building at the University of Toronto. Autumn leaves fluttered everywhere and snapped under their feet. To Maria, the leaves looked beautiful in their red and gold hues, but they were dead too—like the woman they were going to visit.

"I don't think we should do this," she said.

"It can't hurt anyone," Dave murmured.

"And it can't do any good either. Sylvie's dead, and I'm sad, and I'm sorry, but really, you should get on with your life. *Our* life."

"Sylvie died because of what I did to her."

"Nonsense, and you know that," Maria snapped.

They walked past a sign: *Posthumous Neural Research Project*. Before they could go further, Maria grabbed Dave and spun him around.

"Okay, you cheated on her, and you two broke up.

Fine. But I've broken up with lots of guys, and I didn't spend the rest of my life on drugs and booze. What happened to her was her own fault. Let her rest in peace," she pleaded.

"No, I can't—not until I make it up to her."

Maria glared at him, a look of exasperation on her face.

"What are you going to do?" she asked. "Say 'I'm sorry' to a bunch of brain waves?"

TORONTO, TWO WEEKS AGO, OCTOBER 15:

Sergeant John McClure, Toronto Police, watched quietly as the paramedics strapped the unconscious woman to a stretcher and rushed her away. Then he looked at the dead man lying in the corner of the apartment.

The coroner knelt on the floor, examining the corpse. He glanced at the handgun beside the body.

"I'll autopsy him, but I'm sure he died of the gunshot wound," said the coroner, pointing at the right side of the dead man's head. "Looks like a suicide too."

McClure looked at a driver's license and raised his wrist radio to his mouth. "McClure here. Deceased is white male, name: Ben Latz, age thirty."

"And the survivor?" crackled an officer's voice from the wrist radio.

"She's going to Saint Mike's, and no, we haven't identified her yet," he said. He picked up a clear plastic bag of cocaine from the coffee table. "Any information on Latz?"

"Deejay at a strip bar and small-time drug dealer. Served a couple two-year sentences."

"Doesn't surprise me." Only drug dealers, prostitutes, crackheads and derelicts lived in this slum on Jarvis Street. He could smell the sweet marijuana wafting down the street, the rotting garbage in the alleys, and the mouldy plaster of the apartments.

The coroner pointed at a bullet hole in the wall. "Looks like he tried to shoot her too but missed."

"He didn't have to bother about her," said McClure. "She overdosed and probably won't pull through."

He had to identify her. Maybe that rickety wooden dresser held some clues.

He opened it and found lots of lingerie: push-up bras, G-strings, garter belts, and stockings. Combined with the red stiletto heels and black leather thigh-high boots on the floor, they made a stripper's typical wardrobe. Again, McClure wasn't surprised; too many strippers supported their criminal boyfriends.

But a pair of pointe shoes hung beside a mirror on the wall. Their pink satin still shone. They seemed out of place among the sexy lingerie and spike heels. Had he ever seen a stripper wear ballet shoes?

He opened her handbag and spilled the contents out on a table. Lipstick, makeup, comb, money, condoms—and her Toronto Burlesque Entertainer's License. He silently thanked the City for making strippers get licenses.

"I got an ID on her from her stripper's license," he said into the wrist radio. "Real name: Sylvie Courtauld, age thirty. Stage name: Giselle."

"Any next of kin?"

"Don't know yet. I'll keep looking."

He picked up a small black address book from the

handbag's contents and leafed through it. It had the names and numbers of strip bars, but not of people. Friends? Relatives? Didn't she know anyone?

He finally found a name in faded pencil: Dave Tremaine. Not much, but it could help.

"I don't know if this guy's a friend or relative, but he might know who is. Dave Tremaine. His telephone number..."

Dave and Maria walked into Emergency Admitting at Saint Michael's Hospital. Dave looked around, his eyes wide with worry. Maria pulled her husband towards a counter staffed with nurses.

"Is Sylvie Courtauld here?" asked Dave.

The nurse checked her papers. "She's here. Are you her family?"

"No," said Maria.

"Friends, then?" asked the nurse.

"Yes," said Dave.

"Do you know if she has any family? We have to notify them."

Dave shook his head. "Both her parents are dead, she has no brothers or sisters. I don't know if she has other relatives." He paused. "May we see her, please?"

"No, not yet. Please understand, the doctor and nurses need to concentrate on her right now. Please take a seat and wait."

When they sat on the couch, Dave said, "I haven't seen her in five years. *Nobody* has seen her for years."

Maria sighed. "I didn't expect her to wind up like this—overdosed on cocaine."

Dave turned away. *There's something I should've told her years ago,* he thought. *I've missed my chance.*

Then he saw a man, about fifty years old, walk to the counter. He wore a white coat, like a doctor's. Where had Dave seen that gaunt face, that grim expression, and that greying hair before? The newspaper article from last week...

Doctor Jonathan Rand, director of the Posthumous Neural Research Project at the University of Toronto. The so-called brain wave collector. The newspaper called him a ghoul, a mad scientist who prowled in hospitals, looking for the dying. One lurid headline read: "BRAIN WAVE DOCTOR TRAPPED MY DEAD UNCLE'S SOUL ON COMPACT DISC."

Ghoul he may be, but perhaps Doctor Rand had what Dave needed. Dave walked to the counter and moved behind Rand. He overheard Rand talking to the nurse.

"This one will pass any moment now," the nurse said. "Cocaine overdose, she's stopped breathing on her own, and she's on a respirator."

"If we want her, we'll have to move fast, before the brain dies," he said. "But there's no prior consent, no next-of-kin, no family to ask."

"Excuse me, please," said Dave.

Rand turned around, his face empty of emotion. "Yes?"

"Are you Doctor Jonathan Rand?"

"Yes, I am."

It was him, the ghoul. Dave had to ask. "There's a patient, Sylvie Courtauld. Could you please—save her brain waves?"

Rand's stony face warmed into a sympathetic look. "I'd like to, but there's nothing I can do. She didn't sign any consent form, and there's no family here to give their consent."

"She doesn't have any family. But I know her. May I give consent?"

"It's unprecedented, but I suppose it's permissible. We'll have to work quickly; there's no time to spare." Rand flipped to a consent form on his clipboard. "Your relationship to the patient?"

"Former boyfriend."

A half hour later, Dave didn't have to ask the nurse about Sylvie. He could read the look on her face.

"I'm very sorry," the nurse said. "Please, follow me."

They followed the nurse into a room, then to a bed with curtains around it, shut off from the outside world. They were alone with Sylvie—and Doctor Rand.

Rand pointed at a skullcap of metal and plastic on Sylvie's head. Moving his hand, he traced the cables joining the skullcap to a monitor.

Dave noticed a bruise over Sylvie's left eye, as if someone had hit her. He had also never seen her hair so dull and limp, so different from the thick, shiny, blonde tresses years ago.

Maria sobbed softly. Since his mouth had gone dry, Dave said nothing, letting his wife cry. Even if he could talk, he didn't know what to say.

He reached out and felt Sylvie's hand. It had already gone cold. When he raised Sylvie's hand, he saw the track marks on her arm: the sign of years of injected drug abuse.

Doctor Rand pointed at the skullcap again, then at the

monitor. "We're saving the last electrical activity in her brain. Each of those lines is measuring the electric impulses from a different nerve centre of the brain..."

On the monitor, green lines pranced up and down. The lines created jagged hills, and then the hills grew smaller until they turned into flat horizontal lines.

In death, Sylvie Courtauld returned to the people who had loved and missed her. The people of the Metro Toronto Ballet felt aghast that the city could only give her a pauper's burial in a cardboard box. Dave collected donations from them for a dignified funeral. They gave their money eagerly because she was, for a brief time, their best ballerina.

Sylvie had died naked, and the dancers wanted to dress her beautifully for her burial. But all her clothes made her look like a prostitute. After some thought, Joan Silverton, the artistic director of the Ballet, took Giselle's green and white peasant costume to the funeral home.

"It was her favourite role," she explained, smiling as she handed the costume to the funeral director. "Please let her wear it one last time."

After hearing about the Giselle costume, Dave went to the apartment and took the pointe shoes off the wall. Later, at the funeral home, he put the shoes on Sylvie's feet.

At the funeral, Dave and five other dancers carried the oak coffin. With Maria on violin, a quartet played music from the last act of *Giselle*, when Giselle joins the ghostly Wilis.

Lisa Wong, the company's prima ballerina, placed a

daisy on the coffin. The other mourners followed, one by one, each placing a red rose on the coffin: dancers, musicians, teachers, ballet mistresses, choreographers, costume designers, stage hands. Andrei Arslanov, star of the Bolshoi, placed the last rose.

Joan wiped a tear. "She was such a beautiful dancer. She got so excited when she got the leading roles. What impressive debuts. A natural performer. Brilliant technique, lots of stage presence. She would've been a great Giselle."

She was a Giselle of sorts, thought Dave, remembering her show in a strip bar years ago.

"I remember something Sylvie wrote in my *Nutcracker* program book," said Joan. "It had a picture of an angel, and Sylvie wrote beside it: *Dancers are like angels. All dancers go to heaven.*"

"I hope she was right," said Dave.

DOCTOR RAND'S LAB, TORONTO, NOVEMBER 1, THIS YEAR:

The Posthumous Neural Research Project office looked like any other building at the University of Toronto.

"This place looks so ordinary," said Dave.

"What did you expect? Shelves full of brains in jars?" Maria said.

Doctor Rand's assistant, Joleen Smith, prattled on the telephone, telling a friend how she needed more money to pay off her credit card debt.

"I even considered being a stripper at night, but I couldn't push myself into *that* line of work," she whined.

Finally, Doctor Rand came out to meet them. "Good

morning. I'm glad that you can come by."

If he is a ghoul, at least he's a pleasant one, thought Dave as they followed him into his office.

"Did you save her brain waves?" Dave asked.

"Yes," said Rand, picking up the skullcap device from his desk. "I got five minutes of electrical activity before it all stopped."

He sifted through the papers on his desk and held up a shiny golden compact disc. "Her last brain waves are here."

"I hear you've connected living people to the brain waves of the dead," said Dave.

"A few experiments. Sending one person's disembodied brain waves into another person's living brain—joining the brain waves of two people," said Rand.

"Can you really let people talk to the spirits of the dead?"

Rand gave him a thin smile. "The reporters say that. I don't."

"You mean it isn't true?"

"I mean I don't know what really happens when I link a living brain to another person's brain waves. The reporters made up the ghost story."

"But the name of your project is Posthumous Neural Research."

"I changed the name to get more funding," Rand admitted. "It was called 'Recorded Memory Project' and was a lot less dramatic at first.

"I wanted to record memories, and I thought about saving brain waves, the electrical impulses of the brain. It took eight years to develop the brain wave collector." He held up the skullcap device again.

"This isn't just an EEG, which only monitors brain waves and makes graphs. The brain wave collector makes duplicates of the electrical impulses and saves them on these compact discs, which are sort of like batteries. To test it, I saved brain waves from young children, senior citizens, and many people in between. I wanted different types of memories.

"But I had all these brain waves on compact disc and couldn't do anything with them. They can't be replayed like a video disc. So I developed a way to send disembodied brain waves into a living brain. Five years of work. It wasn't easy. I had to find a way to send electrical impulses into a living recipient without electrocuting him or damaging his brain.

"At first, nothing happened. None of the recipients experienced another person's memories. They got nothing but a headache. But I used brain waves from people who stayed alive while I saved their brain waves. I hadn't used brain waves from someone who had died during the collection.

"Several people wanted me to record a death. Every neurologist, psychologist, and theologian wants to know what happens at death. What do people feel as they die? What are they thinking? When does death really occur?

"I found a man who was dying of natural causes. Ninety-five years old. He let me save his brain waves as he died. Then I linked his brain waves with a living recipient. The result was unexpected..."

MONTREAL, THREE WEEKS AGO, OCTOBER 8, *SCIENCE PROBE* TV INTERVIEW:

SCIENCE PROBE: Last year, student Kate Evans volunteered to be in an experiment by Doctor Jonathan Rand, a psychiatry professor at the University... Ms. Evans received the brain waves of Derrick Carp, which were saved as he died... What did Doctor Rand expect to happen?

KATE EVANS: He said I should have experienced one of Carp's memories, from his point of view.

SCIENCE PROBE: By memories, do you mean something that happened to him in the past?

KATE EVANS: Yes, but that didn't happen.

SCIENCE PROBE: What happened?

KATE EVANS: I was at a cottage near a lake, and there was an old guy standing at the end of the tunnel... He walked down to me... and he said, "Kate, my name is Derrick..."

SCIENCE PROBE: It wasn't one of Derrick Carp's memories?

KATE EVANS: No. I never met him before, yet he knew my name. It wasn't a memory, not mine, not his. It was something new.

SCIENCE PROBE: What happened next?

KATE EVANS: He said, "I haven't seen my family since I died. Tell them I'm okay."

SCIENCE PROBE: He knew he was dead?

KATE EVANS: Creepy, eh? But he didn't seem to mind. Sort of like retirement...

DOCTOR RAND'S LAB, TORONTO, NOVEMBER 1, THIS YEAR:

"I saved the brain waves of five more people as they

died. Then I linked the brain waves of each dead person with a different live recipient. Each recipient reported similar results: they didn't experience the memories of the deceased. Instead, they say they talked to the deceased, and the deceased knew they were dead."

"Then it's true that you've captured their spirits on compact disc?" asked Dave.

Rand shook his head. "I don't know *what* I've saved. All I know is that I've saved the last electric impulses of some dying brains. There's nothing that means I have their spirits, souls or anything with a consciousness."

"But your test recipients don't get anything from a living person's brain waves. They have experiences only with the dead," Dave argued.

"Yes, the religious groups noticed that. The living aren't ready to give up their souls, so my brain wave collector didn't get them. There's something extra in the brain waves of the dead, and it's the human soul. Or so the clergy say.

"But perhaps the recipients were actually having hallucinations. Maybe there's something in the brain waves of the dying that makes the recipient think he's talking to the dead."

"Well, that's a sensible explanation," said Maria, finally speaking up. She turned to Dave. "It's all hallucination, dreams. Nothing more."

"I want to be a test recipient," Dave said.

Maria sighed.

Dave took off his shirt and lay on the table. After adjusting the switches on the skullcap, Rand placed it on

Dave's head. Next, Joleen taped sensors to his chest. She pointed at a monitor.

"We'll be monitoring your heartbeat, respiration, temperature, blood pressure, brain activity—all the vital signs," she explained.

"And we'll disconnect the link if anything odd happens," said Rand. "Comfortable?"

"Yes," said Dave. "How long will it last?"

"The links have lasted thirty seconds to five minutes. Sometimes the recipient simply wakes up. Other times, I've had to stop the brain wave flow and force the recipient back awake when his vital signs went bad."

Maria stood by the table and held Dave's hand. She nervously made a fist with her other hand.

"Be careful, wherever you're going," she warned.

"I'll be back, darling," he said.

"Come back soon," she said.

Lying back on the table, Dave remembered his years with Sylvie, starting when they were both fifteen years old...

TORONTO, FIFTEEN YEARS AGO:

The building had light brown brick, large arched windows, a short flight of steps to the front door, and a row of plain white columns facing the street. For decades, that elegant building had housed the National Ballet School.

"*Demi-plié*, rise up, *grand plié*, rise up in first, arms up, take a balance..." recited the teacher as the young students went through their exercises at the barre.

In this rare mixed class of both boys and girls, Dave

Tremaine got more than music and movement; he also got Sylvie Courtauld. To Dave, Sylvie Courtauld had more than sparkling technique, grace, poise, and vitality. She also had her pretty face, silky blonde hair, long legs, and slim body, so tightly wrapped in her black leotard.

If he had been any less dedicated to ballet, Dave would have melted in class. But he had already dedicated four years of his life to dancing, and he could weather distractions like the blonde girl in front of him. Still, she had such fine lines...

There would be more time to daydream about Sylvie later. Banishing thoughts of Sylvie from his mind, he concentrated on the *battement en cloche*, throwing up his leg up in unison with the rest of the students.

After class, they staggered to their rooms to change into the school uniform: he in white shirt and black pants, she in white blouse and dark green tartan skirt.

The School was a combination of boarding school and ballet school. After the dance class, the students went to classes in the usual academic subjects—science, math, history, geography, French, English—then another dance class, dinner, homework, and lights out.

But on Friday nights, the girls and boys sneaked out to downtown Toronto. By eight o'clock, Dave and Sylvie had slipped onto Yonge Street.

They walked past the Zanzibar, possibly the oldest strip bar in Toronto. A decrepit brick building painted pale yellow, it had photos of half-naked women all over its front. Its marquee boasted: 100 GORGEOUS DANCERS, ALL NUDE EUROPEAN-STYLE LAP DANCING.

"Maybe I can work there after I graduate," Sylvie said,

giggling.

"I'd go watch you," said Dave.

They headed into a music shop. Inside, they found Maria Carrera listening to the latest hard rock group.

"Maria, we were looking for you," said Sylvie. "We were going to ask you to sneak out with us."

"I guess I jumped the gun. I snuck out on my own," said Maria.

"You're still wearing your school uniform," observed Dave.

"Yeah, I know, why don't I change into normal clothes?" Maria said. "A lot of guys think the schoolgirl look is really sexy, that's why." She lifted her skirt up to her hips and bent her leg saucily.

They left the music store and stopped at a pizza place up the street.

"We shouldn't do this," warned Sylvie as they each grabbed a slice of pizza.

"You don't have to worry," said Maria. "You metabolize your food so quickly. I do too. We're lucky that way. We don't have to be anorexic."

Dave nearly choked on his pizza. Maria the rebel violated the School's prim and proper norms. Teachers had threatened to expel her for various offences, including growing her hair to the wrong length, chewing gum, and kissing boys.

"What did you do to get called into the director's office today?" Sylvie asked mischievously.

Maria grinned. "Kissing boys again. Stupid rule. I mean, kids in schools anywhere else don't get in trouble for kissing. I swear, someday, I'm going to take a guy to the lawn of the Red Lion and do him."

"That sounds like fun," said Sylvie.

"Well, it's part pleasure, part research. I'm actually doing a scientific experiment for the good of the dance profession—I'm proving that male dancers aren't gay."

"Where do I volunteer for the experiment?" asked Dave.

Sylvie turned to Dave and said, "I *know* you're not gay. I know what *you're* thinking during class."

Dave, caught off guard, rolled his eyes up and whistled.

Then Sylvie turned to Maria. "He's straight and has the hots for me. You don't have to experiment on him."

"Oh, but it's all in the name of science," teased Maria. "So how about it, Dave? You and me at the Red Lion tonight?"

"Screw off!" cried Sylvie as she slapped Maria's hand. "He's saving himself for me. *I'm* going to be his first one."

Summer evenings like this continued for one more week until the summer break began. Dave, Sylvie, and Maria said good-bye and went back to their families and hometowns.

Dave returned in September, and so did Sylvie, but not Maria. None of the students knew what happened to her. When Dave asked the teachers, they didn't know either. But he noticed that her absence didn't worry them.

"I don't think she got expelled," said Dave. "She had really good marks."

"And she was a good dancer too," Sylvie added. "She couldn't have been kicked out for bad dancing."

They both missed Maria, but Dave took her

disappearance especially badly. He became listless and quiet, coming alive only in ballet class.

Later in the month, Sylvie tried to phone Maria's parents without success. "The number's disconnected. I should've phoned her during the summer."

"I should've too," said Dave.

PARIS, TEN YEARS AGO:

Three more years passed, and Dave and Sylvie graduated from the National Ballet School. Shortly afterwards, they joined the Metro Toronto Ballet.

Dave and Sylvie rose quickly in the new company. Joan Silverton, its artistic director, paired them in principal roles: Romeo and Juliet, Siegfried and Odette, Florimund and Aurora.

"In a few years, you'll be as popular as Karen Kain and Frank Augustyn were in the last century," Joan told them. "You're a hot pair."

Their relationship got hotter off-stage too.

It finally boiled over when they went to Paris to perform *Le Spectre de la Rose*. In this one-act ballet, a girl brings home a rose from a ball, falls asleep in a chair, and dreams that she dances with the spirit of the rose, now a vibrant male figure. In the first half of the ballet, the rose dances a series of spectacular leaps and turns in the air. Then he lifts her out of her chair, and they dance a romantic *pas de deux* around the room. Finally, he gently returns her to the chair and leaps through a window. She awakens, still under the spell of the dream.

"Such grace, such beauty," Joan said. "You're the most beautiful couple in Paris tonight."

After the performance, they walked down the Champs Elysées, arm in arm, against a warm summer breeze. They had been friends since their teen years, "officially dated" since their last year in the School, and now, as Dave smelled her soft rose perfume and felt the smooth skin of her arms, he silently told himself what he had known for years: he loved this girl.

After returning to their hotel, Dave walked Sylvie to her room. But he didn't leave her. Tonight, it seemed right to linger by her door.

She kissed him on the lips. "There, I've kissed you good night." But she didn't want him to leave.

"Sylvie, we've known each other since we were eleven years old," he said. "That's nine years."

"A long time."

"And we've been officially dating for three years. I want to ask you—"

"I know what you want, and I want it too." Her eyes flickered with excitement. She moved forward and licked his ear.

"Isn't it about time that our relationship got more serious?"

"It's about time." She grinned.

Dave felt a rush of relief. "Why did it take me so long?"

She shrugged. "We were both kind of shy when we were young."

"That's it? Just because I was too shy to ask? You could've helped me along..."

Sylvie laughed and fidgeted. "That wasn't the only reason. I had these schoolgirl ideas about love. I thought it would be really romantic if I lost my virginity to you. And I wanted you to lose your virginity to me, not to some other girl. I was just waiting for the right, romantic moment. And it's now."

She held his hand and slowly pulled him into her room. Although they had two hotel rooms, they used only one room that night.

They returned to Toronto two days later, the same day the new orchestra musicians arrived. Dave saw a woman carry a violin case into the studio and sit down with the other musicians.

No, it couldn't be, not after all these years, he thought. But she had the same straight, black hair. About twenty years old, the same age as he, Sylvie and...

"Maria," whispered Sylvie when she saw the violinist.

Maria looked around the room. When she saw Dave and Sylvie, her eyes grew larger. She walked to them and smiled.

"You're probably wondering why I didn't come back after the summer," she said.

DOCTOR RAND'S LAB, TORONTO, NOVEMBER 1, THIS YEAR:

Dave watched the monitor. The upper half of the screen showed green lines: his brain waves. Another set of lines moved up and down on the lower half of the screen: Sylvie's last brain waves.

"Sylvie Courtauld's brain waves will be flowing into your brain," said Rand.

"Five, four, three..." Joleen counted.

Maria squeezed Dave's hand.

"...two, one..."

The two sets of lines moved to the middle of the screen and merged.

Dave felt a jolt. He gasped. All the light in the room suddenly shrank into a pinpoint in the dark.

The pinpoint exploded into a grey haze. He floated through a dense fog. A feeling of nausea came over him.

INSIDE DAVE'S MIND, NOVEMBER 1, THIS YEAR:

"Are you okay? Here, have some water."

Dave shook his head. Who was that?

"Okay, everyone, take five minutes! Dave, have some water."

He felt someone nudge him. He looked up and saw Joan bending over him. She put a cup of water in his hand.

"Tired? Okay, we'll end rehearsals now," she said. "You had us all worried when you fell."

"Fell?" he asked.

"During the *fouetté*. Don't you remember? You lost your balance, fell, got back up, but you looked dizzy."

"I've had a rough day," he said, dazed.

"Go see the doctor; you might be coming down with something." She patted him on the shoulder and walked to the piano.

As Dave drank the water, he noticed that Joan wore a T-shirt that read "QUEEN OF THE WILIS." The publicity department had made that T-shirt especially for her when she started planning the Ballet's first production of *Giselle*.

He also saw a newspaper on the floor; the headline read "PAKISTAN AND INDIA AT WAR."

That production of *Giselle* and that war occurred seven years ago.

"Dave, do you want to go home?"

He turned and saw Sylvie sitting beside him. She wore her rehearsal clothes: a black leotard, a pink dance skirt, and pointe shoes.

In a grey T-shirt, black tights, and ballet slippers, he was dressed for rehearsal too. He felt confused; he remembered Joan's T-shirt and the newspaper headline, but he couldn't remember being in the rehearsal back then.

"We're rehearsing *Giselle*?" he asked.

"Yeah... Are you okay?"

He became more confused. "And you're dancing the role of Giselle?"

Sylvie raised an eyebrow. "I hope you didn't get amnesia from that fall. Don't you remember I'm Giselle?"

"And I'm Albrecht."

"Of course. Listen, dear, if you're really not feeling well, we'll go home. Don't push it."

"No, I'm okay," he said, regaining his composure. "Just felt a little tired for a while. Let's continue."

"Okay, let's start from the daisy scene," Joan called out.

The pianist started playing from *Giselle*, act one, again. Sylvie pranced to a bench and began plucking the petals off a daisy.

They were acting out the daisy scene: Giselle plays the game of "He loves me, he loves me not" with the daisy to see if Albrecht truly loves her. He loves me, he loves me not, he loves me... the answer is "not," sadly for Giselle. However, Albrecht convinces Giselle that he truly loves her, and they dance together happily.

Sylvie dropped the daisy on the floor, rose from the bench and turned slowly away from Dave.

Dave turned her around and smiled. She smiled back, and they embraced. Then they danced across the floor in a series of lighthearted *ballottés*, steps that rocked back and forth. This happy *pas de deux* came from act one, when Giselle and Albrecht celebrate their love, before Giselle meets her tragic end.

Dave danced vibrantly, but he felt confused. Had he travelled seven years back in time? Joan directing the ballet, her "Queen of the Wilis" T-shirt, the Indo-Pakistani war, Sylvie as Giselle: everything was the same.

Except one thing. Seven years ago, he did not play Albrecht. Rather, a Russian dancer named Andrei Arslanov had danced the role...

METRO TORONTO BALLET STUDIO, TORONTO, SEVEN YEARS AGO:

Dave watched Sylvie and Andrei dance a series of *ballottés* from act one. They dance well together, thought Dave. How lucky of the Metro Toronto Ballet to get the visitor from the Bolshoi.

Dave had wanted to dance the role of Albrecht, but Joan had other plans for him. He and a few other dancers would bring *La Sylphide* to rural Ontario for the next two weeks. They had to go on the rural tour to get more government funding.

Maria walked in and watched the rehearsal.

"Ready for the tour?" asked Dave.

"Yep, got the violin packed," she said, looking at

Andrei hold Sylvie by the waist as she spun in a *pirouette*.

"She's good," said Maria. "All those years in the school. If I had stuck it out, I too could have been a ballerina. Now I'm not any type of dancer."

"But you became a violinist," Dave reminded her. "You're still an artist."

"Yeah, and music was safer, well, at least for me. After my nervous breakdown, I knew I couldn't survive in the School. I couldn't stand the stress and competition in ballet... But you, on the other hand, enjoyed your time at the School because you had Sylvie."

"True, but it wasn't just Sylvie," said Dave. "I really wanted to be a dancer. The School was important. I learned a lot there."

"You learned a lot outside class too," said Maria.

Dave winced and looked back at Sylvie and Andrei. The rehearsal was breaking up.

Sylvie walked to Dave and kissed him. "So, honey, are you going now?"

"Yes, but I'll be back for the opening night of *Giselle*."

"You better come back," said Sylvie.

"You must be so thrilled to dance Giselle," said Maria.

Sylvie smiled and nodded. "Oh, yes. Every ballerina dreams of dancing Giselle. Giselle is to the female dancer what Hamlet is to the male actor."

DOCTOR RAND'S LAB, TORONTO, NOVEMBER 1, THIS YEAR:

An explosion of noise and light blasted through Dave's mind. A jolt ran through his spine. His mind shifted back and forth through time: his teen years at the ballet school; the years with Sylvie at the Metro Toronto Ballet; their trip to Paris; and a time that never existed, when he danced Albrecht to Sylvie's Giselle.

He opened his eyes. He was no longer watching the *Giselle* rehearsal of seven years ago; he lay in Doctor Rand's lab in the present. Confusion spun through his mind.

"Sylvie Courtauld's brain waves are separating from Dave's and flowing back into the storage disc. Link severed successfully," announced Joleen.

Dave rolled his head and saw the brain wave monitor. One set of lines flowed up to the top of the screen, another set of lines stayed in the bottom half of the screen: Sylvie's brain waves separating from his.

Doctor Rand quickly pulled the skullcap off Dave's head while Joleen peeled the sensors off his chest.

"How are you feeling?" asked Rand.

"Uhhh—" said Dave drowsily.

When he tried to stand up, Dave stumbled. Rand and Joleen caught him and helped him move to a chair.

Maria rushed to him. "Dave, what happened? Are you okay?"

"They're normally drowsy and disoriented after they come out," said Rand as he lifted a glass of water to Dave's lips.

"Dave, your heartbeat and respiration increased rapidly near the end, so I stopped the brain wave flow and severed the link," Rand continued. "You were linked to the brain waves for the longest time so far."

Dave gulped the water. "How long?"

"Fifteen minutes."

"It felt like fifteen years squeezed into fifteen

minutes."

"Did you experience Sylvie Courtauld's memories?"

"No. They were *my* memories, from my point of view. But there was a strange one. A rehearsal for Sylvie's first time as Giselle, with me as Albrecht."

"But that didn't happen," said Maria. "I remember that production, years ago. You didn't play Albrecht. Andrei Arslanov did."

"Sounds like you didn't experience an afterlife as much as you experienced an alternative life," Rand said.

"If I had continued in the link, would Sylvie have played Giselle?" Dave wondered.

"You mean she didn't play Giselle in real life either?" asked Rand.

Dave shook his head. "She rehearsed for the role, but she never danced it on stage."

TORONTO, SEVEN YEARS AGO:

Sylvie stopped and caught her breath in the rehearsal of the Mad Scene. The Mad Scene: Giselle discovers that Albrecht had been courting her while also engaged to be married to Princess Bathilde. Stunned by the discovery, Giselle goes mad, swings Albrecht's sword in the crowd of villagers, and dies of a heart attack. Act one ends there, and act two begins with Giselle as a ghost, a Wili.

"Okay, Sylvie, put more intensity, more pain, more madness in it," said Joan.

Sylvie pulled off the ribbon that had kept her hair tied into a bun. Her hair fell to her shoulders, the traditional way of showing Giselle's anguish.

"Grrrrr, arrrr," growled Sylvie.

Andrei laughed. "We producing opera now, not ballet?"

Joan shrugged and clapped her hands. "Okay, it's been a long day, and we're all a bit tired and getting useless, so let's go home early."

"Thanks," blurted Sylvie. She put the sword back on the floor.

"Remember, only two weeks until opening night!" said Joan.

Nodding silently in exhaustion, Sylvie, Andrei, and the villagers staggered away. Now they were in dress rehearsals. So much practice, and in only two weeks.

At least Dave has returned from the rural tour and is taking some time off, she thought as she walked home. She needed to feel his warmth, his caresses and kisses, his body against hers.

She entered their apartment. "Honey, I'm home."

No answer. Maybe he went out. No problem; she would wait for him.

She walked into the bedroom. Dave lay in bed, naked.

Maria lay there too.

They stared at each other.

"What!" cried Sylvie.

Maria blushed red, got up from the bed, and bent down to pick her clothes off the floor. "I better leave," she mumbled.

She hastily pulled up her panties and skirt, buttoned her blouse, and walked past Sylvie without looking at her.

His face awash in despair, Dave turned away from Sylvie and looked out the window.

"How, why?" Sylvie asked, tears running down her

cheeks.

Dave still looked out the window. "I was trying to relive something... Maria was my first lover."

Sylvie nearly choked. Now she felt more baffled than angry. "But—but I was your first girlfriend."

"Girlfriend, yes, but not *lover*," said Dave, his voice trembling.

Sylvie sobbed. "I don't understand. You were my first. I thought I was your first too."

"It happened years ago." Dave cleared his throat. "A long time ago. Remember that summer, when we all went home, but Maria didn't come back in the fall..."

TORONTO, FIFTEEN YEARS AGO:

Dave was packing his suitcase when he heard a knock on the door. It was Maria, casually leaning against the doorway.

"I've already packed, and I've got nothing to do, and I'm feeling a little bored," she said. "Do you want to go for a walk?"

"Sure," he said. Sylvie had already gone to her parents, and the packing bored him. "I can finish later."

They walked into the night, talking about school, dancers, summer vacations.

"Have you and Sylvie done it?" asked Maria.

"What do you mean, done it?" said Dave.

"You know what I mean. *It.*"

"I still don't know what you mean," Dave lied.

Maria giggled. "Do I have to spell it out? S–E–X! Sex!"

"Oh, God, why on Earth are you asking me that?"

"Oh, no reason at all, just curious. I want to know

whether you boys brag about the girls you've done."

"I'm not telling or Sylvie would kill me."

"But don't you boys tell all the dirty details to each other? So what's it like with Sylvie?"

"Oh, lay off me. No, I'm not telling anything. Besides, I should be more worried about what she's telling you!"

"She doesn't tell me much about the sexy stuff. Probably because there isn't any sex."

Dave didn't say anything.

"It's been a rough year for me," said Maria, changing the subject swiftly. "When I was a little girl, the only thing I ever wanted to be was a ballerina. But now, it's so much stress on me. The classes, the competition, the teachers, the exams, the tests, who gets to play Clara in *The Nutcracker*—it's all so awful."

"It's hard on all of us," said Dave.

"I guess so. But—this is going to sound awful—I've been doing things to relieve the stress. Kissing boys. Playing with myself—"

"Oh, God."

"And then—I did it with one of the boys," Maria confessed. "It was my first time, I think I was his second girl. I was frightened, I was nervous, but it felt great."

Dave listened silently in both embarrassment and awe.

"Every day, I stretch and bend and move my body, my arms, my legs, my neck and head, trying to look like a beautiful, graceful ballerina, but all I feel is the pressure building up. Sex was scary the first time, but I felt so much joy, so much *relief* go through my body.

"We did it again, in secret, in the middle of the night, in one of the dance studios. It was so sexy because we could see ourselves in all those mirrors," she said wistfully.

"Wow," murmured Dave.

"I hope you don't think I'm a slut. Please don't think that way about me because I'm not. I'm not doing it because I'm a nympho or lonely or drunk or stoned or whatever. I'm doing it because I need some relief from my problems. Okay, maybe it's all related to feeling rejected and unwanted in the School, to not being a good dancer like the other girls. But I swear I need to do it. Oh, God, maybe I'm not cut out for ballet school."

"Are you thinking of going back to a normal school?" Dave asked.

"Did you listen to yourself? '*Normal* school'! As if we aren't normal." Her laugh had a trace of bitterness. "We're special all right, but sometimes I wish we weren't. Sometimes I wish I could be like ordinary girls back home."

She reached out and held his hand lightly. "Dave, I like you very much."

He pulled his hand away. "Maria, I don't think we should be talking like this."

Maria grasped his hand again. "You haven't done it with Sylvie, have you?"

Silence.

"You haven't done it with *anyone*, have you?"

More silence.

"Then—then learn from me. One day, Sylvie will want to do it. She deserves a little bit of experience from you."

"No, I don't think so."

"Dave, I know you're not gay." She gazed into his eyes. "You've wanted sex for a long time."

"Maybe..."

"I know you've wanted it. I've seen how you've looked at her."

Dave moaned softly as Maria pulled him towards the Red Lion, an old mansion that had been converted into a pub years ago.

"Oh, no, not in front of the Red Lion!" cried Dave.

"It's okay, the customers are all inside, and they're all drunk." She pointed at a bush. "Nobody'll see us behind that bush."

They scrambled behind the bush. She started swaying her hips sensuously. He watched, dumbfounded.

"I'm a stripper," Maria said, giggling as she unbuttoned her white blouse and played with the straps of her black bra. Seconds later, her skirt fell to the grass. Then she pulled him closer.

"You've craved her all these years, haven't you?" Maria asked. She kissed him. "Pretend that I'm her."

She slowly unzipped the fly of his pants and pushed them down. "Nice briefs," she cooed.

Dave fumbled with his shirt buttons.

"Oh, let me help you," Maria said.

They fell on the grass. She unhooked the front clasp of her bra and let the cups fall away. Then she kissed his neck hungrily.

He smelled the sweet perfume that she wore around her neck. Soon, he was groping the smooth, soft skin of her belly, her legs, her loins...

TORONTO, SEVEN YEARS AGO:

"...She had a nervous breakdown that summer and quit the School," said Dave.

"And you learned to make love from her—at the Red Lion, of all places?" Sylvie asked.

"Yes. I wanted sex desperately, but I was too nervous to ask you. I really wanted *you*. And she liked me, and she was so sexy. We were teenagers."

"But you aren't teenagers anymore," said Sylvie, harshness coming into her voice. "Why now? How long's it been going on?"

"This is the first time."

"But why? After all these years?"

"A man never forgets his first love."

"You mean his first lay," Sylvie spat.

Dave sighed. "Okay, first lay."

"So why did you get it on with her again?"

"We became friends again during the tour. One thing led to another..." Dave trailed off.

Sylvie sighed. "I thought I was the first, I thought I was the only one. I didn't know I was the second, and now I'm the second one again!"

Sylvie walked to the living room and collapsed on the couch. She was still crying when Dave walked out with his suitcase.

Joan Silverton shook her head when Sylvie missed another cue. Only a couple days ago, Sylvie had been the most passionate and graceful Giselle in years. Now she danced wearily with neither passion nor grace.

"Sylvie, more energy, more spirit! Giselle's supposed to be young and excited and in love with Albrecht," Joan called out. She knew what to do with a dancer who had a broken ankle, but what should she do with a dancer with a broken heart?

And less than two weeks before the premiere? Joan watched Sylvie go through the motions of a *pas de deux* with Andrei. Without a good partner, he danced poorly too.

"My dear Mademoiselle Sylvie," said Andrei, "please be my lovely Giselle again."

Joan smiled in approval of Andrei's kindness to his languid partner despite his disappointment, obvious in the sadness on his face.

But Joan had given her enough slack already. The time for grieving and sympathy had run out.

"Stop, take a break, five minutes," Joan called out. After Andrei walked away, she went to Sylvie and put a hand on her shoulder.

"I know something wrong has happened. But you're still a ballerina, and you'll still perform your best," Joan said. "Save your sadness for act two."

"I'll try, Joan," Sylvie mumbled softly.

Five minutes later, other dancers arrived to play the villagers. The pianist began playing the music from the Mad Scene again. Sylvie picked up the sword and swung it in a circle past the feet of the crowd.

Then she began crying and tearing at her hair as she danced. She had a look of agony on her face. Her dancing, the movement of her legs, her body, and her arms: all showed pain and loss.

Oh, that's real, thought Joan.

At the end of the scene, as Giselle dies, Sylvie sank to the floor but did not lay still and quiet. She lay face down and quivered and cried.

Joan walked into the crowd of dancers and pulled

Sylvie back to her feet.

"Take her to the lounge," she told two dancers.

I have to make the tough decision, Joan told herself. She took a deep breath and turned to a young Chinese girl wearing a peasant's costume.

"This doesn't happen to understudies very often," Joan began.

She grabbed the girl's wrist and steered her towards Andrei.

"Andrei, meet your new partner, Lisa Wong," she said.

"New partner?" said Andrei.

Joan turned to Lisa. "I'm rehearsing you for the part of Giselle now. You might have to dance it on opening night."

"What about Sylvie?" asked Lisa.

"She'll come back to us when she's ready." Joan clapped her hands. "Okay, break's over. Now, girls and boys, we have no time to waste."

Sylvie cried the night *Giselle* premiered without her.

She stopped taking daily classes with the company, and Joan removed her from the remaining ballets of the season. A month later, Joan stopped Sylvie's pay; the company couldn't support an idle dancer. After three months, when Sylvie still hadn't returned to classes, Joan quietly fired her. But they met one last time.

"If you need anything or want to come back, call me. Our door is always open to you," Joan told her.

They hugged, and Sylvie walked out of the building. Before crossing the street, she looked back. All her happy memories of the ballet studio seemed so distant now.

I'm not special, I'm not Dave's first and only love, she thought. What a mistake. She would never save herself for one man again.

When Dave returned to their apartment, Sylvie and her belongings had gone. He sat down and stared out the window for the rest of the day, hoping that she would walk through the door, but knowing that she wouldn't.

TORONTO, SIX YEARS AGO:

In the Ballet's cafeteria, Dave thought about Sylvie as he stirred his coffee. The spiral swirling of the sugar and cream reminded him of her graceful, endless pirouettes.

He let out a heavy sigh and sipped the coffee. One year. Sylvie had been gone one year. Nobody had heard from her.

Maria walked into the cafeteria and sat down beside him. She hadn't talked to him since their afternoon fling. At first, she looked him in the eye, but she shifted her eyes away, as if trying to avoid his gaze.

"I miss her too," she said.

"Yeah."

Maria finally looked at him. "I'm sorry. We shouldn't have hurt her like that. It didn't make any sense, that afternoon. It's my fault."

"My fault too. I wish I could tell her how sorry I am," said Dave, stirring his coffee again.

*   *   *

TORONTO, FIVE YEARS AGO:

Dave grunted and put his sword down on the stage. A few feet away, Andrei Arslanov, his shirt soaked in sweat, lay on the floor and panted. Nothing exhausted them more than the sword fight in *Romeo and Juliet*.

Andrei rose back on his feet. "Good rehearsal. Time to relax." He paused for a moment. "Dave, before you married Maria, did you have—uh, what is it called—stag party?"

"No," said Dave, amused that Andrei had learned the less dignified North American customs.

"Ah, you did not see strippers?"

"Andrei, why are you asking?" Dave's eyebrow shot up. "No, I didn't see any strippers."

"Then you feel deprived, yes?" Andrei asked. "I suggest we go to strip bar."

Dave chuckled. "This is more for you than for me."

"You are very smart. I have spent the past two years in Russia. Getting paid in worthless money, living in lousy apartment, eating bad food, and all the good-looking women are girlfriends of gangsters. And good strip bars are rare there."

A half hour later, they were walking towards the Zanzibar, which still looked as dilapidated as it had in Dave's youth. Its marquee still promised 100 GORGEOUS DANCERS, ALL NUDE EUROPEAN-STYLE LAP DANCING.

"Lap dancing," said Andrei, grinning. "Not what they taught at the Bolshoi."

Like all strip bars, it had very dim lighting, which reflected off the brass and chrome railings. Body parts of old store mannequins decorated the walls. A stripper danced on the stage, and like stages in all strip bars, it had a vertical metal pole in a corner. Throughout the bar, naked dancers gyrated in front of customers at their tables.

They sat down at a table, ordered their drinks, and waited for the next stripper to get on stage.

A new song started. "Gentleman, put your hands together for Giselle," announced the deejay.

"Hah, clever name for a stripper," said Andrei. "Shows she has sense of humour."

Dave looked up. A slim girl with long, attractive legs strutted onto the stage. She wore a bra, G-string and high heels, all in red.

She grabbed the metal pole and swung around it. Then she walked back to the centre of the stage and danced some turns and steps.

"Those are good turns and steps, a lot more sophisticated than what strippers usually do," said Dave.

"Perhaps she had some dance training," said Andrei.

Dance training? Is that where Dave had seen the girl's movements before? When the stripper twirled in a *pirouette*, he suddenly recognized her.

"Andrei, that's Sylvie!" he said.

"Oh, God," said Andrei, stunned.

"Giselle" danced her first song with her clothes on. She removed her bra in the second song. And in the third song, she took off her G-string and danced naked, her graceful turns and steps combined with the lewd grinding of her hips and rump.

She put her clothes back on after the third song and walked off the stage. Then she started walking from customer to customer, asking them if they would like her to dance at their tables.

"Gentlemen, put your hands together for Giselle," said the deejay, "and Giselle can be yours for a table dance. Don't be shy, call her over!"

"I do not know if we should leave now," Andrei said.

Sylvie walked from table to table, quickly approaching theirs.

When she got to their table, she stared at them, then she opened her mouth in surprise.

"Dave, Andrei," she gasped. After a brief hesitation, she sat down beside them.

"Mademoiselle Courtauld," replied Andrei, embarrassed. "How nice to meet you again."

"Sylvie," Dave stammered. He didn't know what to say. He wished he could read her thoughts, but he couldn't. Her face, like a mask, had no expression.

"My stage name's Giselle," she said. "Do you like it?"

"Nice," said Andrei. "Very classy."

"I'm a classy exotic dancer," said Sylvie. "Do either of you gentlemen want a table dance? Or a lap dance?"

"No, thank you," said Andrei.

"Well, what about you, Dave? You've enjoyed this body before. Come on, I'll give you a lap dance for free."

She pushed his knees apart and dropped a small, white towel on his lap. Then she eased herself onto his lap, leaned back, and pressed her butt into his groin.

"Have you ever had a lap dance before?" she asked.

"No."

"Well, baby, this time, *I'll* be your first."

She gyrated her body, slowly grinding her butt against his groin. Slowly, she pressed her back into his chest.

Then she turned herself around and rubbed her belly

against his nose. She smelled sickeningly sweet, like a cheap perfume.

She rose away from him, swayed her hips, and slowly fondled the clasp of her red lace bra. It unhooked in front, and she let the cups fall away, exposing her breasts.

Dave looked at Andrei, and Andrei stared back, silent and dumbfounded. Then he looked back at Sylvie.

She tugged at her G-string, which had plastic clasps at the hips. Swaying with the music, she undid the clasps and pulled her G-string off. Now she was naked again.

Like a ballet student, she wore her blonde hair in a bun tied in a red ribbon. She pulled the ribbon off and let her hair fall down. She looked so erotic when she swept her hair.

There was a daisy tucked by her ear. She plucked it and gave it to Dave.

She sat in his lap again and ground her butt harder and harder against his groin.

"I can feel you getting excited," she said. She raised the palm of her hand backwards and stroked his cheek. "Poor boy, don't you get anything like this at home?"

"No."

"Then maybe you should come here more often," she cooed. "Share me with the other customers. As for me, I've had lots of guys since I left you, mostly strip bar deejays: Jimmy, Ron, Tim, Jimmy, Allan, Jimmy... why are so many strip bar deejays named Jimmy?"

When the song ended, she rose away from him and put her bra and G-string back on.

"Like I said, that one's free," she said. "I hope you enjoyed it."

"Sylvie, is this what you've been doing for the past couple years?"

"It's what I'm good for," she said impassively. "I'm a star here."

Dave didn't know what to say. This girl used to dream she would be the country's prima ballerina.

Sylvie stood silently beside their table, looking at Dave and Andrei at first, then looking around the bar. None of them said anything.

A ragged man, reeking of foul body odour, walked to them. He tapped Sylvie on the shoulder. Curling her lips down dejectedly, she turned to him.

"Who's that?" Andrei whispered to Dave.

"I think he's the deejay," replied Dave. "Saw him in the deejay booth."

"I'm going out now," the deejay said. "Give me some money."

"I already gave it to you, Ben," she whimpered.

He grabbed her chin, pushed it up, and stared into her eyes. "That was before your stage show. What about after the stage show?"

"I haven't done a dance since then."

"Are you lying to me? What did you just do for that guy?"

"That one doesn't count, I did it for free." She turned away from him.

He grabbed her arm and pulled her around. "You bitch! You gave it away for free to that guy? You're so useless, you're lucky you've got me. Nobody else wants a trashy slut like you!"

Ben shot a quick glare at Dave and Andrei. He mouthed more obscenities and dragged Sylvie away by the wrist.

"Should we leave?" asked Andrei.

"Let's go," said Dave, still holding the daisy.

A week later, Dave returned alone to the Zanzibar, but Sylvie and Ben Latz had gone. A waitress told him that they had been fired; the manager suspected Latz of selling drugs, and Sylvie had showed up drunk for work. A dancer told him that Sylvie was now drifting between the sleazier bars north of the city.

Dave did not see Sylvie again until he had to identify her body in the hospital.

TORONTO, NOVEMBER 1, THIS YEAR:

"You gave us quite a shock," said Maria. "Your breathing and heartbeat got really fast at one point, but then you returned to normal."

They walked back out into the autumn cold, leaving Doctor Rand's lab behind them. After a few minutes of silence, Maria spoke.

"Do you really think you met Sylvie's soul?" she asked.

"I don't know for sure, but it felt so real. I think that really was her soul," said Dave.

Later that night, Maria walked up to Dave from behind and put her arms around him. "Dave, I need you."

"Not tonight," he said, moving away from her.

"We haven't made love for two weeks," she pleaded.

"No, leave me alone," he grumbled, walking away, leaving Maria frowning.

Two weeks, she thought. Not since Sylvie died.

Four days later, when sifting through their mail, Maria saw a TV producer's logo on an envelope.

"Look, it's from that TV company," she said as she slit open the envelope. "*Dear Mr. Tremaine, for acting as consultant to our series, The History of Modern Ballet...* yes! You're going to get paid."

"That's great," said Dave, empty of feeling.

"Great? Is that all you can say?" She waved the letter at him. "They're finally going to pay you a year after you worked for them. Can't you feel something?"

He forced himself to smile. "I feel great."

Sure you do, Maria thought. She grunted and turned away.

Two days later, Maria put her arms around Dave from behind again. "I have needs," she hinted.

"No, I've been busy, and I'm tired," he said.

"This is about Sylvie, isn't it?" She already knew the answer.

"No, it isn't about Sylvie, it's—well, uh—" he began.

Maria held up the palm of her hand to stop him. "We haven't made love since Sylvie died. It's been three weeks."

Dave gazed away from Maria.

Maria continued, talking to his back. "I know you felt guilty about Sylvie becoming a stripper, and you've felt more guilt since she died. I'm sad too, and I miss her too. But I don't feel guilty, and you shouldn't either."

No reply.

"Dave, you wanted to apologize to her, tell her that you're sorry. When you were connected to her—soul—did you do that?"

"No, I didn't," he said, the disappointment obvious in his voice.

"Then what are you going to do?"

"Go back."

DOCTOR RAND'S LAB, TORONTO, NOVEMBER 8, THIS YEAR:

"I didn't expect to see you again, especially not so soon," said Doctor Rand.

"I want to be connected to Sylvie Courtauld's brain waves again," asked Dave.

"Why? You experienced an event that you know didn't happen in real life. It was neither a new experience nor an old memory. It was a dream or hallucination. You didn't actually meet the soul of Sylvie Courtauld."

"I know I met something. That's why I have to go back."

Rand looked over to Maria and hoped she could help him. "What do you think?"

Maria's eyes were sad, lifeless. "I don't want him to do it. But he's obsessed with something in those brain waves. He won't come back to me until he does what he needs to do, so let him do it."

Rand turned back to Dave. "And just what do you have to do with Sylvie Courtauld?"

"Talk to her."

Rand nodded. If he could make this couple happy again... "Okay, but the same rules apply. If any of your vital signs become dangerous, I'm pulling you back."

An hour later, Dave felt Rand attach the skullcap to his head again. Maria leaned over the table.

"Don't stay there too long," she warned. "You had us scared the last time."

"No, I won't stay too long," he promised.

Joleen began the countdown: "Five, four, three..."

Maria reached out and held Dave's hand.

"...two, one..."

Dave felt a jolt when his mind merged with Sylvie's brain waves again.

INSIDE DAVE'S MIND, NOVEMBER 8, THIS YEAR:

Dave stood in their apartment—his and Sylvie's apartment.

"You can turn around now," said Sylvie from behind. He turned.

She stood there, dressed in a red babydoll. Dave could see through the skimpy silk garment that left her legs completely uncovered.

She shot him a lewd smile and struck a pose that accentuated her legs. "Do you like it?"

He leered at her. "Do I ever."

She pulled up the hemline and tugged at her thong panties. "And do you like this?" she asked as she turned around.

"Oh, yes, I do," he replied.

Then he noticed that she wore red ballet slippers. Ballet slippers, not high heels—a cute touch.

There had to be a reason, an occasion, for this show.

She walked to him and licked his ear. "Happy Valentine's Day, honey," she cooed.

Valentine's Day. The day for lovers.

She held two flowers out to him: a rose and a daisy. He

knew the symbolism: *Le Spectre de la Rose* and *Giselle*, their two favourite ballets they had danced together.

He took the flowers and kissed her.

"To my favourite prince," she said. "In Russia, they still give a bouquet of flowers to the danseur as well as to the ballerina at curtain call."

He smelled the flowers. "That's nice; we should do that in North America too."

She led him to the couch and sat him down. "There's something I've always wanted to do," she said.

She turned on the CD player, and rock music blared out. She began gyrating her hips slowly. Then she sat in his lap and writhed.

"Remember when we were kids, we always passed by a strip bar on Yonge Street? I've always wondered what stripping in a bar would be like. If I weren't a ballerina, I would be a stripper. More than that—a lap dancer." She laughed.

Dave shuddered. It had happened in the real world. "You would be good at it too," he said.

"Enjoy your fantasy."

Sylvie had tied her hair into a bun with a red ribbon again. She pulled at the ribbon, the bun unravelled, and her blonde hair cascaded down.

She ground her butt into his groin. Then she stood up, and still swaying to the music, pulled the babydoll over her head and wrapped it around his neck. Next, she pulled her thong down to her ankles and kicked it off.

The strip dance lasted a few more minutes. Then, taking him by the hand, Sylvie pulled Dave off the couch and led him into the bedroom. She slowly unbuttoned his shirt and pulled it off. Dropping to her knees, she unbuttoned and unzipped his pants and pulled them down. Then she pulled down his underwear and kissed his intimate parts.

"You want more?" she asked between kisses.

Moaning softly, Dave pulled Sylvie up to her feet and eased her to the bed. She rolled on her back and stretched herself out, her arms and legs sweeping over the bedsheets.

He pressed himself down on her, and he kissed her mouth, then her belly, then her breasts. She ran her hands all over his back and neck. He rubbed his body against hers, and she rocked and swayed in rhythm with his rubbing.

They kissed and caressed each other fervently, and then he gently pushed her thighs apart.

They made love passionately, and then they screamed out in pleasure together...

DOCTOR RAND'S LAB, TORONTO, NOVEMBER 8, THIS YEAR:

Dave's mind reeled from the clashing sounds and sights. His vision jumped between the bedroom and the lab, and Rand's and Joleen's voices mixed with Sylvie's. One moment he was making love with Sylvie, the next moment, Joleen was pulling the sensors off his chest.

Dave gasped and moaned. The furious pounding of his heart began to slow down. He felt hot and sticky with sweat all over his body.

He heard Rand talking. "Any loss of Ms. Courtauld's brain waves?"

"No loss," Joleen said. "They all flowed back into the

storage disc."

"Good. I was worried. We had to break the link pretty quickly."

Rand turned to Dave. "The link lasted twenty minutes. Twenty minutes! Your heart and respiration were going wild. I had to disconnect you."

"You're also the first person to yell out loud," said Joleen. "We didn't know what was going on. And then—well, uh—" She stopped talking and walked away.

Doctor Rand walked away too, leaving Dave alone with Maria.

Maria, frowning, loomed over him.

"Maria, I'm back," gasped Dave.

"So you are. What did you do with her this time?" she asked wryly.

He didn't answer. How could he tell her?

"You don't have to tell me," she said. "I know what you did. We all saw you do it. But tell me, was she good?"

She pressed the palm of her hand against his groin. He felt wet and sticky there. A large stain covered the front of his white underwear.

They walked home in silence. Maria did not burst out until they entered their apartment.

"So, is she just as good dead as alive?" she spat. "Was it good for you? Does she scratch your back like I do? Does she howl like a dog? Did she come too?"

Dave didn't answer.

"Talk to me, damn it! I'm your wife, for Heaven's sake! What the Hell is going on? You won't make love to me, but you'll have sex with a ghost!"

"It's not as if I had sex with another woman," Dave murmured.

"So she's not a woman if she's a ghost? Or it's not sex if you do it with a ghost? Which is it?"

"Neither, I mean, it's not as if I had sex with a real flesh-and-blood woman."

"That doesn't matter. If there really is a ghost, then you're having sex with it. And if it's all a dream, then you're jacking off on a fantasy about her. Either way, you're not getting turned on by *me*."

"I'm sorry, Maria, I don't know what happened."

"These trips have got to stop," she demanded. "Did you finally apologize to her?"

"No."

Maria glared at him in silence.

"Go change your underwear," she said.

DOCTOR RAND'S LAB, TORONTO, NOVEMBER 15, THIS YEAR:

Doctor Rand couldn't believe that they returned to his office again.

"You're becoming our most experienced test subject," he said, "but I don't recommend another session."

"I've had the longest links, and I've had two, which is more than anyone else," said Dave, his voice shaking. "I've experienced things that no one else has. You can learn valuable information from my experiences."

Rand shook his head, unable to believe Dave's desperation. "You're right in saying your experiences are unique. But they've been risky too. Of all the test subjects, you've come the closest to serious harm."

"I survived unharmed both times," Dave reminded him. "There's no medical reason to refuse me."

Rand looked at Maria. Looking distant from the meeting, she hadn't said a word.

"Ma'am, are you okay? May I get you a coffee, a tea?" Rand asked her.

"No, I am fine," she murmured. "Just let him go one more time."

Rand blinked. "Ma'am?"

She looked at him, her eyes hollow and empty. "Let him go one more time, so he can get her out of his mind once and for all."

Doctor Rand looked at the sad couple. Yes, he could learn why Dave's experiences differed from everyone else's. And strangely, Maria wanted a third session too, so he had the wife's agreement.

But in both times, he had to pull Dave out of the link before it killed him. However, Dave had signed the liability waiver...

"Against my better judgment, I'll connect you to Ms. Courtauld's brain waves again," he agreed, "but only once more."

An hour later, Joleen attached the sensors to Dave's chest again and started the countdown: "Sylvie Courtauld's brain waves are ready to flow. Flow to start in five, four, three..."

This time, Maria did not hold Dave's hand. Instead, she sat in a chair and stared at him.

"...two, one..."

INSIDE DAVE'S MIND, NOVEMBER 15, THIS YEAR:

Under the full moon, Dave and Sylvie walked down the street. Autumn leaves, dying and brittle, snapped under their feet.

She laughed. "I'm so excited. *Giselle* opens next week. My first time as Giselle!"

Giselle opens next week. Dave smiled. In the real world of seven years ago, Joan had already dismissed Sylvie from the role. But here, in his mind, her spirit could enjoy a life she never had.

He had to keep coming back. He owed it to her.

"*Giselle*'s my favourite ghost story," she said. "All those ghosts of women who died of broken hearts and came back to make their men dance to death."

She swept her arms around and pranced on the sidewalk. "When I dance the second act, I feel like a Wili, a ghost."

"You're really getting into your role. You should tell ghost stories to kids," said Dave.

"You think this is all an act? You don't believe in the Wilis?" she asked. "They are real. They talk to me."

"Oh?"

"Yes, I hear their voices. And they like us, Dave. They like *you*. They've been watching us dance together all these years: in *Swan Lake*, *The Sleeping Beauty*, *Le Spectre de la Rose*. They want us in their world."

"*Their* world?"

"A world where everyone lives forever. Nijinsky, Pavlova, Nureyev, Fonteyn—they're all dancing there. I'm ready to go anytime, but I don't think you want to."

She was taking her story about a heaven for dead ballet stars too seriously, Dave thought.

"So you don't believe me?" she said.

How did she know his thoughts?

"You better watch out. The Wilis share their powers with me, and I can make you do whatever I want."

"Like what?" Dave said.

"Like dance," Sylvie ordered.

Suddenly, Dave danced a *pas de bourée*, a three-part step.

He hadn't intended to do it.

He looked at her. She grinned at him.

"Simple, wasn't it?" she said, her eyes lighting up. "But let's do something more complicated."

Dave danced a *pas de chat*, which, despite its name, looked like a jumping goat. He shivered.

"God, what are you doing to me?" said Dave.

"You know the legend of the Wilis. They make men dance until they're exhausted and die."

"Sylvie, you're scaring me."

"You must believe me, even just a little bit, by now," she said. "Okay, let's see some jumps. Sixteen jumps in first, sixteen jumps in second, eight *changements*, eight *échappés*."

Dave did the forty-eight jumps on the sidewalk. After jumping on the hard concrete, he felt a mild pain go up his legs. He staggered away from Sylvie and rubbed his calves.

"Hurts a little, doesn't it?" said Sylvie. "Let's continue with our class. You know the individual steps, but the true essence of dance is to combine many individual steps into one fluid movement. For example, Albrecht's dance in act two, when the Wilis are making him dance to death."

Dave immediately started dancing the series of jumps

and turns in the air, repeating the sequence again and again. He could not stop.

Each time, he leapt higher than before, and his turns grew more frenzied. Sweat flowed down his back. His heart pounded erratically, his lungs gasped for air, and a sharp pain shot through his legs.

"Let me stop!" he cried.

Sylvie smirked at him.

He danced the solo over and over. His body felt as if it were splitting into pieces. He felt nothing but the heat and the exhaustion and the pain in his legs.

His heart pounded to a frenzied beat that did not match the music. A force like a heavy weight pressed upon his chest. And yet, his legs and feet could not stop dancing.

I don't control my body anymore, he realized, horrified, as he collapsed on the ground and fainted.

TORONTO, NOVEMBER 15–23, THIS YEAR:

When Dave awoke, he took a while to notice that he lay not on Doctor Rand's table but on something softer. He still felt sensors taped to him, however.

"Dave."

Dave stirred. Maria's voice?

"Sshh." Another voice. "Don't wake him up. Let him get his rest."

Dave slowly opened his eyes, squinted, and tried to adjust to the light. Where was he?

In a hospital room. Maria sat beside his bed. Behind her, a nurse talked to a doctor.

"He's awake," said Maria.

The doctor and the nurse walked to the door. "We'll be back in a minute," the doctor said.

Maria looked impassively at Dave. "You probably want to know what happened.

"You were connected to Sylvie's brain waves for twenty-two minutes, then your heartbeat became irregular—not just fast, but beating to an irregular rhythm. Doctor Rand thought you were having a heart attack, so he disconnected Sylvie's brain waves. You didn't wake up, so we called an ambulance."

Dave let the story sink into his mind. Finally, he said, "How long have I been here?"

"About three hours. What happened?" She sounded genuinely worried, not bitter and sarcastic like last time.

Dave told her how Sylvie had forced him to dance, and Maria listened without interrupting him.

"You can't do this again," she said. "You'll die if—"

Before she could say more, the doctor returned. "Go home, you won't have to stay here for observation," he said. "But be careful. I don't think you had a heart attack, not even a mild one, but something affected your heartbeat."

Just as the doctor walked out, Rand marched into the room. He went to the bed quickly, without any greetings to Dave or Maria.

"I'm ending your participation in the experiments," said Rand. "It's getting too dangerous."

Rand reached out and shook Dave's hand. "It was a pleasure to conduct research with you. Take care, and goodbye."

Rand left as quickly as he had entered, leaving Dave and Maria alone.

*   *   *

When they arrived home, Maria found a letter in their mailbox. "Dave, it's from the TV show," she told him. "Quick, open it!"

Dave opened the letter and took out the seven thousand dollar cheque.

Maria squealed and threw her arms around him. "They finally paid you."

"Nice," Dave murmured.

"Nice?" asked Maria. "Is that all you can say? Nice? This is fantastic. Dave, let's celebrate."

"Whatever you want," he said.

An hour later, they went to his favourite restaurant, an Italian place with elegant white tablecloths and polished brass chandeliers. Soft, quiet music and the aromas of different pizzas and pastas wafted through the dining room.

Dave languidly picked at his food.

Maria looked at Dave's linguine, which he had barely eaten. It's now or never, she told herself. Now that Doctor Rand had ended the experiments, she had a chance to bring him back into her world.

She put down her knife and fork. "Don't worry, we're in a restaurant, so I'm not going to yell."

Dave let out a small laugh. "You're going to tell me not to continue the experiments? You don't have to worry. That's not my decision anymore."

"But I can tell you wish Doctor Rand hadn't stopped them. You still want to talk to Sylvie's spirit again. Stop it, Dave, and not just because it's getting dangerous."

"What other reason is there?"

"Getting on with our lives," said Maria. She took a sip of her wine. "You've been wracked with guilt ever since she died. Well, enough of it."

"She might still be alive, if only we hadn't—well, you know."

"All this talk about Sylvie. Don't I count anymore?"

"I'm sorry. I didn't mean that. You've been a wonderful wife and partner."

Maria smiled and reached out to hold his hand. "I've been waiting to hear that for weeks."

"What I meant is that Sylvie didn't have to die. Her death was preventable."

"Yes, it was, but *not by us*. Yeah, I shouldn't have slept with you either time. And you shouldn't have tried to relive your first time with me. Both times, we were young and didn't know any better. We hurt her."

She took another sip of wine, needing it to continue talking. "Maybe our afternoon fling started the events that ruined her life. But Sylvie made all the decisions that ruined her life. She had choices. She could've dumped you. She could've found someone else. Or she could've tried to get you back. I bet that if she had tried, she would've won. I was only a one-night stand back then."

Dave grimaced. Encouraged by his shock, thinking he might finally be listening, Maria continued.

"Sylvie was young too, inexperienced, maybe flighty. Maybe that's why she ran away. But she didn't have to go into stripping and drugs. She could have come back to the Ballet; Joan would have taken her back, and ex-couples have danced in the same company before. Or she could've danced with another company. She didn't have to run away from everyone and everything she loved.

"Dave, we hurt her, but anything she did afterwards was her choice and her fault."

She quickly gulped down her remaining wine. "There, I've said it. Neither of us have anything to feel guilty about, so stop torturing yourself."

Dave's eyes shone briefly. "I guess you're right. I should stop blaming myself."

"It'll be nice to have you back," said Maria.

Dave began eating his dinner again, much to Maria's relief.

Another week passed, and Maria walked up to Dave from behind again and slowly put her arms around him. Maybe by now he would want her.

"We should make love," she whispered.

"We should," he agreed, already taking off his clothes.

He pulled her into the bedroom, stripped her naked, and threw her on her back on the bed. Without any foreplay, with no gentle caresses or tender kisses, he forced himself into her.

He had never taken her so viciously. Maria shrieked with each heavy thrust of his body into hers. After weeks without sex, she was getting this rough play.

It was primal sex, neither elegant nor romantic. She knew he had only one goal, to relieve his urges upon her. There was nothing for her heart.

But she had physical needs too. At least she got that. Drenched in sweat and panting furiously, she blocked out all thoughts of love and surrendered her mind to her body's pleasure.

When his body began to tremble, Dave let out a long

groan.

"SYLVIE!"

Maria screamed and began to cry. *He's pretending I'm her.* She beat her fists into his back, then his shoulders.

Despite her hitting and crying, he did not get off her. He stayed intertwined with her as he finished satisfying himself.

Finally, he pulled himself away without kissing or stroking her. Turning away from her, he sat up and put his face in his hands.

Still crying, Maria stared up at the ceiling rather than look at him. "You bastard! You were pretending I was her. You don't love me anymore. Get out! Get out!"

"I'm sorry," Dave said softly. He got up and walked into the living room without saying a word.

When Dave woke up on the couch shortly after dawn, Maria had already gone, the earliest she had ever left. Her violin was gone, so he guessed she had gone to the studio. He should go there too; he had a new ballet to rehearse.

Before leaving home, he took the TV company's cheque with him. He could stop at the bank before going to the studio. A half hour later, while waiting in the line to the teller, he remembered Joleen, Doctor Rand's assistant.

Hadn't she needed money? And doesn't she know how to use the machine?

Instead of putting the entire cheque into his account, he kept one thousand dollars in cash. Then he turned away from the path to the ballet studio and returned to

Doctor Rand's lab.

Joleen frowned when she saw him. "Doctor Rand isn't here. He's at a conference. Won't be back for a week."

"I want to be linked to the brain waves again," Dave pleaded.

Joleen didn't look up from her newspaper. "That's over. Doctor Rand's orders. You don't have to come back anymore."

Dave looked at the page of the newspaper: Help Wanted.

"You've been working as Doctor Rand's assistant for a long time," Dave said.

"Years."

"So you know how the brain wave collector works; you've watched him enough times."

"Maybe I do. Look, Doctor Rand's not here, but I'll tell him you came to see him."

"Research assistants usually aren't paid a lot."

"It pays the bills," Joleen said, irritated. "Are you going to leave soon?"

"You need money," Dave said.

Joleen looked up from the newspaper. "What makes you say that?"

"You've said so before, and you're reading the 'Help Wanted' ads in the newspaper." Dave paused, as if gathering courage for his offer. "I can help you."

He took five one-hundred dollar bills from his pocket. Joleen stared at the money.

"You really want it, don't you? No, I can't do it. Well, maybe for a thousand dollars," she said, laughing.

Without hesitation, Dave took out another five hundred dollars. Joleen stopped laughing and grabbed the money.

"Remember, you were never here, and if you tell anyone, I'll say you're lying, but just in case you don't leave alive—uh, just in case anything happens, sign this waiver. You know the routine."

They repeated the routine, and when she put the skullcap on him, she said, "You must love her."

"I did once," said Dave, "but now I don't know."

"Well, don't do anything strenuous, don't do anything silly," she warned him as she attached the sensors to his chest. "I'm out here by myself, so don't give me anything complicated to do."

"I'm just going to talk to her this time, nothing else," Dave promised.

When the instruments started humming again, the brain waves of both Dave and Sylvie appeared on the monitors.

Joleen took a deep breath. "Brain wave flow to start in five, four, three, two, one…"

INSIDE DAVE'S MIND, NOVEMBER 23, THIS YEAR:

He stood on the stage where Sylvie had rehearsed *Giselle* years ago. Behind him hung the backdrop for act two: a dense German forest in the evening. Giselle's tombstone sat off in a corner.

He heard footsteps against the wooden floor. Turning around, he saw Sylvie walking to him. She wore a veil and a white costume with a tight bodice, small wings on her back, and a long, layered Romantic tutu: the Wili Giselle.

She pulled the veil off her face and smiled. "Welcome

back, Dave. Do you remember when we made love again?"

"Yes," Dave replied.

"Then you'll want to join me forever." A glint appeared in her eyes. "I know you want to; that's why you keep coming back, that's why you call out my name when you made love to Maria."

"You know about that?"

"I do. Our thoughts and our feelings are one. I know everything you think, everything you feel."

Dave noticed that *he* didn't know what she was thinking. Only the ghost seemed able to read minds.

"You've devoted your whole life to dance," said Sylvie, "and you can dance forever in my world. And you can dance with the best." She raised an arm and looked up.

Faint, ghostly images, like the flickering of an old movie, appeared high in the air: Marie Taglioni, Auguste Bournonville, Vaslav Nijinsky, Anna Pavlova, Rudolf Nureyev, Margot Fonteyn, and dozens of other dance stars of the past, still dancing.

"Why, I've already taken classes with Pavlova. Think of what you could learn, what you could do with them," said Sylvie.

"I can't go," said Dave.

"Don't make me force you. It'll hurt more if I have to force you. Remember when I made you dance Albrecht's dance from act two?"

Dave started dancing, and he felt his heartbeat rise.

METRO TORONTO BALLET STUDIO, TORONTO, NOVEMBER 23, THIS YEAR:

Maria knew there was trouble when Joan Silverton rushed over to her.

"Where's Dave?" Joan asked.

Maria shrugged and poured herself a coffee. "Isn't he here yet?"

"He's two hours late for a rehearsal. I tried phoning your home, but I got no answer."

Maria put down her coffee. Would Dave really go back to see Sylvie again?

And if he had, why should she care?

INSIDE DAVE'S MIND, NOVEMBER 23, THIS YEAR:

Pain engulfed Dave's body. He felt so hot that he thought he would burst into flames. Sweat poured all over his body. Every muscle felt like a twig about to snap. His lungs, panting for air, were going to explode.

Under so much stress and pain, he thought he would collapse on the floor. But something made him keep dancing.

If he fainted, would he collapse and live? Or would Sylvie keep his unconscious body dancing until his heart, lungs and muscles wore out and died?

He desperately wanted to pass out. Sylvie could kill him after he fainted, but at least he would feel no pain. But he felt her forcing him to stay awake.

"Why do you want to sleep now?" Sylvie asked, reading his mind. "Shouldn't you stay awake during your solo?"

"Please let me stop," Dave croaked.

"Not yet, honey, not until you're in the land of the Wilis."

*   *   *

TORONTO, NOVEMBER 23, THIS YEAR:

Maria remembered Dave's story about his last meeting with Sylvie's ghost, that Sylvie had wanted him to join her in the land of the Wilis.

The land of the ghosts, thought Sylvie. He's gone to die.

Finally, after all these years, Sylvie was fighting for her boyfriend—from beyond the grave.

I'm not losing my husband without a fight, Maria told herself as she rushed out of the studio.

When Maria walked into Doctor Rand's office, she saw nobody at the desk. She heard the humming of the brain wave collector and went into the lab.

Joleen stood by the monitors. She looked pale and haggard.

On the brain wave monitor, the two lines were enmeshed and furiously making jagged peaks. Never before had Sylvie's and Dave's brain waves been so erratic.

Covered with sweat, Dave's body convulsed, and his legs and feet moved. His eyes, open and shifting, had a glassy, dilated look, like an open-eyed coma.

"He's never moved like this before. Or opened his eyes," said Maria, trembling. "What's happening to him?"

Joleen looked at the monitors and shook her head. "Heartbeat is up and irregular, his respiration is up, he's got a fever, and his brain wave activity is erratic and abnormal. He went into convulsions about three minutes ago."

"Cut the link," Maria ordered.

"I can't. His body's under a lot of stress. If we break the link, he might die from the shock."

"And if we keep the link, he'll die."

"Not unless his vital signs go back to normal first."

Maria looked at Dave's feet. They seemed to be moving in a pattern.

"He's dancing," she said, surprised. "He's dancing!"

Maria reached out and grasped Dave's hand. Breathing deeply, she knew she couldn't panic now that her husband's life depended on her.

Leaning over him, she said, "Dave, this is Maria, your wife. If you can still hear me—Dave, don't die. Dave, come back!"

INSIDE DAVE'S MIND, NOVEMBER 23, THIS YEAR:

Panic gripped Dave. He didn't want to die.

"Dave, come back!" The voice echoed through the theatre.

Now he was hearing Maria's voice. The endless dancing had stolen more than his strength. It had stolen his sanity too.

But Sylvie flinched, as if she had heard Maria too.

The voice boomed from above. *"Dave, come back! Don't you dare die!"*

"Ignore her!" Sylvie snapped.

Dave gasped for air and kept dancing the series of leaps and turns, still unable to stop.

DOCTOR RAND'S LAB, TORONTO, NOVEMBER 23, THIS YEAR:

Maria squeezed Dave's hand. A single tear went down

her cheek. She wiped it away; she couldn't break down and cry now. She had to be strong this time.

"Dave, I love you. And I love Sylvie too. We were such good friends long ago. Remember we used to sneak out of the School together, do things together...

"Sylvie, if you can hear me: I'm sorry for sleeping with Dave both times. Stealing your boyfriend once is bad enough; stealing him twice is unforgivable. I can't say much, only that I was young and confused both times. But that's not an excuse. There is no excuse. I'm sorry. Please don't punish me by killing him."

She sighed and looked at the monitors. Dave and Sylvie's brain waves still jumped in a frenzy, and his heartbeat, breathing, and temperature were still high and irregular.

"Dave, you have to talk to Sylvie. Sylvie was always a nice girl. She doesn't need you to die. She never wanted anyone to die, no matter how much they upset her.

"Maybe all she really wants is for you to apologize, to tell her that you're sorry for cheating on her. Dave, please do it this time."

INSIDE DAVE'S MIND, NOVEMBER 23, THIS YEAR:

"Sylvie was always a nice girl... Dave, please do it this time."

As he leapt again in his endless dance, Dave looked at Sylvie. Her face hardened into a stern mask, but her lips trembled, and she shed a single tear.

Dave's throat felt sore and dry, and his lungs were going to burst, but he managed to gasp his words:

"Sylvie, I'm sorry."

Sylvie turned and looked at Dave, and her eyes widened. Slowly, she smiled.

"Please stop dancing," she said.

Dave collapsed on the floor.

DOCTOR RAND'S LAB, TORONTO, NOVEMBER 23, THIS YEAR:

Joleen tapped Maria on the shoulder and pointed at the monitors. The lines became less erratic, more regular.

Dave's convulsions slowed down and gradually stopped, and he lay still again, his eyes closed.

"His heartbeat's going down, his temperature's dropping, his breathing's becoming regular," Joleen said. "If he keeps improving, we can break the link."

Maria smiled and squeezed Dave's hand again. "You can do it! Don't give up!"

INSIDE DAVE'S MIND, NOVEMBER 23, THIS YEAR:

Dave slowly stood up. His legs still felt sore, but the feeling was returning to them. Although his ribs hurt, he could breathe again. He felt his body cooling down as his fever broke.

Her eyes cast down, Sylvie slowly walked to him. No longer a proud, strong Wili, she now looked like a little lost girl in a ballet costume.

"Dave, please hug me," she begged.

Dave embraced her, and they held each other silently for a long time. Dave felt the warmth of Sylvie's body, so surprising for a ghost.

Finally, Sylvie broke the silence. "Do you really mean

it?"

"Yes," Dave replied. "I really am sorry. I'm sorry for being unfaithful and hurting you. I really did love you. I didn't mean to hurt you, I wasn't thinking, I was a jerk. Will you forgive me?"

"Yes, I do. That's all I really need." She sighed and hugged him harder.

"Dance with me?" she asked.

"Sure." They started dancing a slow waltz in tight, little steps, barely moving.

"I missed you so much all those years," she said. "I always thought about you. I was angry at you, but I never stopped loving you. I wish I had the courage to stand up to you, to fight for you. If I had, I might have gotten you back. But I was young and insecure."

She sighed again. "Dave, I was selfish to bring you to my world. You still belong in the land of the living. I'm sorry."

"It's okay," said Dave.

A jolt ran down Dave's spine, the same jolt he had felt just before Rand pulled him back into the world of the living.

"Sylvie, I'll have to go soon."

"You're going to leave me again?" Sylvie said sadly.

"I have to."

Sylvie pulled herself away but kept holding his hands. "Go back to Maria. She was my best friend in the School. She's a bit confused—well, maybe not anymore—but she's really a sweet girl. Your life is with her now. Go make it a good, long life."

"Thanks. And what will you do?"

Sylvie looked up. "All dancers go to heaven, and it's

time I went there too."

She kissed him on the lips. "Thank you for letting me dance with you again."

Dave felt himself slipping away.

DOCTOR RAND'S LAB, TORONTO, NOVEMBER 23, THIS YEAR:

"God, I hope there's no permanent brain damage."

Joleen's voice. Dave knew he was coming back to the world of the living. He felt like a fish rising to the surface of a lake, floating in the water, leaving the dark depths, getting closer and closer to the light.

Someone was holding his hand. He knew its warmth and its texture. Maria, his wife.

When he opened his eyes, he saw Maria's face first, a face tight with tension.

"Are you okay?" she asked.

"I'm back for good," said Dave.

"Welcome back," said Maria, and she smiled, bent over, and gave him a deep, long kiss.

A week later, Doctor Rand returned for new experiments on his collection of disembodied brain waves. He slid Sylvie's disc into a disc player connected to an EEG.

"Now, let's see what you're doing," he said, as if Sylvie could hear him.

The EEG's monitor flickered on. Nothing appeared.

METRO TORONTO BALLET STUDIO, TORONTO, DECEMBER 24, THIS YEAR:

Colourful Christmas decorations hung all over the studio. Christmas carols and *The Nutcracker Suite* flowed from the sound system. Most of the Ballet's staff had already left for Christmas Eve. Dave was getting ready to go when he saw Joleen wander into the studio.

"Joleen, what brings you here?" asked Dave.

Joleen held up a golden compact disc, the disc that held Sylvie's brain waves. "I thought you might want to know about this."

Maria walked up to Joleen. "About what?"

"There's nothing in it," said Joleen. "The disc is empty. It's like a dry battery—no electrical activity."

Dave took the disc from Joleen and examined it, turning it in his hands.

"A leak?" he asked.

Joleen shrugged. "Could be, but I tested the disc, and it's still good."

Maria smiled. "Maybe Sylvie was right. All dancers go to heaven."

About "All Dancers Go to Heaven"

The late Aaron Yorgason started a short-lived publishing company called Oortworks Corporation, which published science fiction novellas and story collections in chapbooks.

Sylvie's funeral, with a quartet playing music from the ballet *Giselle*, was inspired by Rudolf Nureyev's funeral at the Opera Garnier.

Thanks to Aaron for publishing "All Dancers Go to Heaven".

Publishing credits

"The Siren Stone"
Published in *Space Inc.*, edited by Julie Czerneda, DAW Books, 2003. Finalist for the 2004 Aurora Award for Best Short-Form Work in English.

"Transubstantiation"
Published in *Northwest Passages: a Cascadian Anthology*, edited by Cris DiMarco, Windstorm Creative, Port Orchard, Washington, 2005. Winner of the 2006 Prix Aurora Award for Best Short-Form Work in English.

"XY-Girls"
Published in *Space and Time* magazine, issue 133, spring-summer 2019.

"A Girl Like Us"
Published in *Space and Time* magazine, issue 137, summer 2020.

"The Barbecue Battle"
Published in *Speculative City*, issue 13, summer 2022.

"Software Update"
Published in *Clarity*, edited by J. Scott Coatsworth, Other Worlds Ink, Sacramento, California, 2022.

"Willpower"
Published in *Eeriecon Chapbook Ten*, Buffalo Fantasy League, Buffalo, New York, 2011.

"Flying Devils"
Published in *Shanghai Steam*, edited by Ace Jordyn,
Calvin D. Jim and Renee Bennett, Edge Science Fiction
and Fantasy Publishing, Calgary, Alberta, 2012.

"The House of Hagfish"
Published in *Immersion: An Asian Anthology of Love,
Fantasy, and Speculative Fiction*, edited by JF Garrard,
Allan Cho, and William Tham, Asian Canadian Writers
Workshop and Dark Helix Press, Vancouver, 2019.

"All Dancers Go to Heaven"
Published in a chapbook by Oortworks Corporation,
Toronto, Ontario, 2000.

Derwin Mak's story "Transubstantiation" won the 2006 Aurora Award for Best Short Fiction. *The Dragon and the Stars*, an anthology that he co-edited with Eric Choi, won the 2011 Aurora Award for Best Related Work. *Where the Stars Rise*, an anthology that he co-edited with Lucas Law, won the Alberta Book Publishing Award for Speculative Fiction Book of the Year in 2018. Derwin also founded the cosplay competition at Anime North, Canada's largest anime convention. He has degrees in accounting and military history and was the first person to capture a Pokémon inside the Royal Canadian Military Institute.

If you enjoyed *XY-Girls and More Stories*, try...

See all 50+ titles at brain-lag.com

www.ingramcontent.com/pod-product-compliance
Lightning Source LLC
Chambersburg PA
CBHW031210310726
48969CB00001B/288